MUCH LEFT TO RIGHT

ANADI

Leadstart
INKSTATE

ISBN 978-93-90463-59-6
Copyright © Anadi Sharma, 2020

First published in India 2020 by Inkstate Books
An imprint of Leadstart Publishing Pvt Ltd

Sales Office:
Unit No.25/26, Building No.A/1,
Near Wadala RTO,
Wadala (East), Mumbai – 400037 India
Phone: +91 969933000
Email: info@leadstartcorp.com
www.leadstartcorp.com

Disclaimer: The views expressed in this book are those of the Author and do not pertain to be held by the Publisher.

Author Disclaimer: This is a work of fiction. Names, characters, businesses, places, events, locales, and incidents are either the products of the author's imagination or used in a fictitious manner. Any resemblance to actual persons, living or dead, or actual events is purely coincidental.

Editor: Vaibhav Pathare
Cover: Ami Parekh
Layouts: Victor Patali

THIS IS FOR YOU, SAADHYA

ABOUT THE AUTHOR

Anadi likes to read and know about geo-politics.

Though an avid student of history, for sustenance he took shelter in present day economy when he found a job.

And after becoming a people manager, he got ample opportunities to dwell in his interest every day - the people and the places - which has led to his debut novel - MUCH LEFT TO RIGHT.

Acknowledgements

To my mother, Sneh Lata Sharma. Her lifelong endurance made us what my siblings and I are today.

My sister, Pinchu, I am eternally grateful to for being my first editor and critic. Her frequent guidance and many critiques elevated me to the point, I could finally write my first novel.

My love, beautiful and gracious, Priyanka who made me believe I could become an author. She remained the force every day when I struggled to keep up and ensured I kept going.

Contents

Chapter 1 — 9

Chapter 2 — 21

Chapter 3 — 44

Chapter 4 — 61

Chapter 5 — 69

Chapter 6 — 83

Chapter 7 — 105

Chapter 8 — 118

Chapter 9 — 135

Chapter 10 — 147

Chapter 11 — 165

Chapter 12 — 172

Chapter 13 — 182

Chapter 14 — 192

Chapter 15 — 199

Chapter 16 — 207

Chapter 17 — 219

Chapter 18 — 233

Chapter 19 — 243

Chapter 20 — 252

<h1 style="text-align:center">CHAPTER 1</h1>

The meeting place was one block away. He took the stairs down to the lobby. He felt suffocated in that alley just like he felt trapped in his Hindu lineage.

Malik Kafur was dominating his mind, and so was Rani; Bhansali had won him over.

As he breathed in the ambience, he perceived overwhelming to his senses, he felt he was betraying his identity. *Tejo-Mahalaya* was engaging and intriguing.

The face across was without emotions as always. "It is true Anant and my community has a sigh of relief that despite living beside the majority Hindu community, Muslims live in peace. Surprisingly, there is sparse communal antagonism and more harmony," he paused for a few moments pondering. The audience was about to get flabbergasted, "But had we been in majority," his eyes penetrating, "it would be a catastrophe for Hindus, make no mistake." There was a resolve in his voice teen could hardly be mistaken with.

It was the year 1998. This forty-something was just twenty.

This would always be said next – "It is a matter of time and you will find us back in the majority," and pausing momentarily the speaker who was wearing a *safed topi* would end his harangue with a sigh, "Until you land in Middle-East, you continue to fail to realize."

"And what is that Fahad?" the young would ask wearing a heavy smile, crucifying him for ages.

"There is no need to be pleasant, a Hindu could be equally harsh–truthful–you meek." His inner being would taunt him. It still does to this day.

"A Pakistani is not that welcoming. And we belonging to the same religion gathers no special respect among Arabs, that millions here are so sure about."

Fahad's agony would be vivid, "I learned it the hardest way Anant."

"A lot of others to learn it the hard way, I reckon."

"Shoaib is in our neighbourhood and also there, across the border, right? So, what's the ho-halla about if we celebrate their cricketing success? Pitch does not matter, why to give it a nationalistic tone?"

Sarai was just half-a-mile away. He was limping, and so he had all the way through; A mile looked an eternity. Steps were getting shorter - he must find shelter now–they were just behind trailing him. Shahjahanpur loomed large and imminent, he diverted. The upcoming meeting was the crux of the leap, Anant the project manager with a software firm was taut.

Time wasn't medieval, he was just time machined to.

"Huzoor!"

Spine felt the vibration and tongue the senses.

Despite being in his thirties, Naved looked hazy in his outfit and his mind was lost in something.

Subordinate had begun a brief to the Director on the escalated matter, "Sir..." when Anant entered the cabin.

Boss, moments ago, had unleashed depiction of a torrid time at the hands of the customer in the recently held review meeting.

Cutting him short, the Boss said "Why was this not reported earlier, and in time, Anant?"

Anant being the seasoned project manager had the medicine ready and said, "I have had a discussion with the customer a few hours back and Naved will soon implement the solution which was agreed in the discussion."

IT world was steady as usual, but slow. Anant, the IT professional, felt slowing down evermore.

The cabin adjacent to him had been turned into a prayer room was filled to the brim, though it had a few namazees he still felt that it crowed his senses.

The Boss issued instructions to the coder and moved to the next task on hand.

"500 USD project, would you be there, Anant?" Director S.K commented while getting up.

"Yes," said Anant

"Good," replied Director S.K.

"Not sure," he muttered, turning back to the lobby.

His phone buzzed. Instant messaging service delivered the expected, 'Customer has arrived.'

Gearing for strides, he swiftly parked the crisis–the haunting thoughts–Tejo Mahalya, Shahjehanpur, and of course some Shoaibs. A wrong has been done to his community, he firmly believed. That is why all such thoughts are on top of his mind every day every hour. Yet, he treats his work and career equally or even more important. It was hard yet he has learnt how to manage overpowering thoughts to focus on his work and not let them affect.

Panipat rural, Haryana, in 2018.

The window had barely opened and the area which he could see was crowded, he persuaded a few by waving the precious chit in the first chance he got.

For a day and a night, the young farmer was at the APMC *Mandi*. He had to sell trolley loads of wheat sacks, waiting for his turn, amongst hundreds of framers.

He was up early. Sacks, he was still feeling, were pinching his back as the last night and the second in a row were spent enduring those nips; eyes were fighting the drowse.

Scrambling, mustering all his strength, the sturdy lad eventually reached the window. White kurta and blue jeans, his usual attire, had gathered dust and dirt. Last season's bumper harvest led to abysmal market prices this year. Every farmer in the region was at the *Mandi*, chits were out, his turn was due any time. Selling the produce via MSP (Minimum Support Price) scheme was the only hope that summer to collect enough money for the winter sowing. The unseasonal heavy downpour had every nook and corner floating with wheat.

The clerks were yet to settle fully; morning gossips and usual officers bashing were being given the finishing touches.

"One trolley, fifteen ton," he pushed the weight certifying chit through the grill, hand barely reaching the clerk. Chit was issued at the *Mandi's* official weighing point last evening.

'Would he get his chance today?' a scary thought hit him at a lightning speed, he shrugged that off at a greater pace. Anxious still, his head would now and then turn towards the trolley. Sacks were loaded to the brim, body feeling the weight, a nervy look crossed his face.

"Last window… get the quality check done," clerk stamped this chit while making a register entry.

Grabbing all the important pieces of paper, the farmer swiftly made his way to the far corner of the gallery.

Mandi aadhati (wholesale trader) was shouting his way through the chores, commotion, and innumerable transactions. Wheat framer pleaded for attention amongst ten others scrambling for space. *"Chhatrapal sa yo, Sarpanch kaa sa* (he is Chhatrapal, Sarpanch's son)," some attempted to nudge the man in command.

A sarpanch's son, yet no respite and patronage that he could hope for, "Bloody BJP," he gushed.

After some time, he got lucky. His turn came up. The quality check began. Couple of *aadhati's* assistants climbed on top of the tractor-trolley. They quickly took samples randomly from the sacks. Samples were adjudicated, sub-standard ones were marked, good ones were offloaded simultaneously. In about forty minutes the exercise was over. He was handed over the stamped chit which had number of sacks and total quantity passed - only half of the stock could get through!

"Aadhi bhi koni (not even half made it)," he was disappointed. One more trolley full of wheat was back at home, waiting to be toed while only half of the supplied stock passed the quality check that day.

He had spent the last night over the sacks and now to bear the weight of the sacks while limping back home, is *Chhattar* you should have been careful; harvesting, threshing, and cleaning were not adequately carried out," farmer was livid with himself.

But an immediate and a greater worry had by now clouded him. He had forgotten to register the MSP amount. Realising the potential loss, in a flash, he turned back and briskly returning to the window where he must get the MSP amount registered. For the next two months, he was certain not to receive the payment from the *aadhati*. He had gotten tired – a farmer was exhausted. BJP had repeatedly assured the opposition of swift collection and swifter payments to the farmers at the earliest. The farmers were hopeful. This one was no exception.

Later in the day…

Chhatrapal Singh returned home, en route was deputy commissioner's office, which had many important works to cater for. His was related to the rural and ex-defence and so - hardly counted and the government office certainly considered that mundane. He was not disappointed; he had gotten used to it. And partly because, his mind was still occupied with what happened at *Mandi*.

House was big and was situated in a corner of the village. Its gate was huge and consisted a small entrance and a wide one to allow easy entrance of a tractor. He alighted from the tractor; entered inside the house through the small entrance and opened the wide entrance from inside.

In the next few seconds, trolley bearing unsold sacks was carefully parked. He did not want anyone in home to talk about – Why the sacks were not accepted? How would these rejected sacks be sold now? Can these be sold in the open market? Etcetera…etcetera.

He diverted his mind towards planning another trip to *Mandi* to sell the rest of the produce. 'Dharma must have by now sacked the wheat up,' he mumbled to himself.

Courtyard was huge; A couple of cots were lying in the centre, on the left side a buffalo was tied with her calf; in the adjacent corner a series of dung *uplaas. "Laado, paani." He felt thirsty.*

"Your *Laado* is in Gurugram." It was his wife. And It was said, in an annoying way, as always.

"How could she when I asked her to stay?"

"Leave her to her wishes," handing the water jug she advised and not for the first time.

"She can find her way, just support her - she earns now." The mother remarked, making her way to the courtyard.

Little away and further from the cots was the veranda leading to a couple of rooms which were one beside the other. The doors were wide open and the marble floors had aged. Next to each room adjacent and opposite to each other was a kitchen and utility area. The kitchen was modular, yet the floor was deemed to be the best portion to hold the gas stove and some utensils near it. The clothes were all piled up on the floor in one corner.

"Home science would suffice, city jobs are not meant for us Ma, are they?" said he.

"Where is Baapu?!" settling on the cot, he noticed his father's absence.

"Someone from panchayat's office came, he went with him," answered the wife.

"Who?" asked he.

"Tyagi ji," mother helped.

Chhatrapal 35, until a few years ago was an Army Captain and now a farmer in tatters. Last season the produce had fetched almost a treasure but this year it was only a tiny yield–he was devasted – "I must find a right crop," the pensive farmer gushed.

Assembly constituency Panipat Rural had just recently held its Panchayat elections which were intensely fought with a sense of urgency. An election atmosphere like this was never witnessed in any Panchayati election. It saw heavy usage of money and muscle power which were used to fiercely fight, an eyeball-to-eyeball campaign which resulted in violence on the polling day. As a result, the region and its people were left to grapple with fragile peace. Father Sahoo Sigh was victorious, the third time, thanks to his age-old goodwill and integrity.

"Baapu need not indulge any further… high time… politics has hardly done good to any." Anxious he was almost running to the other end of the village where the panchayat office was situated at. And it was certainly rare to find a *Jat* concerned for safety. State's polity since the 2014 General Election, and more significant later in the years, changed owing to BJP's landslide victory in Assembly Elections. *Jats* have always been the ruling class dominating politics at all levels. Most of the state chief ministers have been *Jats*.

A Punjabi, in the thirteenth state assembly, for the first time and many predicted that for the last time too, became states Chief Minister heading the first-ever BJP government. Political experts and social scientists termed that as a start of a political era when castes might start playing a significant polarising role in Haryana electoral which had never been exhibited. The 2016 March *Jat Aarakshan Andolan* riots turned this fear into a social underpinning. All contests and the campaigns would thence be motivated by.

The polity of the state had thus taken a fierce, eyeball-to-eyeball, round-the-clock verbal, visual, pervasive contest.

Farmers in large numbers, by the time he reached, had begun to gather at the Panchayat Office. The news had spread like wildfire. This young farmer of Bawani Khurd was not curious to know the genesis. District Panipat's Deputy Commissioner was on the dais. An address was expected to start any time when Chhattar stepped inside the large hall with his eyes scanning front rows desperate to locate Baapu.

Dais was a temporarily built structure consisting of three or four wooden *takht* (large bed like bench), laid next to each other with no gap in between them. These were covered by a red and white carpet omnipresent in every Harynavi *byah* (marriage). A few plastic chairs in a line placed some feet from the wall, with a small table in front.

Occupants were staff from the Collector's Office. BJP's representation of the State government was through a few cadres. Some policemen were in the company behind and on either side of the dais. In front of the dais were a few rows of plastic chairs, followed by many farmers standing eager to know the crux. The first row had the eminent ones purposefully invited; among others was his father - the frail - die-hard Congress veteran Sahoo Singh, clad in stainless white kurta payjama and shining black jutti.

"Price per acre will be decided later," shouts and the context welcomed his ears as he entered in the large hall, "Faujji, you must be knowing," someone enquired, "what does Sahoo reckon?". He ignored as always, lurching furtively, zigzagging his way towards the dais.

The announcement began gingerly. Deputy Commissioner sounded reluctant, body language was fearful, expression was staid, the tone was monotonous, and his tongue was grappling to utter right words.

"In the Masterplan 2024, this area has been identified for industrial purpose. Industries are to be set up here, which will produce equipment for our armed forces. For years this land has produced farmers and soldiers, this land has satisfied hunger and served armed forces."

"What is the price that the government will give for an acre?" someone jumped the gun, was too curious to wait and wanted to know the windfall size.

Many in the crowd and on their toes waiting for this moment agreed. Their voices in chorus demanded the essence be announced first, rest are merely the details no one was interested in.

In the front row:

"Ram-Ram Inderjeet, finally our MLA could find an excuse to visit us."

BJP MLA from Panipat rural constituency, Inderjeet Singh had just entered with a large entourage in toe.

"Jai Shri Ram Sahoo and I am sure my people are happy to see their Sevak."

"Nah...they are feeling blessed, guess a few words are in order of a minute?" Sahoo said, looking towards to the struggling speaker, "don't you think it is a waste of energy and our time."

"Well, plenty to think I guess, and time shouldn't be an excuse, a year later Sahoo. 2019 is just a few months away," smirking MLA replied.

"Nah Inderjeet India is just not shining."

"Rural India is shining," patted back of one of sarpanch aide, "Ask them whether they any longer feed pigs every morning. Pucca latrine they relieve themselves in, if you don't know."

"I feel for pigs...I wonder what they live on now...stray cows in abundance too... a war is raging in the fields."

"General election will slay competition... once and for all," said the BJP MLA before swiftly ascending on the dais as the address was going on unabated.

"Now, this land will produce what is needed to let our soldiers fight with the best equipment. On this noble occasion let me ask for everyone's help," the commissioner said, "we need to make this process easy and fast for everyone."

"Land belongs to farmers, first right is reserved with them," Sarpanch Sahoo Singh intervened, "So, they must be heard first commissioner. And, I only heard of a Railway freight corridor," he asked, smiling.

"Committee has been formed keeping the interest of the farmers only Sahoo ji," commissioner replied.

"And yet we get to hear for the first time this master plan!"

"Our office and central ministry had the information dully made public through announcements in the newspapers," the voice was made up to sound and facial expressions to look surprised.

"Newspapers like the national dailies, commissioner sahib, who reads the English ones? I saw one of them. Too little information - perhaps could only serve the purpose of the rumours."

"Still, you find me here, with earnest intent that all can witness themselves."

"Committee is to visit very soon and will hear everyone's opinion."

"I want, my people must be apprised the details by the committee first before the committee can come here and do the necessary recce."

"I will do my best to arrange for the same, yet I can at best try, the final decision will be conveyed to us."

"My farmers are not at the mercy of any committee-," a frail voice thundered.

But was cut short, "Pranaam Sahoo ji," BJP MLA took the position next to Deputy Commissioner.

Curious and thus silent so far, the crowd had multiple opinions in shapes and mediums - whispers, murmurs were going up a notch every second.

MLA hand nudged the officer from the side, the commissioner swiftly hopped two steps back.

"*Prannam bhaaiyon,*" the voice was commanding Chhatrapal adjudged, requisite attention was brought about and effectively that very moment.

"*Inderjeet ka pranaam,*" murmurs faded, "Modi Sarkar since day 1 has been committed to the welfare of the Farmers," few were impressed though, "Be it farm insurance, be it loans at subsidised rates, be it Minimum Support Price-".

"APMC act implementation is 'The-Way-Forward' MLA, a wheat farmer needs consistent MSP," shouted one from the crowd.

Wheat and Rice are the major crops grown here. Haryana is self-sufficient in food production and the second largest contributor to India's central pool of food grains. MLA tried to calm the protesting voice down "*Mandi* is open and operational day and night bhaiyon. And Modi Sarkar is making all the arrangements."

"Aadhtis are a nuisance, payments are hard to come by," a voice complained.

"We are…"

"Payments take months to reach us," another from the back shouted cutting MLA short.

"And that too in installments," many voices then shouted in chorus.

"MLA Ji, if the government is so serious about us the farmers, what is the need to take away the lands?" some first-row occupants raised the opposing view and agenda of the day.

"At least some insurance will be at our disposal and we can use it to fall back upon," Chhatrapal murmured.

"No one is taking away any one's land," MLA made a timely retreat, "Only the agreed ones will have their lands taken away and be paid *Ati-Uchit Muavja* (fitting compensation)," signalling the assistant to do something.

A haphazard map with abstract details was hung on the wall quickly the next moment, mindful of not covering the leadership faces in the backdrop.

"Look at this," said the MLA pointing at the map, "Master plan envisages only select few areas," eyes penetrating at Sahoo Singh, "We are not others," staring at the veteran congress worker, "who are after whatsoever they could have from the bottom up to the top and not before the thirst of near and dear ones is satisfied too."

The message was clear. Some chuckled, music to ears in power, MLA hoped to have instilled the finality now. Sarpanch was up in a dash. "Bhaaiyon, land bill 2014 waapis aa gaya hai!! (Land bill 2014 is back)" The timing had a much-needed effect to tame the tempo.

MLA was taken aback.

"The Year 2014, ordinance after ordinance were brought out to bring to effect this slavery bill yet they could not defeat the people's will in the parliament," looking back straight into the MLA's eyes, "nor they could on the streets and in the farms."

"This is diverting tactics, my brothers," MLA retorted at the top of his voice, "State governments in the consultation with farmers are authorised to carry out any land acquisition. Land bill is history!!!"

"Land bill was abandoned - they left it - BJP had to!!" Sarpanch thundered, "farmers will not be crushed, farmers have neither let you do that on the floor of parliament or outside and same will be the result here!"

"Party is working to fulfill every wish," response was quickly hurled in, "as I said," MLA took two steps aside to bring himself face to face with the farmers, stepping out of the confrontation he was fast losing, "Only whosoever agrees, will be part of this grand welfare scheme."

"Welfare scheme?" Sarpanch followed him to the side of the dais, "Land taken away can only take a farmer to doomsday."

"Every acre will fetch *muaavjaa* (compensation)… that too as decided by market prevailing rates on the day of signing. It is not me," wearing a sweet smile, "or some officer will decide… nah!"

Murmurs were back and made MLA believe, a lot were curious to hear the details.

"The map can guide you about the potential areas," MLA encouraged and now cajoled, "Not every farmer will have to necessarily agree. if not at least some number of farmers are willing - this scheme will be rolled back and instead be offered to the adjacent region of the state," penetrating the Sarpanch's eyes, and challenging, "but farmers will not be overlooked."

"Is it the final map?" the Sarpanch etched his next move.

"Committee is working on the finalization - this is just a draft!"

"Then what's the guarantee here that only shown areas will be included, and what's the point of basing your entire message on this mere draft?"

MLA could not afford to fumble, at the very crucial moment moved to the centre of the stage, "Potential areas…um…as I said multiple times over most likely to be the finalized ones."

"Okay…let's say…" old man swiftly ascended onto the dais. Lathi in the right hand was now pointing to the most interesting area on the hanging big size map, "You are right. Your Sarkar even honest…"

"And transparent!" MLA interjected, both hands out pointing towards the crowd.

"Zaroor-zaroor it is for the people," Sarpanch added as he began to prepare the final salvo.

"For the people, for the common man, for the farmers," MLA's voice was up by two notes.

"Sabka Vikas, right?!" Sarpanch added.

"Sabka Saath Sabka Vikas, it is for the welfare our country and everyone will benefit," a BJP MLA corrected him.

"So why do the lands around the highway and the railway line appear in your map and that too for 1 km on both sides," veteran shouted waving the lathi towards the designated areas.

For a second or two, BJP MLA was speechless.

"Mere bhaiyon, which industry requires 1 km wide lands and that's too only on either side of the railway line and highway?" energy lifted the otherwise a frail body, "why not next to the oil refinery?!" The famous Panipat refinery was being referred to.

"If constructed there, all the required logistics would be found in place. The first and foremost need of transportation is already operational and effective," eyes attempting to reach all the onlooking pairs, "even tens of vacant plots reserved for industrial needs from during the time refinery was build can be availed!"

Then turning towards and addressing the MLA, "If so, what is the need for fresh land then?!!"

Turning to the audience and then in a swift move to centre of the dais, he stopped midway little dramatically, his eyes were scanning the audience and he was just waiting to clasp at the right moment. Letting curiosity attain the zenith and he yelled- "This is a LOOT and a PLUNDER mere bhaiyon…2014 land bill…2014 land bill has footprints are all over it!" voice at its highest pitch, lathi dangling, "this is the first step in the grand scheme…" and then he countered eyeballs of the rival with penetrating glare face beaming in confidence, "…Grand Scheme of BJP!"

Murmurs were back…louder and abound. MLA looked sideways, some aid was needed and needed fast. Party cadre…aide… vociferously chatted trying to assess the best point and way out of this. The opponent had scored, their leader had been embarrassed.

Deputy commissioner swiftly stepped in, "There are legal obligations to fulfill, those plots next to the refinery are allotted ones, many of the allotters have submitted the proposal to avail the SEZ benefits, we have a number of factories already under review and will be set up."

"And that is why we have this plan - the party does not harm citizens of this country," MLA supplemented.

"We have no objection", the voice had come from the first row. One in his forties, donning a *laal topi* emerged, "if these areas are selected, especially those adjacent to railway lines this will benefit the community we have devoted our lives for the welfare of," person belonged to a political outfit known to aid and have terms with pro-Muslim national parties and was perceived as pro-Muslim.

The region was situated around the Yamuna, one side falling in Haryana the other one in Uttar Pradesh. Not many were happy at the intervention. "How much of the land do they own in those areas?" Chhatrapal mumbled, startled, "to claim and be representative of?!". Amidst the eyebrows, growing every second, a man with laal topi added, "Sabkaa Saath Sabka Vikas," smirking, "Would you not be hearing the marginalized ones Sahoo Ji?!"

CHAPTER 2

Another week passed and the usual agony started again.

She was standing at the bus early in the morning., In the mist known and unknown faces she planned to catch the sole morning bus between Bawani Khurd of Bharat and Gurugram of India. The hundred km journey seemed rather an eternity. Seats were easily available; the struggle was to start afterwards.

Eve teasing has many contours. And on a crowded bus, they unleash multiple facades. Sapna Singh was wary. In India, the females have learnt to circumvent the usual volleys and regular attempts of eve-teasing. A few men already had their eyes revolving around. Female sixth sense had sensed and had spotted potential troublemakers.

This young lady in her mid-20s took the seat in the second row from the front door. Senses had her wrapped with the best poise they could, the sitting posture being the most disciplined one and that did the heavy lifting. The bus took its course carefully.

And, she began to divide her attention between the stares and the weary mind's constant nudges forcing her to reassess her path and the way forward - something that she would do a zillion times every day.

'Chacko could be the next, or...may be... Zuber?' She wasn't sure who could be next between her colleagues at Billysoft. 'It's been a year, even after performing steadily she was not thorough with the work and technology,' she craved for the possibility, 'Could I be among the front-runners next year... nah?' to be away and be in some foreign city is common greed amongst the Indian ITiens - the large aspiring middle class feels the awe of - a few million, the quintessential cogwheels of the world's software services powerhouse.

"Gurgamma?! - EK? (one ticket?)" voice pierced her thoughts. Haryana roadways conductors are men-in-hurry. "Ji – ek (one)," said she, handing over a hundred rupees note.

Friends, relatives, neighbours, everyone seemed to doubt her calibre. 'Perhaps she is shooting too far, isn't she?!' was a common expression ridiculing her all the time. For her while the start was always a foregone conclusion, she wanted the continuity to be sustained, and 'Would she be able to?' An abrupt end would be her worst nightmare, something that her dreamy countenance kept a promised distance with.

"So beti - It means BPO naa?" another day, another acquaintance and old nuisance.

"It-IT!!" some million-pound sound effect was gushed out.

"Uh- the same thing beti."

"IT is an altogether different industry. It is NOT BPO."

"Ya - Bill Gates banegi. (You know she is the next Bill Gates)" Sarcasm rural Haryana is utterly apt at and jibes are always in plenty.

It was certainly an irritating hour that day could start with.

Shortly an hour elapsed, and the bus now was overloaded brimming over with occupants, her senses noticed subconsciously - they made another quick recce around.

Conservative family, rural life, social conservative strictures for women had turned her to what she was that day. Post her primary education in the village, she did her secondary education from a nearby city. Permission from the patriarchy was hard to come by. Some similar strife from other villages and Ma unyielding underpinning paved the way eventually. Staying away, in the hostel, she completed her graduation.

And now in Billysoft, she wanted to make the best of the start - even if it meant some hook was necessary. Her face would have a determined look and apparent earnest desire - she again reminded herself and would so many times over day and day after.

'Ah!' She felt a hand - a hand at her side, fingers scrabbling, groping. She swung herself around and gave it all she could muster, daring the offender at the top of her voice,'"Apni Ma ke kade haath laaya sae? (ever tried touching your mother's?)"

It was a blot, came out hard and at lightning speed, the offender was almost on the floor - slap had the raw strength that a Haryanavi girl is known for.

The bus screeched to a halt the very next moment. The tormentor shamed, scrambling for leeway crushing everyone between him and the exit, was out in no time and sprinting. Disgraced and never to attempt again. The sincere eyes following him flee could only presume.

For a minute or two, crushingly slow, she felt nowhere. Her senses battered, she lost control of her being. To be proud of one's decisive act–this feeling was no longer was anew. The agony of dealing with these, every other day, had lately begun to be the sole after-effect instead. 'Must get back to be where you have to be,' she reminded herself.

A few old people came to her support, "Koi baat naa beti - ye kutte toh marange (have faith, they will die a dog's death)." The Prying eyes around were still unaffected and followed every move as her body

A young lady was devastated, but for only a minute and to come back and retain her ascendency - she was not to lose, give up - Indian females can't -they have to go on with her journey.

A few hours later, at Billysoft, in Gurugram:

The Kick-off meeting for the project of the year had the agenda to lay out a rosy project plan, which will be optimal to describe, rosy to incite–It was better to delay the inevitable - a fraught project and a dejected customer. He had adopted the style to breeze through kick-offs, the fifth year in this avatar he was now experienced enough to manoeuvre the tricks of the trade. A cursory glance was necessary - boss appeared easy so far, which was an encouraging sign to continue with the adapted facade - sooner the meeting ends better will be the objective met. 500K USD was at stake, the customer had hired the best consulting service Billysoft, the investment made sense, guaranteeing top of the box–ROI. A few on the customer side, thus, were excited and overly so. Consultants could sense and smile to each other, 'Not the first one to get trapped in, guys!' They jumped the line to tell their experiences and consultants must take a leaf out of their book. Their expression made it clear. The smiles on the other side could only get wider. In awe of the famous vendor was the culprit to cause this spontaneity, they pitied.

The seasoned ones were the manager and the director SK who yielded the best consultancy words, reassuring to the wise ones across, and the customer geared back. Proud and stupid were the mumblings, one more tapped, curtains were drawn, pleasantries exchanged!

Little later:

The Project Manager had a team meeting scheduled last week. He was in the meeting room and was the first one to arrive as always. The team had begun to gather - Zuber Malik, Chacko, Sapna Singh, one after the other, and in the end, came Naved.

Zuber would not sit next to the lady. Kashmiri always found it hard to bear the dour of her sweat of the lady. As he could not appreciate the trouble an average rural bhartiya undertakes to reach urban India and become part of that room. But they complemented each other.

She frowned a Muslim's presence - his dress up - round white topi, beard, and ankle-length patloon (trousers)- was intimidating to her, 'He must learn to lead as Naved does,' who was rather a modern Muslim to her eyes.

"Kick-Off meeting went okay," and the manager began his brief, "and in the next 2 days we are supposed to get over with the first round of requirements gathering and related discussion."

"Anant, if you can please pass on the customer contact details?" Senior coder Chacko requested.

"Hmm…bulls eye, let me send you now," the manager quickly typed the message and added, "we all must be wary of schedule and as always stringent," eyes penetrating towards the wards, "any delay at any point in time must be brought to my attention right away."

All faces nodded in affirmative.

"Sent…his name is David…sounded a tough one."

"Who would lead from our end?" experienced coder yet a newcomer in Billysoft, Zuber asked.

"David has preferred to engage with me at this stage. Shortly, we shall have team composition decided, don't worry."

Certainly not music to his ears, so gingerly, "I have lead team from onsore once for UK customer, so…"

"So?" snapped the manager.

"I will be available to offer the best of my experience," the newcomer said wearing a smile.

"No doubt as we all have to," the manager looked away.

"Schedule has quite limited time allocated to the first phase," Chacko commented.

"To win the contract, the sales team had to cut corners."

"Hmmm. Can we have the analysis started as early as we could?" asked the most experience and the best amongst all reporting to Anant.

"Yes please, the practice head has been notified already."

"Thanks, his help would come handy."

"We are a team," manager reiterated the routine IT slogan, and asked, "So when can we have the draft ready?"

Members searched for the perfect answer, "Functional Specification Document - right?!" excited Zuber pitched in.

"Or would you give me the code itself?!" manager pierced as the team almost burst into a giggle.

"Anant is talking about the deliverable of this phase and yes the Functional Specification Doc," said Chacko.

She was keen to know him, her eyes were noticing the things she was eager about - his soft skills, body language, the content he has to offer in all the meetings - amazing isn't it? 'And looks?' voice inside her prodded, 'shut up!' yet she confessed, 'not bad!'.

"Every week we shall have two meetings. So, bi-weekly we all are meeting to monitor the progress - Way to Go!" said the manager wrapping the notes.

"Definitely Anant," all responded in one voice.

The lunch break had arrived, in groups, all headed in the basement grand cafeteria.

Zuber would sit somewhere near to Naved, he felt an urge to know him.

Girls would notice a never-changing demeanour of the new joinee Sapna, who had just spent a few months in Billysoft.

Chacko was determined to top it all, to be in front, and be the flag bearer for the managers.

She was alert, to her needs...no... aggressively in knowing her wants. Her demeanour would never change, who would know the genesis was an urge - a burning urge, kept infuriated by everyday struggle, the emotional trauma of still being subjected to typical rural social onslaughts she should have escaped long back given now she was an earning hand and earning in a city - yet to come back every week and bear the touch, the stares, someone prying everyone corner of the city? And to top them all - An omnipresent look on all and sundry claim she is one of them and will always be.

Morning episode had of course not shaken her, but she was certainly getting tired.

"You hail from?" asked Zuber, with naughty eyes.

"Hyderabad," Naved replied, "You seem new to Billysoft?"

"Yes, joined only last month."

"Good, glad to meet you. Kashmir must be beautiful, I heard a lot, someday would like to visit."

"Yes, it is indeed. Otherwise, why would two nations fight?"

A bit unconvincing argument to many in attendance.

"You live in Srinagar?" Naved asked.

"Yes, downtown Srinagar," Zuber replied.

"Awesome."

"How is it nowadays?" asked the young lady.

"As ever – beautiful!" Kashmiri uttered emphatically.

"I mean - militancy still around?" she queried further.

"Street fight as was the case in the 90s and until 2003, is not the case now but you never know."

"Yes, the coalition government does not look too stable," Naved commented.

"Blame BJP and their right-wing polity," Kashmiri sounded firm.

Naved said, "I guess, it is more to do with the historical backdrop and reasons."

"If you occupy an area and play with the lives of the people - things could hardly be peaceful and both played mercilessly," the voice was two notes higher and intense.

"Both who?" the youngster asked.

"Pakistan and India," Zuber snapped.

None said anything. A few moments passed by. Chacko kept on eating showing no interest.

"Your Hyderabad and my Kashmir were alike once," Kashmiri nudged.

"Hyderabad? like Kashmir?" The Muslim from Hubli swiftly wore the mask of ignorance.

"India occupied by force." Eyes static, gaze piercing, fellow-Muslim felt caged.

"What about PoK?" retorted the young Jat lady.

He ignored. "One born in the valley is a Kashmiri, not an Indian." Incessant gaze was still following the captive soul.

There was a sense of invincibility in his tongue, body language, his facial expressions. The Indians were taken aback by his bragging expressions - she felt insulted. He was either smiling or smirking or perhaps both. 'He can read us. Our faces are revealing our mind right now,' young firebrand cautioned herself.

Chacko was conspicuous by his silence. He had kept eating all that while unaffected. 'Country does not exist for many.' She seethed.

"Is that so bad?" Naved shouldered ingenuity.

"What are you doing here then?" agitated young lady snapped.

"Gandhi, Nehru, Patel - what they were doing in the UK? Were advocates in the UK - had their careers in the commonwealth," Zuber retorted.

"They were not murdering people," Young lady snapped.

His eyes widened. Plain talk from a rural girl was the last thing he had expected.

"Am I?" said Kashmiri with a half-grin, "Glorifying the invaders and the militants alike."

Shrugging she said, "I don't know."

He shrugged. He found straight talk quite unsettling, "We have seen people dying, community losing generation after generation, you cannot feel the agony of being at the receiving end of everyday harassment and life becomes a joke."

She wouldn't take any of that, "Vajpayee, just before reaching Wagah, in his bus journey to Lahore received a message that 28 Hindus have been gunned down by terrorists in Jammu & Kashmir. Agonised he wondered whether there was any point in further tasks, yet he persevered."

"A joke or gossip…and look who is talking…" both arms straightened out and towards the young lady, "They need reservations…and…um…they can kill you…um…in broad daylight…you know…muscle power dictating terms!"

"Reservation is our right!" Jat lady thundered.

"Jats arm-twisted government…uh…well here we are lucky enough," sipping tea in haste Kashmiri seemed a jittery figure, "that it is not anybody's right to just start demanding and be on an onsite sojourn the next day…you know…just like that!"

"At least not up for a free run by Mulla and militants to get slaughtered and become refugees in their own country" she retorted.

"Pandits were the minority. As always and in every riot a demography number game rather, whichever side has the larger population is eventually the winner," commented Naved.

"Genocide...what happened to Kashmiri Pandits in 1989/1990 wasn't just rioting," Chacko broke his silence.

"No rights for the crestfallen, reservation?? we must be joking...republic turned its back on Pandits," youngster was speaking her mind unabated.

"They can come back...Kashmir is their home," snapped Kashmiri.

"There is no Article 370 for it to become their reservation!"

"370 is our right!" he yelled.

"Kashmir is Pandits' land and right too...you have seized it...370 made it definite - for Kashmiri Muslims its shelter and for Pandits - an imposed exclusion."

"Or a necessary exodus...the night of 19th Jan 1990," Chacko complimented.

"Good knowledge Sapna," remarked Naved getting up, "hope you have equally good skills in coding?"

Chacko stood up too.

She ensured tongue did not wag - wasn't prudent to take on the heavyweights, looked on as both seniors swiftly walked out.

No more words were spoken, it was time to get back and resume the everyday sustenance.

Over on the 5th floor, minutes later:

"Whom would you pick?" asked Director.

SK and manager Anand had little time now left before the project would be in full swing yet team formation was far from complete.

"Naved," answered Anant.

"Naved? Hmmm... okay...but why not the other guy?" queried the director.

"Chacko is needed to lead. At offshore team members look up to him. Naved's technical knowhow and associated brilliance are needed in the 1st phase to win over customer confidence. He cannot lead the team," Project manager Anant justified.

"Okay, but we need to ensure the team can deliver the quality customer expects," director SK cautioned.

"Chacko's unmatched technical skills will be the surety," Anant tried to give a satisfactory reply.

"I perhaps would have preferred Chacko to go, he is calm, composed - technically first-rate!" remarked SK.

"He will be needed to see us through the most turbulent period of the initial phase - once the project enters the midlife phase," Anant said.

"By then you will have to ensure the team is groomed enough to work according to the instructions and directions received from Chacko, who will be at on-site," SK suggested.

"Precisely SK the reason why I'm keeping him here. Naved will see us through now during the first phase and later Chacko's first-rate skills as you said," replied Anant.

Director suggested further, "You ought to see Anant if we can have someone from the team - anyone from the youngsters to backfill if any team member is absent for a considerable period."

"My contingency planning has so far zeroed on Zuber..." Anand shared, but he was cut short.

"Neither is he young, nor he has proven himself," director objected.

The manager realized he has hurried. He had for sure gotten impressed with newcomer's profile.

"Handing him baton will make many believe we have lost faith in the abilities of those who have been around for so many years," director cautioned the manager further.

"My bad, one-two youngsters have shown promise," said Anant.

"There you are!"

"Thanks, SK for your time," said Anant stepping out as the very next moment he hurried onto the war room.

The newly formed team had begun to gather The manager was keeping an eye out to spot any teething problem every inception suffers from and an IT project as well.

"Had your lunch...team? how was it?"

A beaming project manager's face greeted the project members in the first team meeting.

"We managed," many said in a chorus and somewhat shy fully.

"Great, so let me get to the agenda…" said manager getting up and stepping close to whiteboard, "no time to waste."

All settled in, some around the table, a few chose to stand. The war room was now full to the capacity.

"Naved will be…" The manager started his brief, "off to New Jersey, early next month." He was standing straight, his palms clasped against each other.

Some were surprised and one was hurt – Kashmiri. He argued to the inner self – 'I am new, it was expected.'

"Get your tickets done. Travel desk has already been cautioned," the manager continued his brief, "We have less than three weeks in our hands."

"I will Anant," Naved nodded.

"Next…" he stopped and let a few moments pass, looking over to faces if there was any curiosity - a question - none was spotted so he announced emphatically, "Chacko will lead the project!"

None were surprised. If Naved was to be away, who else but Chacko would be the one.

Anant looked around one more time and everyone nodded.

Work must impress, she decided that moment; put in all efforts, strive hard yet be close to lead, may come handy; not that she did not like him.

She had an irresistible exterior. This, five-feet-seven-inches lass from the Haryana heartland. Until she would speak, and every utterance would giveaway her rustic rural background. A look-down-upon expression would follow replacing the recent awe destroying her self-esteem. Wasn't a hindrance? One she was most conscious and sorry about, to anyone and everyone in this world boasting off a gorgeous presence as one young lady commanded? She would ask wondering, only to come back, 'What I will not let it, to bog me down and down to a low that to even forget how killing looks and a figure I have and stop me being spontaneous every time an opportunity passes by for me to impress, and prevail over so to step on to the next pedestal. After all, I'm here with a purpose - right Sapna?'

A non-discrete a regular kind of next-door-guy, Anant had to strive hard to get to the place he was in. No, there wasn't anything spectacular about it - just that a lot many could not hailing from the same abode, pinned down constrained by always thriving set of social-economic-patriarchy mindset hurdles.

He was driving back home later in the day. The consultants and the manager had gotten through the kick-off meeting with certainty.

Etched in his memory were the episodes and a few sentences in particular, '71 was an eye-opener!'

"How?" the popular Pakistani social media video portal hostess asked.

"Always, since childhood times, we looked forward to going to Pakistan once stable with careers," a second class citizen and perceived victim from India said.

He shrugged his thoughts, tuned into his favourite FMs - the Sarkari ones - simple, steady, low-on-voice-volume yet more meaningful. Social messages were the order of that minute alternatively played with 70's Kishore and Asha songs. Builder party had the largest share of advertisement, rest made sense - highway driving best practices sought his attention – since it was Hindi, almost Shuddh, 'devoid of any Hindustani words,' he liked. That message was soon over and was a beautiful one.

He was forced to think, 'how many would have been touched?! After all language does impress you, you identify with it, no? A Delhi Punjabi wouldn't relish a message in Shuddh Hindi - Am I not correct?'

'Which language would you identify and be impressed with?'

He had no clue, scrubbing left him dry, 'no language he could identify with - Haryanvi never belonged to them since he was always an outsider for them - the purbiyaa - chaawal kaa aadmi.'

'Hindustani?!' inner being scrubbed further.

'Do I belong to Pakistan?' he almost yelled.

Anant grandparents migrated from Pakistan during the partition days.

'From when did Hindustani become only form Pakistan?' pertinence was scary.

'This is the irony of these times,' he retorted reckoned.

'Are you sure?' one inside prodded.

'Time for a quest for Identity and pertinence perhaps,' he gushed.

'A sojourn?' equally optimistic in parallel, was the inner being.

'A quandary,' now he was sure.

'A journey,' inside one snapped.

He stood corrected – overwhelmed yet hardened evermore! The journey of our times thence. He felt assured, reassuring has been the Right events since May 2014 and the optimism on Left in its last leg, so he chose to stay with the journey - the Beginning.

'History and Civics' textbook of 7th standard was staring at him or, so he thought. Doorbell rang. It was his sister, Patanjali with her lovely children in the company. 7th grader was ecstatic to see his sisters at home and in no time, the commotion was the order in the 3-bhk. Patanjali slumped in the corner sofa. Anant was sitting on the couch at the opposite end.

Teji, Anant's wife, took the seat next to Patanjali.

Teji, a school teacher, started the conversation, "I overheard yesterday Shruti calling on Choudhary Ma'am - Akbar needs to be taught perfectly."

And I said to myself, "As if only Akbar and Mughals form the entire history, what about Ashok, Harshvardhana and other Hindu rajas, kingdom, and empires."

"They are powerful Teji," said Patanjali in disappointment.

"Who?!" Teji asked.

"Leftists have long overshadowed our academia," Patanjali remarked.

"There must have been campaigns in academic circles, in government executive, no?" Teji was curious.

"For?!" asked Patanjali with her eyes seemingly lost in oblivion.

"To bring about a change - the lopsided history text cannot escape learned eyes for 70 years, right?" Teji said.

"As I said - they are powerful, not many could take on them, whosoever had guts eventually paid the price."

Patanjali Kapoor was a Humanities professor. The late upheaval in him - yes that's what Anant ascribed this phenomenon to -, he had been going through and will last forever he firmly believed - to the leftist wrongdoings. The anecdotes of everyday university staff room. How the leftists dominate and how the meek ones - the majority - give in without a fight - right or wrong doesn't matter. Some are in awe. Some do not wish to be in the line of fire. Others the practical ones would rather prefer to stick to the job.

"A project is being submitted, needs a name of an IT industry professional to be eligible and be able to submit and..." she was cut short.

"And a brother is the convenient choice!" taunted Anant.

"For all and sundry - I am not the sole culprit," sister smiled.

All smiled.

Not much into the conversation, the subject made it the way was the most talked about these days. Anti-India propaganda since ages - courtesy leftists, liberals, and the eternal meek Hindus who are too ashamed of their roots, could never strive to explore the remarkable aspects of the gigantic history.

"Lynching incidents are stains, India is grappling to cope with and come clean in the international arena," Anant remarked.

"These have been going on for ages Anant," Patanjali said in a straight voice.

"Yet, a demographically diverse nation can only ill afford it," Anant argued.

"A flash here and a flash there in media cannot generalize the issue," There was a resolve in her voice.

"Bottomline is, let me sound practical here for a moment, they are raising far too many eyebrows in international media and us-"

Brother was cut short, "This could be your assessment, this country has seen the worse."

"And we are achieving what - a handful of culprits? - that cannot be the difference," Anant tried to defend.

"Change is very hard to come by." sister Patanjali said firmly

"Given the size…you mean?" asked Anant.

"Precisely," she answered in a calm voice.

"That's the whole point," Anant said.

"Yet, while I am not for any lynching, there is a message to be sent - plunder cannot continue, and as the majority remain mute spectators."

Greater Noida areas, where the family hails from, are infamous for buffalo smuggling. Within hours of buffalo jacking beef is produced and packed for potential markets - a trend which has encountered bumps allegedly since BJP seated in power in 2014.

"Still their continuation cannot be ruled out," sister observed.

"An end to it is necessary," Teji felt strongly about the whole issue.

"It still goes on," sister lamented, her face glowing in rage.

Anant was thinking hard, perhaps the most affected of them all, said,

"Could society find a way?"

"You cannot, no one has been able to," Patanjali's irate face across seemed to instil the foresight.

He felt helpless, all are helpless, he felt tired, of this feeling, "A majoritarian feeling cannot be so tame," he gushed out.

"Hindus and evidently meek," sister said disappointedly.

All pensive, silence loomed over, broken now and then by three energetic in the vicinity.

Teji tried to change the subject, "Anant was telling me now a university cab has begun to pick you in the morning and drops back in the afternoon?"

"Yes Teji, and that's a convenience I utterly needed." replied Patanjali.

"Does it get crowded. I mean if there are five to sit?" Teji asked further.

"It does, I prefer to take the front seat. Crowding merely at times, unlike the agony of all travels -" Patanjali seemingly pointed to something troubling her.

"And what's that?" Teji turned curious.

"The one from the elite community, in fact, a few and they are not the only ones." Patanjali said in a straight voice.

The last sentence jerked Anant out of his thoughts, "What's with that?"

"He is quite vocal," her face still failing to conceal the aftereffects of some incident.

"About what?" Anant was turning too curious to wait any further.

Patanjali took a minute or two to gather her thoughts, recalled the subtle parts, began narrating a few moments after. 'Our university has been renowned as you know,' She began describing.

'Yes, we do.'

'And the best shelters for returned diaspora is to seek shelter. I mean livelihood is these knowledge campuses,' she said further.

The couple was all ears.

"For the last five years or so, there are only a few jobs on offer in the west particularly in America," she continued.

"Times are changing," the IT professional knew it the best.

"So, we have a few with us now, to deal with every day, meekness I lament about, of my fellow countrymen – no one dares to confront them,' Patanjali continued

"Okay, but what happened in your cab en route?" Anant was turning too curious.

She continued, "One fine morning, while on the way to university, we all came to know about Muzaffarnagar incident."

"The stone pelting on Ramnavami procession?" Teji asked.

"Yes, the driver had his kin caught in rioting and was in the hospital; he was away for a few days and had returned to duty that day."

"I feel for him," Anant said.

Patanjali continued, "We were 5 in the cab - a recently arrived professor from Bengal; one from Delhi; My department colleague Rekha and I, all being driven by a local Gurjar."

Teji meanwhile went inside to bring order in the ensuing commotion.

Patanjali continued, "This Delhi's elite gentleman voiced his approval, proclaimed – they were planning to take out a procession."

"For what?' I asked."

"'For the Hindu rioting that took place afterwards.' Elite said."

"'But then stone pelting was done by the other community,' I said."

Patanjali continued narrating the incident While Anant was all agog.

"They were some elements, hooligans you know." Elite countered.

"'How can you be so sure?' I was rather surprised at his blatant claim," Patanjali said.

"This is the modus operandi of right-wing polity, you don't know," elite said firmly.

"I countered him," Patanjali said, "What you and we know is the amalgamation of news reports, you cannot be so sure."

"'Yes, I am sure,' he almost shouted."

"'Bengali co-passenger intervened at that juncture, 'Or you have distorted?'"

"'Distorted what?' Elite thundered."

"'The truth.' Bengali snapped."

"'And what is that?' asked Elite."

Patanjali continued narrating the incident and the heated conversation.

"'That it was stone pelting by minority community which triggered the violence as per the news reports,' Professor from Bengal answered in a poised tongue."

"'You are going by reports - half the time a by-product of fake news,' Elite pitched in, in a note or two higher."

"'You cannot hide behind excuses,' Bengali tried to conclude."

"'Elite went back to from where he started, 'These are dark times.'"

Patanjali continued narrating the incident.

"'We still reserve the right to protest, as we will,' said Elite."

"'Right? you must be joking,' said Bengali. The gentleman did not want to appear lame or so I assumed Anant."

"'The constitution of India preserves our rights and we will,' said the Elite."

"'You will what?' Bengali had begun to get utterly rattled now."

"'We WILL protest!' leftist thundered - eyes burning!"

"Bengali thundered back addressing us the ladies and the Gurjar, 'Look who is talking!' pausing for few moments, 'Joke of the day,' and he gushed out, 'CONVERTS will protest!"

"Jibe turned the thundering leftist's perseverance into non-ending mumblings- 'We came from Iran, my ancestors you know? We have our roots elsewhere, we do not belong to this place, do not count us with a meagre percentile, we are from East, you know - you must know - Iran and the sacred land I hail from...'"

"Colleagues of the Elite appeared to call it quits when a shell bombed them all as the most unprecedented thing happened."

Patanjali stopped narrating the incident momentarily.

"Cab came to a sudden halt, next minute Anant. I could notice something is in the making."

"Gurjar turned around and asked, 'So when are you going back to your east?' in a tone best understood by the outsiders - Elite was bundled into his shell – hit to the core, observed Patanjali completing the narration.

"And the Bengali?" asked a curious Anant.

"He had the guts," Patanjali remarked.

"Yes, I am surprised too…not many can be so straight and blunt." Anant agreed.

"I reckon need of the hour." said Patanjali taking a long deep breath.

He felt otherwise, the need of the hour is to bring the truth out, and by the best means, travelling the most distances, to an average household, the truth must travel and the fastest now.

He began to ponder over the most effective carrier.

Patanjali was up quite early, preparations were over last evening though. The England trip had boosted her confidence. The cab was in at the right time. She took the front seat, something co-travellers had gotten accustomed to. Professor Khwaja was sitting on the rear, mumbled, 'pseudo-Hindus and womenfolk's Sita-pan swag.'

Colleague Sengupta looked in distant horizon outside, eyes stuck, all by himself. "Would this be your first paper?" asked Khwaja, the Elite in a subtle voice.

"No," she kind of retorted.

"Would the audience be the first?" he asked further.

"Not sure what do you mean?" Professor in Humanities wasn't interested, or conversation was probably making her nervy.

"First timer - he means Patanjali," Mr. Sengupta aided.

"Some are…" Elite commented.

She would reckon him being party to Lutyens, an elite class forming upper echelons of intellectual, academic and journalism leftist ideologue and the hoppers, of course.

"I heard the majority are…" Elite sounded as if cautioning her.

"Let it be," replied she asserting to herself, "I got to be at my best."

"All the very best," in a rather sarcastic tone said he, smirking.

Co-occupant Sengupta noticed something peculiar, snapped, "Perhaps you already know!"

"What?!" perplexed, Elite asked, looking at him.

"The majority!' Sengupta snapped, smirking.

No words, just another smirk followed.

"How was your England one Patanjali?" Elite tried to change the subject.

"Well received - all I can say - I'm happy at the reception I got."

"Congrats!" voice was subtle not a regular congratulatory one.

"Oh, thanks!" replied in the same tongue terming as if she was a lame duck.

"Would there be details available?" he further poked.

"I have some summary notes."

"Thanks, as much as you can, I am working on a topic; the ingredients at some places are similar to the subject you attempted there," Elite said in a requesting tone.

"I will see to it - the best I can dig out," She said in an indifferent tone.

"Thank you," cab was about to reach the destination the popular university of western Uttar Pradesh.

The conference hall was not far off, she took the staircase to her cabin first. The laptop was to be readied with last-minute presentation touches, five minutes later she was ready and briskly walked towards the ground floor conference room.

Someone called her name – "Patanjali!"

She stopped, turned around. The Head of the department was standing at the far end of the corridor.

"I had a glance at the material," said he, walking towards her.

"How was it?" she was eager.

"Content is rich," they both walked towards the staircase leading to the ground floor, "yet I advise you tone down the presentation."

"I fear losing the crux," Patanjali found that quite bizarre.

"And I fear losing an excellent teacher," The man sounded concerned.

"The other side seems to enjoy no brakes," Patanjali said, sarcasm was vivid.

He smiled, "perhaps they came on course, very early."

"And mine is still in infancy?" asked Patanjali

"Modi-Shah will take some time, or perhaps in the last year already, who knows Patanjali?" he remarked.

She thought for a second or two, and the replied in great hope, "Discourse and activism must remain steadfast, organized thrust is not a necessary sustenance Sir."

She smiled, turned around, and ambled her way inside the chambers.

Dignitaries were about to arrive, the audience was yet not fully in attendance, emerging in ones and twos in the far-right side corner entrance.

Humanities professor settled herself on the stage, laptop hooked at the projector with the first slide welcoming the attendees on the big screen.

The topic was 'Non-European Roots of Mathematics,' flashing large, loud, and clear for the audience to become talkative already.

In the audience, there were students in a number the hall could accommodate, faculty members from various departments, and a few hailing from the other eminent universities and institutions.

She began with a brief introduction to Newton and his famous work on gravity only to quickly shift to the mathematics and the subject of Calculus.

"The Newton's work at the end of the seventeenth century has a great reputation and is significant especially it's remarkable work on Calculus algorithms," she continued, "However the equally great component of Calculus - The Infinite Series was discovered in Medieval India, especially by the scholars of Kerala."

Murmurs were beginning to be heard.

Professor continued, "For some reason, this has gone unnoticed and probably there were deliberate efforts to suppress the fact that the knowledge in those times and time before that travelled from East to West," she paused for a moment of two and resumed, "My paper and the study associated shows that the infinite series discovery has wrongly been attributed to Sir Isaac Newton and G. Leibnitz."

Murmurs were steady by now, the speaker continued though conscious of the time in hand.

"The paper is based on various works carried out by eminent scholars from the University of Manchester and other parts of the academic world."

Voices went down by a note perhaps surprised to hear the reference of a western university. It was hitherto unknown and rare to quote in seminars and paper presentations. Some of the slides were flipped though, Patanjali subtly elaborating on the content of each slide, content highlighting and emphasizing the significance of these works and the conclusion they had arrived at.

Humanities professor added further, "Kerala school and other south Indian academic communities of 14th century A.D. worked extensively on Pi series."

And then she paused for a moment gauging anxiously at the audience especially the first row and resumed, "They not only devised but also calculated correctly the Pi up to 17 decimal places."

Some had begun to make notes by now preparing for salvos later.

"The beginnings of modern maths are attributed to Europe but the significant work in medieval India in 14th,15th and 16th centuries has been overlooked."

One interrupted, "So Ma'am, are you suggesting the whole of Mathematics originated from Indian?"

"Is that what you have come to understand so far and thus summarize so?" she asked gently.

"The text and sentences we have heard in the last few minutes, certainly suggest taking us in that direction," he added.

"Would it be feasible for you to wait until I finish," she had to retort politely.

"Would by then we may not be wasting our time Ma'am," professor of the eminent university had certainly dug in.

"Why would you be not willing to hear until the end, the way you were in the first place to get here in time and be in attendance," duel was on some suspected, indifferent lot hoped to get entertained.

Another from the front row intervened, "Ma'am...um...your good name please?".

Speaker pointed to the top of the slide.

"Ah...oh sorry – Yes...so Ma'am Patanjali, I would like to add to what Mr. Nair has been trying to put across."

She listened attentively.

"We believe in your earnest work as we would for all our colleagues and fraternity cutting across the institutions, thus we are here, however..."

"However?' Lady speaker snapped and purposefully so, "However at the prospect to eventually get wasted in this nonsense for another whatever no of minutes - does merit an objection? To look at and understand the work done by not me alone, but also by the eminent scholars will eventually get you closer to the truth if you are willing and just be patient?"

"We will have to spend a lot more time, I am afraid to conclude Newton was a chor (plagiarist)," he retorted.

A few laughs followed and intentionally with thumps on desks.

She could easily deduce, Elite's smirks were a dead giveaway that he had the company whipped much in advance, she, therefore, decided to retort in no time, "There were many reasons for not acknowledging contributions made by non-European civilizations in medieval times."

"Such as?' questioner asked, co-occupants in the row smirking - some chuckling - she noticed through corner of her eyes.

"Ignoring, overlooking and neglecting scientific ideas emanating from the Non-European world - a legacy of European colonialism and beyond," she remained firm on the face of the collective leftist onslaught.

"We are going no-where, are we?" one fellow objected, others joined the chuckle.

"Human beings everywhere have been capable of advanced and innovative mathematical thinking," she answered, "to believe it cannot be the case just because only whites have been capable and other races could never - is amounting to negate the very basic strength of human beings."

"And what is that?' the questioner and his company were not too sure what she was suggesting.

"That is not about what but rather a question of why?"

Relentless onslaught for a moment ceased - had no clue.

Juggernaut went on from the dais, "for the known reasons to act to be in the haze and to keep others in the haze of..."

"Haze of?" asked spontaneously, the front row was completely lost apparently.

"Haze of age-old stories faithfully told and without due diligence so from the teachers their students in every phase of modern history..."

"To?"

"To keep the leftist propaganda alive!"

All hell broke loose as the session at that moment went berserk. All in the front row were up. All were speaking the same time, fingers waving, Glares and stares were out in open - elite was startled and his fellow ones utterly rattled.

Moderator came up on the stage, brought about the much-needed decorum, and appealed all to speak in turn, one-at-a-time.

Patanjali Kapoor stood her ground, preparing her thoughts for the next set of sentences - a lot was to be told and told now - as subtly and effectively she could - she musters all she had and resumed.

"Works such as this and a number of them before this one and some," looking straight at the front row, "even from the University of Manchester vividly describes and proves the multicultural roots of mathematics in the medieval times."

Patanjali Kapoor was speaking unabated.

"Deep influence that the Egyptians and Babylonians had on the Greeks, the Arabs' major creative contributions, and the astounding range of successes of the great civilizations of India and China," speaker had the momentum by that time, "Mathematical ideas travelled from east to west," and she concluded thereafter, "If you believe and I doubt hardly, that it's work...um..," smirking, "rather a figment of some right-wingy, nationalist imagination then look at this work by University of Manchester faculty named Joseph."

Elite sprang up, yelled, "This Joseph gentleman," addressing the audience, "was born in Kerala, he is an Indian."

"So, does that make him incapable?" She snapped.

"It does make him prejudiced," Elite retorted.

"Wow..." she burst into laughter, rattling Elite and the company to the core, retorted, "he grew up not in India but did his education in England, he is no RSS man," expressions ridiculing the lefty group.

She turned back - quickly flipped through the slides and flashed the slide bearing the comments on Josephs work from those entities the front row and Patanjali's leftist keep great regard for, "and this is what he has received from, you all have been so willingly hearing and reading from."

'Enthralling . . . After reading it, we cannot see the past in the same comforting haze of age-old stories, faithfully and uncritically retold from teacher to pupil down the years. . . Invaluable for mathematics teachers at all levels.'--New Scientist.

'What is valuable here is the unified approach that Joseph brings . . . and the non-technical clarity that the attempt to reorder historical priorities and educate his readers out of their European prejudices requires.'--Times Literary Supplement.

She was smirking and held herself short of an ever-urging chuckle.

Moderator thrust himself back in action, energetically requested the audience to take their seats all along nudging the speaker to conclude.

"Surely Sir," said she, settling her nerves thoughtfully Patanjali resumed.

"I will conclude with what learned as Joseph had said, I am quoting those comments and…" directing every word to a select few as if addressing solely them, and they were getting rattled, "..and not mine sir to make this presentation a subject appreciated and well received."

"And we all are eager and patient," an impatient moderator snapped.

Professor gathered her thoughts for a moment and, uttered at a high pitch her concluding remarks.

"These scholars through their work have found evidence which goes far beyond that: for example, there were plenty of opportunities to collect the information as European Jesuits were present in the area at that time. They were learned with a strong background in maths and were well versed in the local languages. And there was strong motivation: Pope Gregory XIII set up a committee to look into modernising the Julian calendar. On the committee was the German Jesuit astronomer/mathematician Clavius who repeatedly requested information on how people constructed calendars in other parts of the world. The Kerala School was undoubtedly a leading light in this area. Similarly, there was a rising need for better navigational methods including keeping accurate time on voyages of exploration and large prizes were offered to mathematicians who specialised in astronomy."

"Again, there were many such requests for information across the world from leading Jesuit researchers in Europe. And Kerala mathematicians were hugely skilled in this area."

Courtesy: https://www.manchester.ac.uk/discover/news/indians-predated-newton-discovery-by-250-years/

CHAPTER 3

Sahoo Singh was standing proud and scrupulous. The day had arrived and the number was swelling every minute. Would farmers hold on to the land or make a killing by selling that off, positions were hard to guess. The survey committee could come calling any day. Maha-panchayat must sense the farmers' pulse and set the spirit in motion, for 2019 is just not an opportunity opposition could afford to park until 2024.

Time, career politicians must dig in. It was the opportune time that the politicians would want to make the most off.

"Bhaiyoon, Apke aane ka bahut bahut dhanyawaad (Brothers, thank you very much for coming)," Sarpanch began his address.

Elaborate arrangements were put in place from supplying chilled water to uninterrupted production of milk-chai to the constant filling of trademark hookah dotting the cots and chairs which occupied the mammoth courtyard of Bawani Khurd Panchayat office. A lot many had taken the seats on the roof while rest who could not get in the premises ascended on to the tractors and trolleys to be at vantage points. Draped in a white, the cotton cloth was saving his face from the heat. Eyeballs were fixed in one direction scanning the attendance to find his Baapu. He took a corner seat, and in the very next moment stood up. Tall and sturdily built six-feet-one-inch ex-army man wanted to avail the vantage point. Sarpanch was just a few yards away, 'should be by his side in no time if the need arises,' he said to himself. Any mob had begun to make him nervous since 2013 Muzzaffarnagar riots.

"This is not a political gathering as rumours doing the rounds would make you believe," Sahoo Singh's roaring disclaimer was in. He stopped for a few seconds for the massive crowd of farmers to take notice. The words calmed the din. Hundreds of eyeballs were now fixed at him "We are here today because we all are about to lose our land." The conclusion is drawn by all inflicted by deafening silence in an already heavy atmosphere.

Sarpanch roared again. "Who does not know that the Modi government has taken all the steps necessary in the last 4 years to make my community landless." The Maha-panchayat had Panchs; a few congressmen and a person no one in the crowd has seen ever were sitting on the dais.

Sahoo Singh said his next carefully chosen words. "Recall 2014. We had to spend sleepless nights and rush to Jantar Mantar every week to make this callous government hear our voice and to shun the 2014 land bill." A few policemen had by then positioned themselves at the usual places. "And the other day you all heard how cunningly same 2014 Land Bill is being thrown at us." The spirited voice was up to an intensity equalling the event's massive opportunity.

"Would you?!" he poked pointing at one set of the audience.

"No way!" some shouted.

"Are you going to?!" The seasoned politician wanted to seize the hour right from the onset of it. Arms stretched, he yelled, pointing at the other side now.

"Nah...nah," a louder response echoed his call.

"Or Would you?!" he roared at the top of his voice to engage the farthest in attendance. "Nah Ji Naaaahh!!" thunderous chorus admitted the leader's plea.

"But then how would you, me and us all ensure that these thugs do not get away with what they are coming for?," he asked, moving his upper half from one direction to another, "Only by exercising our democratic rights," nudging with his eyes for a response and anything would be welcomed, one arrived, "Chalo Jantar Mantar!" Stalwart snapped, "Nah, not again – We are to fight for our land from our land - this time Bawani Khurd will be the centre of our protest!!" A roar of supporters and excited farmers followed. No guard was to be dropped, the Sarpanch who had swiftly moved to the centre of the dais, retorted:

"Across the country you hear of farmers' protest. Maharashtra saw 1000 farmer families marched on foot to Mumbai to get their voice registered," pushing his voice to a note higher with every sentence, "Lakhs marched to Delhi at the start of this year in protest of lopsided policies - We will protest as they have! We are in solidarity with the plight of the farmers of this great land!"

Pausing for a moment, sipping in half glass of water as farmers impatiently waited for stalwart's next words.

since 1947, to climb the social ladder and live life with an average level of subsistence."

"Zamindars have been from all communities - to say Muslims and backward classes only had the smallest of land parcels is misleading, so probably…."

"Probably you seem not to understand the precious opportunity the marginalized ones have now. The zamindars can keep their lands. I am a Samajwadi. We need farmers and zamindars, so as the marginalized ones, to make the best of the opportunities coming along. While the Annadatas are to sow, cultivate and harvest and be proud of their lands and good amount year after year from the yield, the marginalized ones can bank on the education and find a place in society, in years to come, with elevated social status and stature. The only way is to get some money and part with the land which has just kept them the same as how they are today, for centuries now."

With folded hands, he bid adieu quickly descending from the dais, flanked by an entourage of laal and kaali topis.

Through the corner of his eyes, Chhatrapal noticed or as would be the case most of the time - wanted to notice whether his little sister had denim on, it was not. Yes, little for him and will always be.

A relief to his senses – "Jeans invites trouble invariably" - by him or rather by his mindset. Ever since her time away in the city and far from home, he had found himself on tenterhook - always wary and so weary, at times angry, determined not to let her get her way, yet eventually resigning himself and her to fate.

Baapu had just returned to the house accompanied by two Panch's. Hookah was quickly prepared and served in the courtyard.

The conversation was as usual around politics and a long discussion on the probable course and discourse and a hundred other topics off the main ones.

"Yudh's medicines are needed now," Ma Rajrani cautioned.

"Tomorrow morning, I fetch some," replied the elder son.

"All are almost consumed, all are needed."

"Give me a day or two then."

Looking at her daughter earnestly, "Yes, she has found the job and that has gotten me some relief."

Son wasn't inclined to comment, though many times the topic had been visited, Ma's overwhelming desire for her daughter and sister's insistence was hard to counter.

He got up, "let me see," walked out and into the courtyard, reluctantly showing up in the ensuing conversation, "Aur Chhattar...Faujji- all good?" asked one Panch.

He snubbed, settled on one cot facing father. "Two trolleys of sacks have finally been admitted in the mandi."

Chhattar's arrival would signal any entourage to leave - they did so promptly.

"Payment schedule?" Sahoo Singh asked.

"Dharma enquired, perhaps by next month-end," hesitantly added, "Baapu family needs you, spend time with them, at least some."

"Politics has brought us many luxuries, do not discount that Chhattar."

"Has ruined us equally!" Chhattar said in a heavy voice.

"Jittu gets the time. I am fine. He needs affection of all at this age, grandfather gets to spend time with him - you should be happy."

"We are not too sure where your priority lies," Chhattar said in an agitated tone, eyes looking down though.

"Pension has gotten credited?" father changed the subject.

Chhatrapal did not reply, he was pissed off.

"Pension ?!!" father repeated, eyeing his son over the stem of Hukka pipe.

"Perhaps by day after."

"And yours?"

A second or two passed before the reply was uttered, "Nah"

Father murmur curses, and he had been since the time son took volunteer retirement form Army and come back.

Murmur caved his senses, and he didn't have to listen clearly to know – agony peeked.

"There is no point..." son yelled.

"Would have been far easier," said father calmly.

"Away from all this would have led me to..."

"You have deprived a constant income to your family," father said in a disappointed low voice.

"To be away wouldn't let me work, I would have perished someday and returned eventually."

"I would have handled ... things would have fallen in place, nah?" father retorted.

"What you could have you did not."

"Yudh is up," Chhattar heard his wife Anita.

He made haste, was by Yudhvinder's side in no time, picked him up from the bed, and made him sit on the wheelchair. Yudhvinder was Sarpanch's second child, Sapna the youngest.

"Regular Income and stability it would offer, he has been the cost." Sahoo Singh was mumbling still.

"Yudh has been the cost, you couldn't care less," said Chhattar, stepping back into the courtyard.

"I never asked him to go there…participate," father desperately submitted his plea.

"You should have seen that he does not step out," elder son shouted, eyes moist.

"Do you? why do you follow me all the time?!!" father snapped back, added some moments after, "We have come such far, we will get through, things have begun to look up."

"Yudh is permanently disabled, wake up baapu. Until you get over with this petty politics we will never. Your politics cost us Yudh. What else you want now before you give up?"

"Jat Mahapanchaayat was aimed at a show of strength to the Muslim community," The Veteran was talking about 2013 Muzaffarnagar incident.

His face glowed in pride. That fateful day while returning in the evening the caravan of Scorpios, bikes and tractors were attacked by Muslim peasants resulting in a long-drawn battle of wits. Jats winning hands down due to strength and for no fear of repercussions from the law and order. There were losses on both sides, Yudhvinder was one - a lose stray brick brought him down and made him bedridden perhaps forever.

Second Lieutenant with bright career prospects, Chhaterpal decided what would change his life forever, to persuade what Yudhvinder had adopted - family's main source of livelihood – farming! Five years since then now 36, he aimed to bring all in order and had been able to curb the slide much. Be that uncertain income or putting in the requisite efforts to make Yudh's condition stable and not let that deteriorate further or to become an unfailing source of reassurance a family needs from his eldest while 'the eldest' was always busy with politics his first love, the family stood much after.

Angry and anguished, "Sorry that I spoiled your evening, I came out because we need money."

"Where is yours?"

"My pension is still a few days away," he thundered, then said in a low voice, "medicines are needed, Yudh needs to undergo tests too."

"No need to spend on all the medicines how many times should I tell your mother?!"

"How much do you have in your party fund?" he asked in a firm dead voice

"That is for the party."

"I will return it by next week, let me use for now," son pleaded.

"You know my answer, that's cheating, absurd," swiftly, "Sapna betti…?"

"Nah baapu, we must not use her money." Chhattar tried to persuade the father in a low voice. He did not want sister to know of it.

"She is capable and earning as good as your and my pension put together, so no harm."

"She is a girl and we must not use her income, let that be saved for her mar..." he stopped short.

Youngest of the family had presented herself... almost running, bhabhi's chunni was snatched & swiftly put in, "Ji pitajee."

"How much you earn now, last year you said 27 hazaar."

"Ji 27. Only once in year salary is revised."

"Hmm, how many months now since you got this job?"

"Six months," replied the elder brother.

"Are you saving some?'

'Ma has all.' She said gingerly.

"Theek hai…too jaa anader. (alright…go inside)."

She hurried inside.

"Anything else?" father asked.

"Anything else? Where is the cash?!"

The rest two looked at each other. They were certainly shocked.

"Only if you let me solicit the best of your know-how," youngster latched onto the moment.

"Absolutely...Team collaborates, no?" Zuber nudged peers. Leads kept mum, "Come on guys, she needs us, right Sapna?" looking at her, look pushing her to express.

"uh...Yeah...yes," said she, striving hard to keep the fake half-grin on.

"So, who won?" Chacko asked subtly, voice a little raised and quite irritated.

"Who?!"

"Between Kashmir and India?"

"That's...you know...uh," Kashmiri employed gestures to suggest the heated argument the other day was trivial.

"You seem to get along well," turning towards the youngster eyes fixed at hers Lead asked next, she felt trapped, no point rubbing any of the heavyweights, the expression, not tongue could merely say, "With whom?"

"HE!" eyes still locked, index finger pointing at Kashmiri.

"And why not - part of one team and teams do gel and they gel fast...you know," Zuber chipped in with a wide grin.

"Lest it should melt even faster," retorted the lead.

"That's gross Chacko...that's gross," Kashmiri said head shaking and having a wide grin on his face.

"Oh, I had forgotten she is a youngster after all," Chacko snapped.

"My dear...that's the whole..." he was cut short, "Then why don't you..." eyes back at her making youngster even more unsettled, "hang around with Neetu and others – LET the entire team gel?"

An apt choice of words was a necessity of the situation she reminded her of her decaying thoughts, it was merely her first manoeuvre to impress upon the seniors and it was going surely wayward.

"Neetu and...uh," eyes glaring every utterance, she fumbled – "they are... too...Punjabi!"

The youngsters in the project looked down upon her, as most from a young generation would - rural background, fiery attitude, not that she wanted yet she had developed subconsciously to fight everyday odds, and above all no inclination to talk cosmetic stuff from discussing fashion to weekend parties or discussing latest movie plots.

"Punjabi?!!" all three were shocked at the brazen words.

"Jats and Punjabis haven't had the best of social relations of late in Haryana," Naved remarked.

"Oh, I see," Chacko said, "So you hate Punjabis?"

"No, I did not mean that."

"She has obviously not meant that," Zuber jumped in, she felt supported.

"You two can be a good company," commented Chacko standing up, Naved collected his belongings too, "Please carry on," looking at her, "I am sure you can learn a lot from him," suggested Chacko before duo walked off.

"You need not worry...they are too arrogant to let you in," Zuber tried to soothe a harried soul.

She nodded, while quite unsure from inside.

He said further, "Look at me!" She was lost. "Sapna?!" a youngster was fearful of permanent damage her manoeuvre might have inflicted, "Look at me..." he grabbed her forearm to draw her attention.

She employed a strong flick to loosen his grip - it was a spontaneous gesture - a spontaneity her body had developed while travelling thousands of times in packed buses, Zuber's body was almost pushed fully, he could have fallen had it been a little stronger.

"Oh...I'm...am sorry."

"It's okay," said Kashmiri, rearranging himself.

"Look, you have the capability to become part of the core team."

"Core team?!"

"Every project gets a few who are doing just regular pass time job...just sufficient to stick around."

"Okay," she was trying to feel her nerve back in - settled and normal.

"And then a few who carry it on their shoulders."

"And they become core members." she queried, curious.

"Exactly!"

"And who would you have become?!" She asked.

"You are too straight at times."

"I like to be blunt," she said, straight eyes backed up the words.

"A few minutes back one could hardly see anything of that league,' said he half smirking.

Her eyes strayed, "Come back to the main point, Sapna," said he in a hushed tone. She felt that was awkward - no one was there from the team to listen. "Look," a hushed and harried tone carried on," Once Chacko is away at onsite, this core team will be counted upon by all," index finger moving forming an arch from nadir to the zenith.

"You mean even the managers?"

"All," smirk was back.

"Okay." She nodded.

"Whosoever becomes a crore member will find Chacko directing..."

"Most of the work?" she was getting interested.

"Major work items, not most...you see?"

"Okay."

"Grab that, keep on churning the result he is looking at and, stay late, work on weekends...you know what I mean?"

"And?!"

He smiled, "You can decipher yourself from here on now," smirking he got up and gingerly walked towards the door. At the exit he turned, her eyes were following him. She wanted to be sure of what she had just heard, he smiled and turned around and made his way towards the escalator.

She spent a few minutes pondering over, time was limited she had always felt, 'who could be my way?'

Little later, on the 5th-floor project manager's cabin.

"It has bogged down my pace Anant," Chacko hated working in the middle of the project phase - always dragged his career progression down he strongly felt, " Naved hops from one customer to another and I just get stuck."

"How does that even matter?"

"I care for my career. I may be good for the project but cannot see my progression as swift...um...I mean-"

Manger read his mind, "Like that of Naved."

"Yes please."

"Because he gets to learn a lot more by being at many-a-customers...as you said - 'Hop!' - while you reckon you do a marathon at just one customer all along that period."

"You get it now Sir."

"Sir?"

"Please do not get me wrong," he said miserably, the body quite unsettled, he was sitting on the edge of the chair, elbows on the knees and both legs spread out, Anant was leisurely sitting with back reclined on his chair, hands clutched together holding the head from the rear.

"No I'm not, you seem to miss the whole point." said Anant

"If my career is on a -" cutting Chacko short Anant flung his body forward, elbows now resting on the knees, face facing the lead, said he, "And in doing so you are leading a team something Naved doesn't do hence you have an advantage over Naved from organization's standpoint. You can manage customers, be the focal point of contact...be onsite be it offshore...you lead team hence you are a people manager, an average member looks up to you, none of these attributes we find in Naved you are so fearful of losing out to."

"But...um..." words were strong Chacko could not get his head around that very moment, decided to park the topic aside for the moment. He got up, "Okay Anant," tongue could hardly utter.

"Yes, you can go back, and rest assured you are doing well."

He was still thoughtful when his chair collected his stray body. A loose body disconnected from hyperactive mind churning wild thoughts, a wide set of permutations and combinations, he logged in into this laptop.

"I've assigned her my task," was the message on the instant messaging organization's app.

He turned around with fury. Zuber, senior-most among the new joiners possessing almost of his profile was there, grinning.

Lead let go that, "I can still see him later, let me get over with his phase first and Naved," he adjudged and carried on He opened his mailbox.

"I've gotten tickets confirmed," was the mail from Naved to him and Anant.

Over the weekend, he will fly out. The first phase was to get on, the team had already with each other at least. The teething problem every project goes through reckoned the manager - 'Everything will fall in place as they every time.'

Five weeks on, the first phase gets completed in time achieving the laid-out results, Naved moved to another project while Chacko reached New Jersey replacing him at onsite and thence on the Onsite Coordinator.

A team of seven by now, Zuber turned out to be a consistent performer all the way through. Juniors, Sapna, and Jyoti had done well with others supporting them consistently. Arrogantly superior, the lead was looked up to except of course the one from the north.

"I'm wary of this Zuber," manager confided in Director SK one day.

"You need not Anant since he has done well contrary to our expectations, you see."

"No doubt about his abilities, but then human nature..."

"Good manager must be first good people managers, good to see you factoring in human nature." Director said.

"Problem is, too many with similar skills set and experiences are in the project," Anant's problem was vivid to the director, he asked," One is moving out, just two to deal with if I read correctly?"

"Yes sir, but of late Zuber has stopped delivering the quality work."

"I'm not surprised, and then I am sure you will deal with it."

Silence prevailed for some time, both sipped coffees untangling their challenges of the moment.

"Chacko will need support, and I'm not too sure of these two girls," Anant resumed.

"But they have delivered consistently."

"Zuber helped," Anant said in a dead voice.

"Interesting! and why?" Director asked with a grin.

"Will come to know soon, but I am not surprised I anticipated it." The manager replied leaning back on his chair.

"If my manager can anticipate correctly and in time, I have nothing to worry about," getting up, "so excuse me, for now, Anant and keep up the good work."

"Sure Sir." said Anant swiftly getting up.

Little later, "Good morning Chacko, early in today?" call was from New Jersey.

"Good afternoon Anant. I need to spend some time with Naved. Today is his last day here as you know, need to understand the in-progress work items."

"Okay, but there must be something concerning that you called up at this time?" asked Anant.

"About Zuber."

"Troubling you, last delivery I heard David complained about," Manager queried further.

"Yes, But I managed, David has calmed down now," Chacko said.

"Zuber needs to continue; We have none as experienced at offshore as you were," Anant cautioned the onsite lead.

"Can't we get Naved in?" Clearly, Chacko was getting tired of Zuber and his antics.

"I would love to, but he has been booked for another project." Anant said.

"Oh, I feared that."

"You know how it goes."

Chacko did not say anything.

"You speak to Zuber, I reckon," Anant said after a few moments, "sort out the stiffness between you and him."

The lead did not comment.

"You would need him, wouldn't you?" The manager tried to convince his lead, a valuable part of the project.

"Yes, one at least is needed from of shore to ensure timely communication and on-time delivery."

"Or if you can groom these girls fast enough, I will move him into another project." The seasoned manager sent in the challenge and quoted the prize.

"I will speak to you soon, I need to see one way or other, otherwise, I may not be able to pull this off."

"Speak to Zuber Chacko...girls will take time," cautioned the seasoned manager.

He kept mum, a few seconds passed by, "Anything else Chacko?"

"It is two months phase If I'm not wrong Anant?"

"Last when you looked at the schedule my Project leader," remarked manager, "It is little over nine weeks."

"And then advised him in a firm voice," Unless you work twelve hours every day you would need him."

He did not comment, the call was disconnected soon after.

CHAPTER 5

What if the majority turn out to be overwhelming for the law and order to cope with, was the test of the day and the most were anxious about?

The region was on a tenterhook. Thousands were moving towards the site where the committee members had convened the meeting of the farmers.

March was on since early morning, from Bhiwani Khurd situated nine km southeast of Panipat crisscrossing many villages lying en route to the destination some twenty-five km south of Panipat, east of northern railway line, Uttar Pradesh Haryana border was a few km away to the east.

"All are welcome," one in the centre said, "I'm the convener and the chairperson of this committee to look into the land acquisition plan and its smooth execution."

He was cut short straight away, "No compensation that Kissan is looking for, you can wrap up and go back," Kissan Ekta Manch representative Dharma snapped.

Convenor ignored, resumed, "An area of roughly 11 sq. km has been chosen as the site for construction of a massive freight depot for the planned dedicated freight corridor connecting Ambala to Dadri in western U.P. While Eastern and Western freight corridors are to become fully operational by March 2020, situated in the north once constructed."

Outside and a few km distant, leading the grand foot march was Sahoo Singh with slogans chanting mammoth farmers' might in toe. Congress veteran had many party colleagues in the company, each leading a platoon of followers. A strict whip had been issued to keep the protest peaceful.

Mobile was buzzing every other second, constantly engaging protagonist with his state party men in the state capital Chandigarh and nation's capital New Delhi.

"This shouldn't end in a face loss, beware Sahoo."

"Momentum has been built, we will score the point, rest assured," veteran was oozing with energy - contagious to all in presence - spreading far and wide every moment – "Modi Sarkar…" veteran would yell, animated supporters would follow with a fervent - "Hai Hai!"

"No violence is needed yet the might must make its presence felt," was the leadership objective set forth.

"All will lend a hand to the farmer!" assured the mass man in his mid-sixties. "Must be a mighty one so that be taken note of by the people in power," was the bottom line drawn.

The destination SDM Office was about to be arrived at and now a couple of km away, Sahoo Singh and his close associates gathered for a quick discussion, Yadav was arriving from the opposite direction in a few minutes - news had come in.

"He was leading a sizable number of supporters comprising primarily of Yadavs of countryside and Muslim peasants, rest were political cadres donning laal and kaali topi…" - the veteran was quickly apprised by the messenger. Slogans were beginning to get heard now from the eastern side of the Congress march - the anti-kissan Ekta Manch march was in the vicinity now.

Sahoo Singh asked his aides to quickly spread the message to get the supporters to spread far and wide, thus creating a GHERAO at the epicentre in the next few minutes.

Police force accompanied by rapid force battalion in full riot gear had been called in from adjacent

divisions over the night, barricades had been erected at various entrances.

A few hundred meters straight down the road, marching Sahoo Singh could see chauraha on the road leading straight to the SDM office located half a km away – the committee was present in at that moment. Standing there were senior police officers with police personnel deployed in the rear and ahead of them behind a 'two layers' of barricades.

Yadav leading hundreds made a swift entry in the arena from the east, with vociferous sloganeering on.

Inside the SDM office, committee convenor was setting the objective and agenda up:

"This northern freight corridor will feed in these main freight corridors in the south around NCR.."

"Farmer's land is being forcibly taken," protesting representative shouted again, "BJP hai hai," shouted the aide.

"Several new roads to connect major cities of this region such as Bijnor, Saharanpur, Muzaffarnagar, Shamali, Panipat to this freight corridor and the depot were also part of the plan. The expansion of the existing northern railway line connecting Jammu/Amritsar/Chandigarh to Delhi with the addition of the 3rd line, so to connect and starting from the IOCL Panipat refinery at the northern end and freight corridor in its south was also to come up."

"Farmers' Voice is not being heard," duo stood up threatening to walk – out.

"Your presence is welcomed," Convener said calmly, "We shall hear you and your demands," voicing pleading now almost, "All stakeholder's rights will be preserved, let me assure you on the behalf of the state government and the Freight Corridor Corporation of India. Committee will hear the representations today and the pleas will attempt to resolve as many as we can today itself. Our goal is to bring all stakeholders on the table to agree to the acquisition plan, its scope, and most importantly as I believe - to the compensation."

Suddenly earnest knocks began to bang the shut door, "What is going on constable?!!" shocked convenor asked. All present were startled.

"Some civilians from Panipat," a screeching voice replied.

"What are they doing here?!" asked his co-members.

The answer came from an unidentifiable, "You can't get away without listening to us."

Words made many curious. "Let them come in," convener ordered.

Two almost barged in - one lady in mid-forties and the accompanying man over fifty.

Farmers representatives two each from Samajwadi and Kissan Ekta Mach were utterly surprised to find middle-class city dwellers there.

"Must be one of those sitting outside with placards talking about some builder's pre-launch and cheating," Dharma's aide whispered to him.

Almost snapped of all energy, gushed out immediately the moment duo found themselves in, "We are from RWA Imperial City..."

"And what could be that?" was the common expression on all agog faces.

"You got to hear us, no matter what," voices pleaded.

"I am not sure..." said the Convenor.

"This is about our homes - lifelong savings we have invested in," pleaded the lady further.

"You better take seats," said the convenor, signalling the attendant to bring some water.

Sipping in a few quick, "We represent a group of 300 people," apolitical submitter started his submission before the committee, "Who have invested their hard-earned money, provident funds, years' saving in a small part of the land that this committee and grand welfare scheme aim to acquire."

"So?"

"We stand to lose all if the acquisition does take away that it has planned to."

"Please get to the main parts of your plea if you can quickly," convenor nudged.

"The land on the east of railway line, some thirteen km south of Panipat railway station where the 3rd line and possibly fourth and fifth feeder lines are planned to come up that land bank of almost 50 acres was the site builder Prestige Infratech launched Imperial Residency on..."

Interrupted, "Pre-launch," by his partner.

"Yes, it was a pre-launch," stopping momentarily, "Hope esteem members understand this key term of our entire plea?"

Some smiled, "In this era of rapid urbanization, yes these terms are not unheard of, please go on."

"Almost 275 citizens like me and her, had a year ago registered ourselves in this prelaunch scheme by paying," then reading from a file he had in his hand, "10% of the total price and that comes to about twenty-seven crores."

"A steady mind will not invest in prelaunch - too risky!" one member commented.

Other said, "10% is anyway too much for a pre-launch, what would the prevailing standard," asking one other.

"Should not be more than 5% to my knowledge," other added.

"It's a shame," one disinterested pitched in.

"You seem to represent an educated group of senior citizens," convener looking towards the peasants momentarily, "not out of mind, living on the nerve," asked, "how you ended up investing here? Quite strange!"

"It's a long story and may not be necessary we believe," the lady intervened, "we would not like to waste your valuable time either," looking at her partner she said, "we are here to submit our plea."

"Okay - what is that? and in brief please." Convenor said.

"Either the money is refunded with 18% interest or..."

Convener cut short, "or the land of 50 acres be put aside for a builder to construct your dream homes," smirking.

Sloganeering outside all that while was going on unabated.

Every chant of "Modi Sarkar Hai-Hai" was meeting "Modi Sarkar Karo Pichhron Ka bhi Vikas!"

Inside:

"You need to educate yourself," convener told the lady, "this is beyond our purview, land acquisition is done to fulfil nation's need hence all other matters become trifle thus not as important as the nation's need."

Both shot back in a chorus, "We are here to ask, how was the land decided to be part of the plan while the same had been acquired by a private company in the first place?"

Convener though for a moment or two, asked, "Show me the area maps, if you have."

File with maps, some macro some micro was handed over.

Flipping through the pages and comparing one or two with the same set of committee's papers, Convener replied, "this piece has been earmarked for the proposed..." stopping momentarily, "and possible expansion by having 4th and 5th lines."

"Possible expansion?!, does that mean - 4th and 5th may not at all come up and the land is spared?"

"Yes, precisely."

Surprised, they asked: "How early could we know of the final plan, these will come up or will not?" the lady asked in hope.

"May take years," flabbergasted, "or may come to know about as early as in twelve months."

"As you may very well understand, the middle-class citizen cannot afford to live with such a vast oscillation for years to a mere twelve months - we need a concrete answer - a final decision," lady sounded determined.

"You are asking for too much," facial expressions suggesting a lady could only ask never a male could dare to, murmuring, "um…final decision…" then digressing, "4th and 5th lines will not eat into your land, look carefully, depot facility to load and unload, and the road emanating from the depot will," lifting one file and showing them corresponding maps.

Depositors looked at each other, startled.

Convener said, "Depot will be the necessity as you can easily make out to make the line operational, and the 3rd line will come up no doubt."

Resolute asked, "What is the possibility of shifting the depot a few km north or south?"

Stunned at the daring query, convener resorted to smirking, "Depends on them," pointing towards the farmers' representatives," and the agenda they pursue now on!"

Dharma, his chaperone, the representatives from the rival group looked on.

Lady turned towards them, "your land can save our homes if you…"

"Wait for a second," a member interrupted, "What about builder refunding you money? Why haven't you been talking about that option?"

"Looks the most-easy one to me," convener commented.

Dharma commented, "You all must be naive…that company is owned by powerful," smirking, "is the most difficult way out."

Looking on, the depositors seemed to agree.

"You can file your plea formally outside please," Convener signalled to one clerk in attendance to assist the depositors, "And sorry - we do not have all day!"

"Formal submission we will do outside but," Lady said getting up, "Let me deposit the case details, background, and our argument with this committee… you seem to be the last hope," expressions seconding the opinion made by Dharma.

As the two got up and made a slow exit murmuring, discussing, Convener moved to the next agenda turning towards the farmer's representatives, "Who would like to go first?"

"Dhanyawaad. We welcome the plan and the distinguished members of the committee," said Abdul Khan, a Samajwadi party cadre in laal topi.

"We are happy to see both representations here," convener said, "As I pointed out at the start, we are here to preserve the rights of all while executing this public welfare, nation-building scheme as smoothly as we can without adversely impacting anyone."

'We are already," Dharma quipped.

"We are happy," commented the opponent.

"Okay, anything that you have come with and want to place in front of the committee."

"Yes!" Dharma said calmly, "mere two words -" and yelling top of his voice - "Go back!"

Convener ignored, looked towards the opponents.

"Altogether my fellow farmers and peasants hold an area about twenty-eight percent of the total committee is planning at to acquire."

"Khan, you were planning to sow ganna just a few days back, now ready to sell off land. In no time you have made up your mind. What a speed… excellent dedication!" quipped Dharma

Convenor and Khan both ignored the comment.

"We are willing to hand over the land parcels that we own but must receive a good compensation," added Khan.

"Glad that you understand the objective and believe in this nation-building effort. let me request my fellow member to apprise you about the compensation model government has finalized."

One on the right opened a file and read aloud, "We are very happy to receive you here. The prevailing law stipulates 900 rupees per square meter, yet the government has come up with higher compensation and there are two models."

"My fellow farmers would be very happy to hear this, what are those two models, sahib?" Samajwadi Khan asked.

"Under the first model - a compensation amount of 1000 per square meter along with benefits - housing, compensation for the cost of construction (tube wells, houses) on the plot; employment for one member of each family or a onetime compensation of five lakhs…"

"And the second option?"

"Under the second model - a compensation of 1400 rupees per square meter without additional benefits."

"And those who do not want either," snapped Dharma, Kissan Ekta Manch representative.

Convener snubbed him, did not reply.

Dharma looked on, thinking hard, "You contested last assembly election on a BJP ticket- didn't you?!!"

Convenor looked away.

Dharma typed in some words and sent the message, began discussing something with his associate.

"Convenor Sahib," Samajwadi Khan said, "As I said earlier, we are willing, what should be the next step?"

"You will have to submit the forms filled in with all proof documents and most importantly with an affidavit," replied the Convenor while asking one of the members to hand over instructions form.

"Shukriya, any timeline?"

Dharma cut his rival short, "70% consent is necessary for any acquisition," looking at the Samajwadi in laal topi, "your 28% will not suffice."

"Committee is confident of receiving more willing to contribute in Bharat Vikas," Convenor snapped back.

"2013 land bill asks for Social Impact Assessment as well," questioned Dharma's associate.

"All rights will be preserved and honoured," Convenor replied.

"At the moment you do not have 70%, what is your next step?" Dharma asked.

Before Convenor could reply, Samajwadi asked, "Should we wait until we hear from you of 70% acquisition completion?"

"You please get the forms filled in properly," little irritated Convenor replied, "and attach notary stamped affidavits," and then turning to Kissan Ekta duo, "in the meantime we will resolve the rest of land issues - you need not worry!"

"How do you propose to tackle the issues of no payments - First the acquisition happens, the farmer waits for the payments…job…compensations not getting paid to all," Dharma asked next.

"Committee is not sure, which cases are you referring to?" irate Convenor said.

"Pick any acquisition in the last five years in Haryana, you will find pending court cases, never needing wait, no jobs at all."

A circumvent Khan asked, "Convenor sahib, how likely is that to happen if the acquisition target falls short of 70%?"

Convenor ignored, replied to Kissan Ekta Manch duo, "Acquisition may have taken place in the previous regime."

"And if you find a few in your regime?" snapped Dharma.

Convenor was a bit taken aback, one member quickly added, "Government and Corporation have ordered quick resolutions."

Outside:

Sahoo Singh his aides had received the messages sent in by Dharma, quickly loudspeakers blared calling on the followers, "Bhaiyon sirf 700 rupay milenge 1-yard ke...Hummari dharti kaa mol legaa diya inhone (Just 700 rupee for a yard, our motherland has price tagged now)."

Yadav yelled at his troopers, "Mere doston - Kushkhabri 1500 rupay 1-meter ke aur ooper se job aur 1 naya ghar (Good new friends. 1500 rupee for every meter besides a job and what else a constructed home too)."

"Basis what has been the overall experience in other parts of Haryana - me and my Kissan bhaiyon they are willing so don't worry - but wary! So, until the payment happens, a job is not given or in the event of an issue-"

He was cut short, "What type of issue?"

Inside:

"Any issue - so until that is resolved," smirking looking towards the member, "we shall have the right to use our land."

"Once acquisition happens, the land belongs to the government, any usage will be termed as trespassing," Convenor warned.

"Once acquisition happens...payment comes next day...job is given in fifteen days...resettlement happens in a month...land will be yours," Dharma said, almost murmuring.

Convenor retorted, "I think you are not serious. This is not how the acquisition takes place and matter is processed end to end."

Associate snapped back, "Precisely the reason - these issues are being raised."

"Didn't you invite us in the first place to discuss all the aspects?" Dharma added, "and we are serious."

One member yelled, "Any trespassing will be dealt with as a law and order situation."

Associate snapped, "So you will throw us out?"

Dharma typed in a few more words and sent the message, got up, and addressed committee members vehemently, "First you are not taking in 70% consent. Second, you are not willing to carry out Social Impact Assessment either and then you're advocating the use of force and to top all – you want us to be silent - why all this drama of – Sabka Saath Sabka Vikas - Everyone rights will be protected and honoured?!!"

Convenor was at a loss of words for a moment, murmured gingerly, "Compensation disbursement takes time..."

Dharma cut short, "And there is no limit of this eternal wait too many... right?"

"This is a project central government is involved in, this is unlike the short scale project you may have had bitter experiences of."

"Dharti for a farmer is everything, the scale of the project is irrelevant, once taken away - he needs all that has been promised."

"Prime minister office is to supervise the project regularly," convenor tried to reassure.

"Oh bhai - Modi ke bina toh inki koi baat poori hot hi nahin (nothing gets over for them without Modi in helm)," Dharma quipped while his partner added on a serious note, "Eastern and Western Freight corridor are behind schedule by more than one year - for your kind information."

"Let them for a year more, comes 2019 and cometh the hour," both stood up and rushed outside in no time.

Outside:

Pro and anti-land acquisition slogans had by then began to attempt and mow down each other. Cadres on both sides were being egged on.

Every "Zammen pe Vikaas Kamzor kaa bhi Adhikaar" was to be mowed down with 'Mera Khalihaan Mera Samman.'

And every chant of "Kissan Ekta Zindabad," met with vociferous "Pichhada Samaaj Kare Azaadi Ka Aagaz"

In a few moments, as committee members flanked by representatives began emerging out of the SDM office, leaders briskly walked towards the barricades, followers in toe with vociferous chants.

"Leaders are requested to come forward," Senior office announced from the handheld loudspeaker, words barely reaching the troopers, "Committee has heard the representation now the announcement will be made."

Sahoo Singh sent out two of his aides to spread a quick whip amongst by then an animated force. Yadav sent around his trustees.

Sahoo Singh turned around to address the supporters.

Yadav stepped towards Samajwadi cadres.

Speaking at their rhetoric best these two warring opponents, the pro and anti-sentiments were sparked as volunteers all along kept animated sloganeering on.

Rhetoric punches were pitched in vehemently attempting to arouse the sentiments of thousands gathered to the point everything must break loose - nah! – that was hard to come by - potentially may precipitate the undesirable.

The rival Yadav was getting more effective all that time. Samajwadi troopers were growing confident against a startling majority, complacency had begun to play its part.

Eyeballs meeting every other moment – contesting - provoking the other!

Rhetoric attempting the best salvo in every shot.

Sweat sneaking from the forehead down to his eyes, frail Sahoo was now feeling the heat - the heat of the occasion proving too high to sail over.

Yadav was, on the other hand, sending out stupendous salvo, one after another.

The ground was slipping away fast, Sarpanch thoughts cluttered now, his slogans were getting repetitive. His cadres looked around blankly, watching opposition numbers pillaging the majority!

Ekta Manch was almost there - the loss was in sight, staring!

The desperate veteran attempted the salvage shot - signalled to Dharma swiftly.

And the novelty broke the monotony - "2013 ka Aao Bhaiyon - Chukayein Badla," followed by one more – "Ek Dhakka Aur Do…." These last two did succeed in breaking the opposition rhythm, one 'over-enthusiastic' Samajwadi hurt, punched back – "Allah Hu Akbar!"

Yadav stepped up – "Sabkaa Saath…" yearning the mainstream slogan half to be followed with "Sabaka Vikas," rebuked rather by aroused cadres and Muslim peasants- "Babri ki Shahidi Nahin bhoolegi - Nahin bhoolegi."

Lost ground retained now Manch numbers sent in – "Ek Dhakka Aur Do…"

Khan attempted a turnaround flanked by aides – "Zameen pe Vikas Kamjor Kaa Bhi Adhikaar," aroused Samajwadi by then instead shouted, "Ek Dhakka aur do - Kafir Ko Maut Do."

Ekta Manch attempted the last move - a stone was thrown in - hit Yadav's aide.

And with that, all hell broke loose.

Much concerned, Superintendent ordered a mild lathi-charge expecting to establish order in quick time - proved futile - stones had hit many on both sides by that minute, one stray Sahoo on his chest.

"Baapu....!!" shouted Chhattar and held him with his strong forearm, righthand shielding from salvos - a few hit him badly - unnerved he pulled his father out of volleys; aides all along striving to stop bulky body while Dharma egged on - "He needs to be on the podium, he can't leave until Yadav…"

Chhattar paid no heed to political urgency, kept pulling while aides began to push both bodies in the opposite, now.

Superintendent ordered extra hands – intensified the police charge.

The mob began to spread out - stones frequency and intensity went down instantly - letting Yadav stood his ground.

"You cannot…stop it now…let him speak," Dharma pleaded, shattered veteran tried to stand on his feet body pushed and pulled from all the sides.

"Baapu…!" Chhattar cried, face almost on his father's face.

"Chal" pleading, Dharma pulled him aside, then coming close, shouting close to his ears, "We are losing…look at him," pointing towards a smirking, confident, jubilant, sloganeering Yadav.

Chhattar pulled himself aside, Dharma & aides hoped for better now, helped veteran to be on his feet - the moment Chhattar pulled out, he made a brisk run at Yadav - shattering aides wall - he pushed Yadav - sudden and aroused emotions' energy transcending into the gigantic body force - propelled mediocrely sized Yadav off the podium.

Falling many feet on the ground next to the podium, hundreds almost ran in from all directions to save their leader.

While aides started throwing punches on his face - few had bamboos ready by now, Dharma rushed in with two aides.

Chhattar tackled two, rest by the reinforcement - snatched a bamboo attempting to evade all along with the other one, he was now in a dangerous situation - he could be just a hit away - he attempted best of his defence - hit the opponent on the head ensuring shouldn't result in death yet powerful enough to nullify and suspend the attack - it did.

Tear gas shells landed on the podium, prompted Dharma to take the fainted leader in his custody. Chhattar swiftly secured their backs as all rushed towards the parked jeeps a few hundred meters away.

Patanjali Kapoor registered a complaint with university authorities for a hurriedly organized, perfectly disguised propaganda-driven seminar on Kashmir.

"Were they attempting to brainwash the young mind?"

The Head of the department did not pay any heed, kept reading the book.

"Pandey cannot have this," she was fuming.

"Your lecture is about to start Patanjali," head moved to note some points in his diary.

"Would the vice-chancellor take some action? This is outrageous."

Head stared at the book.

"I'm speaking to you, Sir," she almost yelled.

"You need not Patanjali," calmly he said.

She leaned back on her chair, muttering, "Rule mandates a formal request be submitted with the objective of the seminar clearly mentioned."

Moving her body forward, palms clasped on chair arms, she said, "And once permission is granted, the organizer needs to notify everyone through an adequate circular."

She leaned on the chair, "Not that you just mention it an hour before and get on with the proceedings."

Head stopped writing, took off his glasses, and said looking on, "Whether or not an action is taken does not warrant you make yourself the subject of discussion and gossips."

She flung herself on the edge of the chair, "Why not if what is being narrated does not highlight the truth."

An irritated Head remarked, "And who will decide what is truth and what is not. Kashmir issue has drawn many versions and for ages now."

She did not say anything for a moment or two, little later, "All I want…" she stopped, rephrased, "All is needed is to get a committee formed to see into the allegations and reports of misuse of stage and the content lectured there."

"Authority will decide, as they always do, no need to go gung-ho and draw unneeded attention. Just think of your career," HOD advised caution.

She was not listening, lost somewhere she mumbled some words, "Who this Pandey thinks he is benefitting? They are just using him…he is not going to get any paper published and secure some berth in a western university."

"You need to learn to adapt Patanjali," Head advised, "Discourse in public and the course of events can be daunting to one's belief," he stopped momentarily shaking his head in disappointment, said gingerly "of course one cannot always expect to draw home one's point," then vehemently, "channelize you setbacks and anger into creating a forum instead."

Words seemed to affect her.

"With one session here and two there, you cannot take on their might conclusively."

She smirked, "In one session here and two there hardly these meek arrive," sneering her voice gushed out word meek in perfect isolation, "and show courage to even nod, lending strength to a forum is a distant possibility, Sir."

"Then muster the organizational ability Patanjali. A call here and two tweets there cannot turn your crusade, if it is you think it is, into an overnight success."

"Excuse me, there have been many before me and many I know in equal strides as I am to this day."

Head looked into her eyes, "Still, we find ourselves sitting here grudgingly disappointed, and complaining."

"It is just about one session and the rules not followed," she snapped.

"It is about how easily they can have sessions and anywhere in the academia they need to," Head retorted, "The spread translates into a number of souls touched. These steady touchpoints affirm their wide reach and underscore equally the right's glaring limitation."

She got up and walked briskly out and towards her classroom, pensive.

CHAPTER 6

The occasional din associated with card game was soothing, he was lying subconscious. The pain was severe last night, had receded but just, faujji was breathing heavily.

"There have been multiple casualties," he heard, "Bawani Khurd has the most," another voice said.

"Who could be other?" subconscious yet he could feel and fret, "Laado?!"

It had been two days since he attained consciousness only to lose again. Almost 3rd degree was thrown at, since the day he was arrested.

"Faujji hai (he is an army man), any other couldn't survive the salvo," adjacent cell inmate half-drunk would observe time to time.

Cells were 2 in 2 rows opposite to each other, a passage from the middle leads people to the middle part of the Tehsil Police kotwali, rooms housing clerks, constables, and officer's cabin, downstairs.

"You couldn't have done worse," Dharma thundered at the SHO sitting across the table.

"Sahoo is merely a Sarpanch," SHO sneered, "Should have known limits and consequences."

"In case you have forgotten farmers are at stake."

"Never mind. Only once you are back in power," Yadav commented, stepping in.

He was not without an entourage of beaming faces. It was a Muslim peasant killed, and the moment must be seized.

"Still quite a time away," chuckling SHO taunted.

"Matter of a few months," Dharma retorted in optimism.

"Twelve months," said Yadav taking a chair across, "sufficient for us, not enough for you to get away."

"Torture was not necessary," friend's agony was vivid.

"Killing wasn't either," Yadav said in penetrating eyes.

"Chhattar did not attempt it, Zafar attacked first, he was merely defending."

He sounded pleading rather.

"Relax, Sarpanch is doing just fine… can't you see… we could have killed him had Samajwadi intended to, did we?" Yadav smirked.

"Chhattar did not either."

"Only if you can prove."

"I need to meet him," Dharma sounded demanding surprisingly.

"Of course, court orders would suffice," chuckling, SHO protruded at the right time.

"You couldn't even become constable had we not let you in," agony and insult uttered the obvious.

"And what about you? You-"

Samajwadi interrupted, "You can go and meet him," addressed SHO, "No point wasting time, better be ready to deal with Sarpanch."

Dharma anxiously moved towards the gallery housing cells, a couple of constables following him. Hardy ex-serviceman had his body resist every abuse it could, Dharma was stunned, softly held his hands.

"You got in?" tried to bring a smile on.

"Our failure." Dharma could only whisper, could not muster the courage to see into his eyes.

"Nah," pausing momentarily, "Sarpanch's failure."

The cell was stinking, the building wasn't old, the absence of regular cleaning was the genesis, constables chose to move out instead, kept a watch from outside.

"He will be here any time," a teary Dharma tried to justify, "he has been very concerned about you."

A dear friend was not in good shape, Dharma could barely behold the sight, turned around yelled at the constables, "You got to pay a heavy price!"

Chhattar had by now sitting with his back leaning on the wall.

"MLA needs be taken to task," Chhattar said thinking.

"This is not the time...first, we must get you out."

"Will take time," pausing for a moment, moving his upper body close to his friend, Chhattar asked, "Were you able to?"

Dharma tried to decode the words, "Ma had very little left...Sapna has some - making ends meet somehow."

"Nah Dharma, could you visit them, had any word for Laado?" an anxious brother asked.

"I couldn't be there, was to visit today to meet him in person. Sunday last he was not at home met his family." Dharma replied.

"Ma went too?"

"Yes. she has approved the family."

Gingerly, and fearing the worst Chhattar asked, "Did they talk about her job?"

"All could talk were customary exchanges. Nothing particularly was discussed...but..." Dharma stopped short.

"But?!' Chhattar heartbeat raced up.

"But they don't know about you."

"Me?!"

"That you are..."

"Don't worry a matter of time," thinking hard Chhattar suggested, "Boy if you could meet soon?"

"Sapna is yet to be told," perturbed Dharma said annoyingly, "Leave this Chhattar, for the moment we need to see you out."

"That we don't know Dharma," he let a few moments pass by to find his breath, the battered body said moments later, "I'm a lot more worried for her now."

"There is no need, you must not panic, we can't lose!" the friend pleaded.

"Please see if APMC aadhati can expedite and release our MSP payment fast."

He breathed heavily.

"He cannot do much, those close to MLA will get to lay their hands on the first set of MSP payment arriving," Dharma said in a dejected voice.

"Bastards," Utter anguish, despair, and frustration outwitted the body pain.

"Tau is arranging a few thousand, should be reaching any time." Dharma tried to instil some hope in his friend.

"Yeah...why not? Such a grand success, Congress hasn't had such a success for a long time."

"He is not the usual one when you are not around," Dharma said clenching his friend's hands.

"And this is the most unfortunate," Chhattar sighed, "a little regular support is all that I need to get my family a long way."

"He may begin to change post this incident."

"I can only hope."

Both paused.

Chhattar was pensive, injuries causing sharp and steady pain along the waist every other second.

Dharma was thinking hard. "FIR has only named a mob."

"Against a mob?!!," Chhattar was utterly surprised, "Baapu name doesn't figure?"

"Not yet and not even yours."

"That's strange."

"To me as well...perhaps wants to negotiate," Dharma shared his suspicion.

"For what?" Chhattar was surely surprised to think of the remote possibility.

"Agitation has swelled, Congress has been noticed across state and Delhi, we have made a killing."

"Baapu can't stop it now," Chhattar said as he adjusted his back against the wall to try and minimise the pain, "no gain in negotiating, a Sarpanch can have at most a sway locally."

"But then the land they want is here. Protests elsewhere in the state cannot have any bearing on what goes on here," Dharma remarked.

"Use of heavy hand is to frighten the father," Chhattar inferred, "Time will tell – A father survives, or a leader seizes."

"Seizes?!"

"Seizes the moment," he said in a dead voice. No pain a son felt that very moment.

For a few moments, none spoke, the silence was unbearable to Dharna. He blamed himself for the entire episode, wanted to hide behind conversation - any word would do - silence was unveiling his emotions he was at unease.

The friend could read his mind, said, "No one could hold himself. Nobody had the power to overwhelm events on that day. Something was bound to happen."

"Perhaps I could act a minute early."

Chhattar changed the subject, "Tyagi paid a visit."

"Here?"

"Yes."

"That's strange!" Dharma was quite surprised.

Chhattar added further, "Expressed solidarity on behalf of Tyagi and Bishnoi community of Ekta Manch."

"Make sense but to come all the way to see you without letting me or Baapu know is strange."

Constables outside suddenly sprang into action launching themselves in a swift move - almost barging in, held and lifted Dharma by his arms in one swing, and almost took him out dragging, all the way up to the SHO room.

Dharma spotted Sahoo Singh stepping in with the usual entourage.

SHO stood up while Yadav calmly stared.

"FIR is lopsided," Sarpanch said vehemently.

"You are lucky. The mob has been named," SHO said.

"Only Congress workers and Manch farmers are mentioned."

"No surprises, they only created the ruckus," Yadav commented.

"And you hooligans?"

"Think of your son," Yadav snapped.

Elderly gushed out, "He will be out any moment."

"As if the court has ruled."

Courts were closed for a few days due to gazetted holidays, Sahoo reminded himself. Chhattar cannot be out until mid-next week, it was Saturday. Efforts until late Thursday and all through Friday could not secure bail orders.

"Law can decide on its own, I am talking to SSP and will…" his mobile rang, cutting him short.

Sarpanch walked towards one corner, "Ji," listened to the words intently, said, "Chhattar has been taken in."

"Hmmm," on the other side, "Why is that dirt Samajwadi loitering in kotwali?"

He was startled, hurriedly, "His aide succumbed to head injury."

"We need people for Jind by-election rally on Monday," the voice ordered.

"I have asked all to make in good numbers," Sarpanch clarified.

"Keep a watch. We need to be cautious; momentum is with us."

"Ji"

"Don't worry much for your son, he should be out soon," the voice sounded indifferent.

Smothered father wanted to ask, "how?!" felt & fell in line, could merely utter - "Ji," pensive, pondering, "Could this be all he deserved for working hard over the years?!".

He wasn't sure but for sure he was in agony, craving to find his conscience wake up, take a note and be reluctant at the least - 'Could I?' he asked himself, 'Could you ever?' was the answer.

A thundering voice shook him out of his thoughts, "Sahoo?!"

"Ji!" phone almost slipped out of his hand.

"How come the consent numbers be as high as 45%?!!"

"Who told so sahib?!" Sarpanch was shocked.

"Every other block member I speak to, estimate these many already in the bag of the agency."

"I have always been apprised a number not more than 30%" Sahoo Singh tried to clarify.

"Can I ask you to stop the tide?" Voice asked firmly.

"There is no need to panic sahib." Sarpanch attempted to reassure.

"You better be spending time with the block committee," an agitated voice thundered.

"I do sahib," Sahoo replied.

"Yet, this much ground stands already conceded."

A veteran was receiving rebuke as a school goer would.

"Figures I can guarantee are wrong," Sahoo Singh said firmly.

"Engage with cadre, spend time on the ground, apprise with updates every…" voice several notches up now, "you get that?" yelling, "and stop wasting time on your son, he can take care of himself."

The call was cut.

Old-guard was left shocked and bettered. He was alone now with his emotional strength behind the bars - Veteran was in dire straits.

"You cannot have killers by your side and boast to represent common men," retort jerk old man out of his thoughts, Yadav was yelling, "Zuber was the only earning hand in the family," eyes penetrating sixty-five-plus dilapidated face, "You killed my son!"

"He wasn't your son!" Sahoo Singh retorted.

Yadav dropped his voice to a whisper and said, "Now is the turn of another!"

"That will be absurd-," An aging father was frightened.

Complacency was rejoicing, "Your politics rendered us a dead body…"

As all the ranks filled the room Yadav went berserk - a spectacle was on.

"…your son will be the cost," index finger-wagging, tongue vomiting words, mouth overflowing with, "Land will be ours...dead body yours!"

The elderly noticed the phrase, "land will be ours."

"Let politics handle politics," he just answered calmly, "Personal loss will be a loss to all, as has been the case," sounding defiant, "Rest hard work on the ground will drive people around you, me and all."

"Bull shit, you are stuck, and we will see you remain so."

"Going gung-ho will see your back to the wall someday."

"So?" Samajwadi sounded in two minds.

Elderly felt his nerve, "And no one lending a helping hand."

"You will have to survive to that day for that to happen," Yadav chuckled.

"Remind yourself of my days went by and time spent in the region - you will find every reason to the contrary."

Stepping close, intently Yadav whispered, "Only if your son tugs along as he has in the days and time you are so arrogant about."

"Chhattar has always and will." A father's pride yelled.

"A big if!" Yadav chuckled on.

Sahoo Singh turned towards SHO, "Let me talk to SSP in charge here."

"I will file a FIR against your son for committing the murder. Police were present," said SHO, "An open and shut case."

"We will have our witnesses," Sahoo Singh protested.

"There you go," chuckled SHO.

"What is it that you need to set him free?" A tired father asked finally.

"Court orders."

Entourage was surprised to find a sudden outspoken SHO, he belonged to fraternity seldom not to fall-in-line and be yes men of career politicians. Sahoo reckoned an immature, stupid, self-defeating behaviour. He chose to deal with Yadav, held his hand, and took him to one side.

"What is that I can do for you?"

Samajwadi was startled to find the opponent almost pleading, "Years must have gone by seeing you plead."

"Which piece of land you are most eager for?"

"All of that you have fielded your career cards on," Samajwadi enjoyed the moment.

Subtly, keeping the tone and manner consistent, engaging the eyeballs, Sahoo Singh whispered: "Or those 107 acres?"

"Which…Which 107 pieces?" Yadav was taken aback, smirk disappeared

The veteran felt the nerve, "Acres…acres!"

"Whatever it happens to be," ignoring, turning his face away, "marginalized must benefit."

"Or those who keep margins," veteran followed his opponent.

"Margin they keep," Samajwadi pointed towards the SHO and ranks in the room.

"Mere parts - the percentage they get to keep, right?"

Samajwadi felt cornered, "Murderers will not get away," retorted, arms out, hands waving, eyes threatening - the spectacle was re-enacted.

At that very moment, Sarpanch's mobile rang, "Dharna you see to this…I will come back soon," eyes uttering, 'Rascal' and he made a swift walk out with entourage following him.

"And I will see that he remains locked," Yadav yelled at the disappearing opponent.

"Let the sense prevail Samajwadi," Dharma pitched in his advice, "We have to be here forever, elections will come and go, power will keep changing hands."

"Battles must be won," Yadav smirked, "as the War goes on."

"Not at the cost to lose forever."

"Not at the decisive battle...war must be won."

"You are going too far with this," Dharma warned.

"And you, your Sahoo Singh..." He was cut short as a hurried SHO handed Samajwadi his phone with SHO voice turning to a whisper, "Sir wants to speak to you."

Yadav swiftly stepped into another room. SHO signalled to constables.

Dharma could not believe what was getting unfolded in front of him.

A few minutes later Chhattar was being helped to sit on the chair across the SHO table.

In the other room, "Are you nuts, Yadav?!"

"MLA sahib this was the time to nail them in," Yadav sounded jubilant.

But received a rebuke in return – "You are as stupid as you were ever."

"MLA ji, hold your tongue."

"And your berserk ways," MLA Inderjeet retorted him, "we are losing yet you are committing blunder after blunder."

"We cannot-"

"You better shut up and listen...get him..." pausing momentarily, thinking hard, "Where is this SHO?"

Yadav swiftly made his way back. Now, SHO went inside.

The conversation took longer than usual while Yadav peeped in intently from a distance.

Moments later he stepped in too, only to emerge in no time with SHO in tow. They made themselves comfortable on either side of Chhattar. Dharna drew his chair opposite his friend.

"Mob violence will be the case filed," Yadav began gingerly, "Charges will not be imposed on any individual."

In between the lines were read right away.

"But you will have to aid us." Yadav said smirking.

Accused senses felt awkward, "What could be that?" was the expression on both faces.

"Can we not get to know what Manch is up to - at any point in time?" Yadav asked looking at SHO with half-grin.

Friends looked at each other, gaping.

"Let me make it simple and short," Yadav looking for a moment at his aides, "You get us the insider's story."

"And you will keep me outside." Chhattar said in a dead voice.

"Awesome, young blood is wise," Yadav chuckled.

"Dare not you think of us calibrating with your ill designs," Dharma yelled in protest., "Case premise is not strong enough to keep Chhattar inside for a long."

"Let me go home…" Chhattar interjected right hand went up gingerly, "…give me some time to think."

"Shhaabaash," Yadav's chuckle went wider as right arm tapped on the shoulder of the ex-serviceman while friends looked on at the jest, an insult to the core.

A month later.

"She is a turncoat," agitated Zuber had called up at Chacko hotel room. It was quite late in the evening.

"It is too late here Zuber…I will dial you tomorrow morning."

"How can she take over my assignment?!" Zuber thundered.

"Because I asked her."

"And that's why I am calling you, who are you to snatch my assignment?"

"If you do not deliver in time, someone is bound to step in," Chacko replied calmly.

"You stabbed me in the back. I was away for Eid, leaves are my right."

"And what would term your role as, since the time I'm here?" Chacko snapped.

"You spoiled my Eid."

Chacko did not reply.

"A Kashmiri is always subjected to this," he murmured to himself.

"You are wasting my time, I need to sleep."

"Wow you need to sleep today, you stay awake 24X7 and today you want to sleep," Zuber was yelling, "everyone knows what's happening between you and rustic."

"Courtesy you - I learnt a few tricks," Chacko said in a deliberate dead voice.

"She is a turncoat, I tell you."

"Anything else Mr. Zuber?" Indifferent tone cut Zuber in two pieces and he went berserk.

"How long you could keep off with a few hours' sleep, let me see...luck and chance happen to all."

"Grab some water, your words are fumbling now." A smirk was on Chacko's face.

"I will not go out of the way to support the project now on," an exasperated Zuber declared.

But was snapped, "Have you ever, so far?"

"Don't forget I have prepared this rustic girl for what she is today," he was fuming now.

"How can I?" Chacko replied in a firm voice, "And don't ever think it was a favour you did to the project, you needed her to drag me down, and you succeeded."

"And now you want to play that out!"

"You better take care of your next assignment," said the lead in a stern voice, "else..."

"Else what?!" Zuber thundered.

"Your position could well be made redundant," Chacko snapped back.

"Ha-ha, as If I don't know - one out will imply one less billable – a loss to the company."

"Customer needs delivery, individuals do not matter if one is out, 1 another can easily be accommodated." He sounded convinced.

"Of course, you at service 24X7 all can be made redundant," A frustrated

Zuber quipped.

"Yes, thanks to resources like you offshore, that one at onsite becomes the face and the dependency of the customer." Words were firm, deflated the opponent. And he could only blame the providence.

"I lament the day I joined this organization."

"That's your destiny if you could not be here in my place."

"Wow - A Kashmiri does not have a destiny is laughable."

"Zuber, I need to sleep now, Bye." Since he made his point amply clear, Chacko now wanted to end the conversation.

"We have resisted, and I promise you will find this sole one down here no exception."

"You are talking nonsense now." Chacko did not want to get dragged in any political or religious argument.

While Zuber looked at this as an opportunity to score a point and save some face. "Don't forget you an Indian have stabbed me in back."

Egged on Chacko retorted, "I made sure one cannot conquer by ill means."

Zuber recited a couplet: "Ragon mein dorte phirne ke hum nahin kaayal - Jo aankh hi se na tapka wo lahu kya hai."

"Mirza Ghalib," Chacko said in an indifferent tone.

"I'm from the conquering class," Zuber yelled, "not you-" but was cut short.

"devtāoñ kā khudā se hogā kaam - aadmī ko aadmī darkār hai."

"What?!!" Zuber could not recall or relate the couplet.

"Raghupati Sahay, ever heard off?" Chacko asked, grinning.

"There you go, sweetheart; you all can only see from Hindu-Muslim premise."

"You believe one is greater thus the conqueror," Chacko quipped, "this Indian does not."

"Ghalib was an Indian too, you manipulators." Zuber fumed.

"Ha ha ha. Is it Zuber that I'm talking to?!"

"You can hide behind the fake laugh Chacko but for how long?" Zuber shouted, furious he cursed, "You all will have to cope with the reality sooner or later."

"Reality, that you tell us – wow - A born Kashmiri is Kashmiri ever after - never an Indian - right?!'

He felt pierced in pieces, could not find words, "Youuuu…."

"Ha ha ha. Time to reach office, Dear Zuber."

And Chacko disconnected the phone.

He stepped out of his couch, perturbed. Took a cigarette out and lit. 'Outrageous…' he muttered. Calling directly, with an intention to challenge, offshore team lead had gone too far.

He ambled across the length of the living room for as long as he could remember. Perhaps an hour or two had passed by when he noticed half a dozen he had inhaled, 'bad…' he murmured.

Exhaling the last puff, he swiftly moved to the table, pressed keys on the laptop. On the instant messaging app, he searched for Anant. Senior Manager status was green. He trigged a video call.

"Hmmm…looks like something is troubling you, dear onsite lead…" Manager guessed, "it is not usual to find Chacko awake in the middle of the night."

"Um…actually I want to plan my back up at onsite."

"I've no problem and who?" asked the manager, the tongue was subtle.

"Anyone from the youngsters will do," lead said.

"And why not Zuber – the offshore lead? Once and whenever you are away, he would lead…and you know he is keen as well equipped with the experience of dealing with customers, to back his claim."

"His absence will leave a void at offshore. And before I go further…" Chacko was trying to find right words, "my apologies, sir."

"And for what?" The manager could read in between the lines was rather wary of the internal tussle.

"For assessing Zuber skills too early and jumped to the conclusion," he said in carefully chosen words.

"I do not even recall we have had any such conversation, or did we?"

"Not sure…but makes sense to apologies even if it was something only in my mind…certainly must have affected my dealings with him," Chacko was speaking in a naïve tone.

"Go on…who and when?" Managed asked.

"Jyoti perhaps…" he diced.

"Jyoti??!!" Manager was startled, "Not sure if I'm speaking to Chacko I know."

"Or maybe Sapna Singh." He said in a confident voice.

Manager Anant thought for a few moments and then said, "Well, Sapna has certainly done well. Zuber has spent much time grooming her. While Jyoti could be a liability in an onsite role, Sapna with steadier technical hands-on and medium to advance functional knowledge would still need some grooming for this particular role."

"I agree, we can…basically, this is the reason why I wanted someone to join me here for a few weeks." Chacko said firmly.

"Let me consult with SK also…Sapna Singh has spent just a few months… so not sure…I will get back."

"Many thanks, Anant."

Wounds had healed, Faujji was no longer limping.

His illusions long gone, and with the last episode, all the disillusionments had too. Father was closer to his heart for he felt he cared for him evermore since the incident but he couldn't understand why?

Acres after acres were notified by governmental agencies and notifications of acquisition erected on the fields across the belt. Kissan Ekta Manch encouraged farmers not to stop farming - the acquisition was termed as a forced one.

Manch had been demanding the release of documents to prove a claim - by state government and agencies involved - that 70% of the affected farmers' consent had been received.

A number of the farmers were willing to let the land go, should price per acre offered to be increased.

Astute Sarpanch had always reckoned those could play spoilsport and could be the genesis of a good number of consent submission in no time.

70% mark was still a long way away, Manch devised tactics to hold back the rest. Not many were interested, a few in dilemma, politics on both sides attempting best manoeuvre realising momentum howsoever small if gained could swing the battle in its favour.

The ex-army captain had given in to despair, the farm was the place he was seen most of the time. Most of his land had been notified.

Kharif season was on the anvil.

Chhatrapal had always sown Bajra and Jawar, wheat in Rabi season. A meagre income by the standard of the family kept him season after season on his toes. He was desperate this time.

'Income must be sufficient, large enough to sustain all of us itself,' he reminded himself, 'Baapu's pension cannot be made part of calculations with no surety to arrive leads to last-minute scrambling.'

The whole affair was turning quite intimidating. Deep despair had begun to settle in.

And he had begun to ponder over a way out, a permanent one - 'Could a change in farm sowings be the key?' he pondered hard.

'There is no harm in attempting one time,' the young farmer assured himself.

'Could at best be another low-to-medium yield season,' trying hard to feel through and see if he is convinced, 'While even with a moderate return this could be a pivotal juncture to set forth an alternative in hand,' he began to hope slightly now.

'What could be the right crop?' thinking hard, 'What could be…um… Sesame? um…no doesn't yield much…Mustard… could well be yes,' suddenly his memory recalled Expert's word - 'Maize!!' his eyes lit up. 'Returns could be higher if all he said the other day in the rally is true.'

It was getting dark, he headed home, across the horizon under the dusk farms could be seen notified - black hoardings with striking yellow letters - declaring the onslaught on the anvil. Minutes later, Ma was standing on the small gate carved out from the vast entrance to the courtyard. She was much concerned.

"You must keep your phone handy Chhattar."

"Calls irritate me, Ma."

"It gets frightening not to find you around for long." She said closing the door.

"Better If I stay lost in work," he said in a low voice.

She understood the bitterness.

"Maize this time I am thinking to sow," he uttered gingerly what he was thinking over through that evening.

"You would need a lot of water," Ma cautioned.

"Which should not be a challenge, the canal is next to us," He sounded optimistic.

"Would be prudent if you can check at Mandi once the last 2 seasons' prices," Ma suggested. She was at the far corner of the courtyard, next to buffalo and her calf, mending and bringing the livestock's staple food up to the right mix.

"Must be better than Jawar and Bajra," Chhattar said.

"Your call Chhattar - but must not be a gamble."

"I am careful Ma," He said in a coarse voice.

Ma could observe the effect of a tough time on her eldest child, she stepped closer, "You wanted to sell, right?"

He sighed, "Yes, I still want to."

"Why don't you then? - will get rid of the everyday struggle to sustenance in one shot."

"Baapu, and with him politics surrounding our lives, I fear losing everything." The child confided in her mother.

"The way others will get the compensation, we will," she said in a dead voice.

"Only time will tell, for now, we need to toe the line majority has adopted," he sounded unsure.

"Stick to Jawar and Bajara,"the elderly put her warm hand on her son, "not a good time to take a drastic decision."

"Laado marriage will require handsome amount," he kept untangling shoelaces, "perhaps this time we could be lucky."

"Your nana used to sow," Ma said getting up.

"Maize?!" He was surprised.

"Three-four times he did," she affirmed, walking back towards the corner.

"How was the yield? how did he manage water?" he was curious, "Was there a canal nearby?"

"The only well in the vicinity was sufficient those days," she said putting a bucket full of water next to buffalo, "Tube well had not arrived, only zamindars could afford."

"Yields must have been good enough I suppose since he went back to sowing it for 3 to 4 times." He was getting eager and inclined to switch crop this Kharif season.

"Yes, Muslims had the fields adjacent to us; water from the well was equally sourced; they were helpful; in fact, they had begun earlier than your nana. We received many tips," She said going back to mending saani (the feed).

"If I could get some?" he wondered to himself.

"I heard ours have stopped farming," Ma was talking about the farmlands surrounding their farmland, Muslim peasants owned those fields.

"Yes, they toe Samajwadi and you know about them."

"Hmmm."

"Blessing in disguise," The young farmer commented.

"How?" Ma asked.

"I will be the only one in acres needing water,' he smiled.

For a moment she had hoped, was fearful the very next, "only if Agency does not take over the land mid-season."

"Will drag until elections," Chhattar sounded dead sure.

Ma stepped out into the courtyard; time was to prepare another round of saani (livestock's staple food) for the livestock.

Chhattar followed her sat on a cot was pensive, 'It could be life-changing decision,' pondering hard he reminded himself the importance of water, 'one bad season at this juncture, will bring him to knees.'

He was not nervous but anxious to get a way out, "what else could the alternative be?"

"Vegetables," Ma had overheard his murmurs.

"Vegetables?!!" found it ridiculous, "no one does that in the whole region."

"Some do."

"They pop up for a season or two only to disappear. No one has tasted success," Chhattar said.

"One has."

He turned, expressions on the face asking, "who?"

"Tyagi ji." Ma said.

"Tyagi," it was news to him, no other farmer ever talked about it.

"Anita?" Chhattar's better half, belonged to farmer family herself, walked into the courtyard holding a brass glass full of milk. "Saani (livestock staple food) is not well prepared, will become hard for these to produce optimum quantity every day," remarked Ma before addressing son, "For a while, the vital ingredient is not available, much less than desired, can you get some?"

"I know," an irate voice said, "keep the mix as it is, for now, I do not have money to provide best of everything, the priority lies somewhere else."

"Why do you react in the manner you have?" folk woman was running out of patience with baap-beta frustrated disposition, "Can't we keep things simple?"

Chhattar did not react.

"Anita you go inside, someone is at the door," said Ma stepping towards the gate at the far end of the courtyard.

"Ram-Ram ji."

"Namaskar ji," Ma stepped aside, quickly spread her chunni out in a manner to create a veil.

Chhattar spotted leader of Tyagi and Bishnoi farming communities stepping inside. He was surprised to find him visiting the household.

"Namaskar Tau," said Chhattar inviting him towards the cot beside the neem tree standing tall in the centre of the courtyard.

"Ram-Ram Chhattar."

The leader of some prominence made himself comfortable as Ma walked back to the veranda. All were surprised and equally agog.

"I must ask your forgiveness beta,"the old man started gingerly, "I should have been here much earlier."

"You are my elderly, please do not." Chhattar seated himself opposite to him.

"They have not treated you well. No one benefits from personal animosity."

"I have managed to see the worst phase through, hopefully, things will continue to fall in place," Chattar said.

"My blessings are with you, Chhattar," the elderly was speaking in a low but steady voice, "You have been one of the brightest in the whole village. Only time will tell what destiny has for you but had tragedy not struck Sahoo you would make the village proud with your work in Army I am sure."

"Yudhvinder is gradually improving," Ma said.

"Of course, he will. He is still young," then gingerly, "how old are you now, Chhattar?"

Anita stepped into the court with veil fully drawn milk in hand, "Jitti reh (long live) betti," the elderly blessed her.

"Ji paintees (thirty-five)."

"Time flies past," paused as if thinking, "Aadhati called today, my payment has been released."

"When did you deposit your produce?" Chhattar was quite curious and determined to know when his would arrive.

"Much after you," Tyagi replied.

Angrily: "I'm yet to receive any call."

"Blame the protest Chhattar," putting his warm hand on his back said, "Let me try If I could be of any help."

"Ji, kindly see if we can get even if in instalments," Ma said, voice almost pleading.

"You are embarrassing me. I have already sent for." Tyagi said quickly.

"Shukriyaa Tau. I have tried all I could. They are determined to delay this as long as they could." Chhattar said in a low voice.

"You just don't worry." Tyagi tried to assure him of his help.

A few moments passed by. They sipped on the delicious beverage. Little later, the old man asked, "What do you plan to sow this time, Chhattar?"

"Makka."

"Makka?!" veteran landlord was startled.

"Ji, no point running around Aadhati pleading for MSP payments."

"I agree, I had once advised Sahoo to break the monotony," addressing womenfolk in the veranda their veil fully drawn, "The soil also gets fertile if farmer alternates between crops."

"Chhattar is thinking about venturing into Vegetables," Ma disclosed.

"Waah, this is what I was to advise," veteran almost stood up, "finally you are thinking in the right direction!"

"We were merely discussion about the options," Chhattar tried to clarify.

"No harm, so long as you have only the right options to choose one from,"

Tyagi said.

Chhattar was not convinced still, did not comment.

"Vegetable farming earns much better margins," veteran sounded excited, "and you will come out of the vicious circle of APMC-Aadhati-MSP."

"I agree, but to that extent only," Chhattar said.

"Let me know what your reservations are about?" Tyagi asked.

"Vegetable farming will need a constant concentration of labour and resources this is what I have heard," Chhattar said.

"You are right, vegetables grow much faster..."

Chhattar added, "and decay even quicker hence time to market..."

The veteran completed, "is limited."

"So?" Chhattar asked.

"So, one gets a chance to make money in short intervals," the experienced farmer replied.

The young farmer's countenance did not disguise the unconvinced soul inside.

"And why to discount the fact - prices are greater than our regular season's long sowings such as wheat and bajra?" Tyagi added.

"Prices can fluctuate at any time," Chhattar argued.

"Still, you will get the chance to aim at the higher range," Tyagi clarified.

"I am not too knowledgeable about the most fruitful of all, Chhattar said frankly.

"You can sow Brinjal or Cauliflower, rest will not get you the prices you seem to be aiming for," Tyagi advised.

"Onion, potato, or tomato can only support the poor lot," Ma commented.

The veteran said, "I have been doing both Brinjal and Cauliflower since the last 2 seasons in half of my fields."

"What has been your returns?" Chhattar asked.

"'Exact figures my younger son can tell, but for sure if one can manage time to market the margins fetched will surpass the traditional season-long ones," Tyagi replied.

"How many hands do you have at this?" the excited young farmer asked pointedly.

"Good question, you would need at least 2, I have 3 besides me, my both sons," Tyagi answered.

He turned a little disappointed, "We can spend time, you please give it a try," Anita suggested.

"I am sure Dharma will help us too in these trying times," Ma hoped.

Tyagi showed a willingness to support him in the initial days of strife and struggle, "I have developed links and acquaintances over the past few seasons. I will introduce you to them. But you will have to consider the market fee and commission on every sale."

"How much are they?" Chhattar asked.

"6% commission and 1% market fee here in the NCR," Tyagi replied.

Chhattar was pensive for a while and asked after a few moments, "I heard about markets wholly set up by farmers."

"You must be talking about Kissan Mandi?" Ma remarked.

"Yes Kissan Mandi," all were as much surprised as impressed with Ma's knowledge.

"Yes, you avoid these fees if you are one of those farmers. But then the only large farmer can afford the land rates or owning a shop there," the old man encouraged, "Yet it is a good scheme by Modi Sarkar, I must say farmers and farmer producer organisations will be able to meet part of NCR's net demand of 15,000 tonnes of vegetables a day."

"Tyagi ji you have been with Kissan Ekta Manch. It is strange to find you appreciating Modi Sarkar," Chhattar commented.

"It is true many schemes have either been no-starters or had too many shortcomings, yet a few are useful - this is definitely one in the long run," Tyagi observed.

"So, am I still captive at APMCs and Adhatis?" the tired young farmer asked.

"You and I can hope for large private establishments such as Safal setting up these markets in the near future then we can sell to them," Tyagi said.

"Are there none so far?" Chhattar was curious to know

"Not many," Tyagi replied.

Chhattar asked further, "But at these Kissan Mandis at least we will have some outlets which will buy our produce?"

"Chances depend on what you produce and what they are purchasing on a given day. It is a drastically different scenario from the scenario prevailing in APMCs where you can stroll in with the produce and you know someone or other, from the hundred shoppers that will purchase," Experienced man advised caution.

"I understand but Tyagi ji you very well know, from the farmland to the consumer, there is a price build-up of up to 2.5 times because of the presence of several intermediaries," Chhatttar was excited with the potential of Kissan Mandi, "Such Kissan Mandis, I am sure, will cut down these middlemen and give better margins to farmers."

"The practice is yet to reach that stage Chhatrapal," Tyagi cut the story short.

while the young farmer was still eager and "Could we someday?"

"You and me, are to hope."

"And just hope," he murmured.

Soon after Tyagi left.

Womenfolk were delighted to be assured of long due MSP payments and a veteran's help and experience to their aid in farming something considered to generate better and more importantly a 'regular' income.

Chhattar, on the other hand, was desperate.

CHAPTER 7

S ahoo Singh owned a large piece of land running parallel to NH-8 on its eastern side. Jat community had a majority of land in the region. Sarpanch land was bordered from its western end by NH-8, eastern side and southern sides by lands owned by Muslim peasants while in the north was the disputed site of Imperial City - a mega township half-built, rest in litigation. A canal was running through the fields of all from east to west, supplying water from the Yamuna to farmlands in the hinterland of Haryana.

"Water will be pivotal to keep churning out produce after every produce."

Dharma was happy to see his friend after ages, excited, and looking forward to doing something.

"Cauliflower will need a constant supply and this canal has been a boon," Chhatrapal remarked, gazing at the behemoth.

"I feel the need for one more tractor," Dharma suggested.

"I need to verify Tyagi optimism first before investing too much," Chhattar, on the other hand, was cautious.

"I agree, let us see how much every stage grinds you and this time to market. I do not know how you would manage without an additional tractor?" Dharma sounded concerned.

"I will have to employ additional labour too," Chhattar said thinking hard.

"Something you have never done, another area of inexperience," friend added.

"Man can be managed Dharma, a machine can be bought, I'm wary of other factors," the young farmer said. His face was expressing his growing concerns.

"Such as?" asked Dharma.

"Timely and constant supply of water; keeping the water level optimum; timely harvesting," Chhattar called out a few, fingertips counting.

"Most important aspect you are missing still," Dharma cautioned.

"Seeds?" Chhattar looked at Dharma.

"Turnaround time from Harvesting - which will empty your land - that's 1," Dharma said looking intently.

"Okay I count – One," excited young farmer adjusted his posture to sit face to face with his friend.

"To quick loading and swift haulage to market," Dharma resumed.

"That's two."

"To purchase seeds and fertilizers," the friend added next.

"Presumably while returning from the Mandi okay, three," Chhattar nodded.

"To sowing them with an optimum spray of fertilizers."

"Four - that's all."

"No," Dharma said smiling.

"Not yet?!"

"Overlap all these activities if you have two vegetables sown simultaneously and will-" Dharma said getting up.

Chhattar supplemented his concern, "Will make all of us be on our toes... go berserk...round the clock."

"A slight delay in harvesting or hauling could make the fresh produce go stale," Dharma added further.

"Will cause overhead to clear field without earning a penny in hand," Chhattar completed the sentence.

"Lead time to next sowing will increase, offset the next subsequent cycle thus," Dharma almost warned.

"Hmm..." Chhattar was now fretful

"So, stop just looking at the end - of course this will generate larger income," Friend tried to cheer him up and instil some optimism.

"Yet I am to be cautious - I will only go with 1 - cauliflower, no need for 2," Chhattar said in a dead voice.

"Only once you have additional resources to deploy," Dharma suggested.

"Imperative to produce & sustain one vegetable and secure money for that to happen in 3 to 6 months," Chhattar sounded confident.

Dharma was not in favour of a radical shift, "Bhai our Sarkar...," he gingerly began, "is just a few months away; stick to what you know best," his friend perhaps didn't pay heed, dharma held his arm, "no point re-inventing the wheel," or probably worst had convinced ill-fated farmer of a necessity to depart, "bajra will get you the money you need to see this season through" and to depart now; agitated Dharma clasped the friend's arms, pleaded, "Later once we are in power payments will be thick and fast."

Chhattar for sure wasn't listening.

"Hello, Sapna?"

Voice was heavy and not strange to her ears, 'someone she heard before... but who?'

"Hello... um." She glanced at the number, it had +1 as the prefix, 'From the USA?' she mumbled.

Five months since the project start, Chacko called up Sapna Singh on her mobile phone. It was strange. He, the onsite lead would hardly ping her. He would pass tasks brief in team meetings. If there is an urgent message then it would arrive via email, yet here even desk phone was not made any use of, she had been called on her mobile.

"How about Visa... I checked with the travel desk... it is done... right?"

She felt uneasy, "Yes... Ji... Oh!" she felt ashamed, how could she converse in Hindi. She is in the IT world, just recently Visa has been granted to her and Hindi word?

"Ji main... Chacko (Yes It's me Chacko)," the other voice noticed the lull.

"Hi... Chacko," her voice was frail and tattering. Her heartbeats went up several notches.

"Visa?" he asked again.

"Yes, it is done." Words were out in a dash.

"Excellent."

"Login screen is bug-free now," harried soul gushed out. She thought lead must have called to know the status of fixes on the central software component.

"That's okay," He said in a dead indifferent voice.

She noticed he had stopped, 'Perhaps thinking?'

'Uh…'

Another second and one more, 'Definitely trying to recall something I may have done wrong?' she felt on the edge.

"Hi…" he said again.

This was out of place, 'hi? And again? seemingly all over the place,' her sense knocked at her, 'is he?'

"I am sure you must have done shopping for your onsite sojourn." Chacko said in a flash.

"Yes…" she replied at an equal pace, "no…" she corrected, "I mean not completely."

"Zuber… um… appreciated your work," Lead uttered.

They were speaking to each other for the first time. And the hearts trembling.

"So, in the shopping…" stopped short. The topic went back swinging her thoughts wide, 'what about shopping?' she attempted her senses take, if any, there was none.

Resumed he, "must-have… I guess… purchased the formal attire for everyday work here in New Jersey whenever you are here?"

She had tried several stores in Vasant Kunj and Gurgaon. A few shortlisted females were in two minds still.

"Yes… will have business formal Monday to Thursday and on Fridays, business casual," she replied.

"Hmmm", he was not completely out of his thoughts still.

"No," he gushed out loud, he could not control and felt embarrassed.

She stayed quiet.

"I mean… why don't you try picking up a few Sarees?"

'Saree?' she was startled to the hilt. Here she had unleashed a hell of time upon her going wild about how she would carry the attire she had never worn while being in the middle of the most important assignment and the boss is talking about wearing Saree!

"Yes… and also some other ethnic wear…" he said in a dead voice.

"But Chacko… would that not be out of place… they are not meant to be office wears," she spoke her mind.

"Just do as I say,"the voice sounded authoritative, and subtly the very next moment asked, "When are you arriving?"

"Next Monday," she said quietly.

"Have a safe flight."

She was stunned, the call had been disconnected.

A month into the venture.

"You cannot work day and night."

"Who else will?"

The farmer and the friend were arguing.

"I will see tonight through," friend insisted.

"I'm sure - pipe was fully submerged when I left the spot," the farmer was scratching his head.

"You must be sleepy," Dharma was sure.

Shrugging off, irritated Chhattar asked him, "What time will you be in?"

"9 - 9:30."

"You are never in time - be here by 9:30 pm I warn you."

"Where do you keep these snakes," Dharma asked him referring to a mile-long set of pipes to draw water from the canal.

"They are a gem...ready to bend... spine to me," Chhattar said with a wide smile.

"And to your ill-timed adventure," Dharma commented winking.

"Make sure you fully submerge them in the water, at least three-four feet deep; over the night level in the canal goes down as..."

But instructions were cut short, "As, many draw across the belt, I haven't forgotten of the basics," Dharma quipped.

While Chhattar was striving hard to bring the most in his first attempt at farming, he had never done before, adjacent fields were dry. No activity had taken place in the last four months since the time agitation erupted. The Muslim peasants and farmers were dedicated soldiers of Samajwadi outfit, they were hopeful of getting a good price per acre, hoping to get rid of poverty even if temporarily.

Lately, they had begun to run out of patience now. Elections were a few months away model code of conduct will be in force for a couple of months before the elections they knew, hence compensation distribution will be temporarily stopped. The compensation distribution had not started just yet.

A kilometre away, in some bungalow:

"Sahib, BJP could lose elections, Congress or Lok Dal could be in power." Abdul khan sounded appeasing.

"Elections are gamble nowadays; anything could happen Khan chacha."

Muslim peasants, some 50 in number, were at Yadav's bungalow, the request was to expedite the land acquisition compensation payments. Abdul Khan fondly called as Khan Chacha, and widely respected for his honesty was the Muslim peasants' community leader.

"I'm trying but you know sarkari machinery does take time," Yadav said.

"We have heard some have..." Khan spoke in a low voice.

"No...no," raising his left tilted forearm in agreement Samajwadi ex MLA said, "some farmers close to BJP have received...no one else."

"You socialize with MLA, if you could press for our payments," Khan almost pleaded.

"Khan chacha, you all have stood by me, I'm indebted, and I'm committed to getting all the compensation that is due," Yadav assured.

"May Allah bless you," a relived old man said. He could smile now, said further,"You are the sole one seems to understand the Muslims plight."

Yadav stood up, "Marginalized sections have always found Samajwadi by their side, no one has ever been disappointed and no one will ever."

"Insha'Allah." All said in chorus.

"I will speak to MLA and the Convenor once again," Yadav assured the group.

"Last time..." one peasant said.

"Last time what?" Yadav asked in a tone almost objecting at the interruption.

Peasant mustered some courage and utter a few words, "Some were still at..."

He was cut short by a beaming Yadav, "Ahan, good, you made me recall. Last time Agency complained about fields still being cultivated," the eyes staring now, balls penetrating he rebuked, "Even if a couple indulge in farming while have signed over the consent form, the whole 107 acres will not be acquired and no payments will be made."

"107 acres sahib?!" a surprised group leader Khan chacha said, "ours is altogether fifty-six acres."

"Ji fifty-six acres," others said in chorus.

"Acquisition is not about fifty-six acres here and few acres there," politician subtly changed the stance, "every single piece of land will be acquired," then paused momentarily, "Sarpanch land is still being sowed, he has switched to vegetable farming I heard," asked with curiosity.

"Yes, he has," many voices confirmed.

"Oh...hmm....," Yadav talking to himself, 'this is why they are bound by rules, payments are stuck,' mumbling ,' all 107 will be cleared in one go else none will...,' yet at a note easily audible to the first row of peasants sitting on the floor in front of him.

"All 107 acres owners need to agree?!" curious peasants asked.

"Is that some rule blocking our payments?" group leader was anxious.

"Yes, if I understand correctly, it is the case."

"But then what about that consent clause of 70%?" The leader sounded confused.

"70% consent has long been received, MLA announced," said Khan looking backwards over his fellow community folks, received several nodes, addressed the chair in front of him, "Our payments must not be blocked thus."

"Arrey chacha," Yadav said with half chuckle, "do not go by these political announcements, there are many procedures, rules to adhere to..." then stopping abruptly, "Let's not waste time over these rules and regulations," he sprang up, let few moments pass and then, began to address all suddenly and emphatically.

"We must focus on getting our money...do we not have a right to land and fair compensation?"

Village folk stood up, agreed in one voice, "Ji," all voices agreed in tandem.

Raising his voice a couple of notes up, "And a timely one?"

"Ji, no more delay," voices up in volume and pitch now.

Voice raised exponentially, Samajwadi then yelled, "A delay in payment is equal to no payment!!'

"Yes, no payment," emotions roused now.

"Go then, do not demand - but SNATCH your rights!!" The Samajwadi leader yelled!

No one could understand, faces agog, as if asking - "Go? where?!!"

"Capitalists have made us see this day," Yadav continued, farmers confused.

The leader shouted, "Name itself reveals their sordid breed."

None were able to comprehend and as the half began to lose interest, he concluded.

"These contemptible- Imperial City owners."

All were flabbergasted, all in one spontaneous low sound, "Imperial city!!"

"This breed...mere bhaiyon!" Yadav at his best now, eyes penetrating, some frightened eyes stuck in his burning eyes, uttered, "Breed?!!"

"Breed...um… Kutte!!"

"Kutte?!!!!" all astounded.

"Kutte builder bhaiyon," arms stretched out, enacting Alexander calling upon his exhausted troops, "Go then, ask for the compensation!!"

"Why...um… them Sahib?" group leader Khan could merely utter three words, fury was tangible.

"Did you not give the builder your lands to build this city??" Yadav asked pointedly.

"Yes Sahib, in 2010," Old man nodded.

"Have you received the money?" Yadav asked, index finger dangling, stepped closer to Khan.

"Yes sahib," Khan said in a dash, many voices joined of the leader.

Yadav stepped up the tempo and asked, "Have you received the interest?"

"Interest?!" most had begun to feel pain in heads, they hadn't faced riddle so complex all their lives.

"Year after year a land fetch greater price; And if a delay in construction, a home buyer receives delay compensation; flat sold in resale will get a bigger price than the original price." Yadav uttered in one breath.

Interesting thoughts to the many in attendance but made little sense to the elderly.

"Is the city fully constructed?" Yadav asked in a deliberately low voice.

"No sahib," replied some.

"Has your that land..." waving the index finger pointed on the group, "sitting next to your land you are asking for compensation now, being used for construction."

"No sahib," All said in unison and Samajwadi leader exploded.

"So, go and ask for money, your land is yet to be sold - prices since 2010 have doubled - they will construct now and fetch crores extra years later."

The eldest, Khan Chacha, pleaded, "Our payments will suffice to fulfil our needs, not necessary to indulge in...um extortion?"

Alexander of 2018 AD was now calling on his troops.

"Politicians and builders have made my farmers poor. They have been looted, lands snatched on the name of development," stepping close to Khan, uttered, "nothing will happen, you will get some money to see off the time I need to get you your compensation."

Waved toward one side of the veranda, a couple of musclemen stepped ahead, "Escort them, come back soon," folded his hands, "Shukriya bhaiyon!"

She had dozed off.

There was no direct flight from New Delhi. Connecting flight from Abu Dhabi took thirteen hours.

As she struggled to come out of the couch alarm went off. She had set one to be up and be ready in time.

It was 7 pm and she must hurry now. Chacko wanted her to be present in the wine and dine arena, ground floor.

The hotel was not far from the customer's office. New York Skyline was amply visible.

She gingerly stepped in, eyes looking for him, the only as far as the project was concerned. And as far as she was interested.

His penetrating eyes, she spotted at the far corner, were fixed at her. She ambled her way in and sat down across the table.

He kicked himself, 'Come on... be courteous enough... should have gotten up at least... bossy!'

Male ego was all of 33, began to find himself infatuated but the struggle was still on, 'hardly 27... 26 maybe... how could I... shameful,' it would argue.

She was with him for the first time. And so was he.

He leaned over the table.

She adjusted herself in a laidback posture, hands away, and confined in lockdown against the chest. 'Lest… he desires to touch,' she cautioned her inner self.

She was not sure about anything. Her feet were still feeling the alien land, senses still folded in, trying to assess all and live the ambience, the aura of the foreign land and while jet-lagged, the body was ticking in sync with another time zone.

He smiled a little, "the first day you must wear a saree," he said hesitantly.

'What?!' she muttered. But could only nod.

"And…" he started in a low voice, and then said in-dash, "are you carrying high heels by any chance?" eyes away pretending to look for water.

She felt him through his eyes. Every few moments they would glance away only to come back and gaze upon her beauty, "how sweet?" Smashing his face the next moment, 'how dare he?'

"Um… Yes…" she replied finally.

"A Saree is half effective if not worn with high heels," his voice was more steady, eyes lot stable now, "so make sure you wear heels tomorrow."

She was lost for a few seconds. She dug herself out, adjusted her posture. She could not fathom the purpose of this hurried conversation.

He carried on, "Most of the days, you will be in these ethnic wear… these white skin… they are in awe of our traditional outfits…"

"What is that we are trying to achieve here?", bluntly she retorted. She could not stop herself anymore. The riddle had gone on for far too long.

"David… must be impressed by our work and for a long stay a rapport needs to be built." He answered in a firm and a dead voice.

"So, does that imply warning exotic clothes?" She was far from over with it.

"No… a skin-tight shirt and", putting his palm beside his thigh, "a skirt of this length would have served the purpose you think I am on to. While for some other reason here I'm asking you to wear a regular Kurta-Salwar, legging, and Saree with…"

"With?" She could not understand.

"High heels and jutti." Eyes again looking for the elusive glass of water.

She could not stop bursting in laughter. Dinner was served soon after.

"We will meet David first thing tomorrow morning," Chacko kind of ordered.

She folded herself inside her shell, munching the tasteless food.

The very next day of trespassing and brazen demand, Samajwadi received a call from a harried BJP MLA Inderjeet.

"You must have read today's newspaper?" a perturbed voice asked.

"Jai Shri Ram MLA Sahib." An emphatic Yadav greeted Inderjeet.

While MLA carried on in the same tone and manner "Did you?"

"Yes, I did. Anything special for us?" Samajwadi sensed something amiss.

"The circus party you sent has gotten Imperial city the headlines." MLA almost rebuked Yadav.

"I did not want to but then, I feared losing them."

"Yadav, was it necessary to instigate? Do you understand the ruckus they created in the office has gotten us negative coverage," MLA Inderjeet was furious, "while it meant another great show for the opposition to sell this as another low for ruling BJP - the already oppressed farmers now have no choice but to resort to extortion!"

"I never intended that MLA, but you have left us with little choice - the payments must be disbursed now." Yadav defended his action.

"Talk sense Yadav," Inderjeet tried to instil some sense into him, "Whole must be vacated first!"

"MLA - I promised fifty-six acres, delivered months ago," Yadav retorted.

"We are still to get all of 107 do you get that?" Inderjeet thundered

"Not my fault, I need my people to rally behind me," rattled Samajwadi admitted.

"Mere fifty-six you very well know is hardly a landbank agency will convene a meeting to discuss and release."

"Your political rivalry to blame," Partner was getting exhausted now.

"Don't be absurd Yadav."

"I will do everything to keep my followers intact," A firm voice sounded challenging.

BJP MLA retreated, let a few moments pass by, resumed: "Office has sent few lacs, they will lie low for some time, don't worry."

"But why did office-bearer reveal at all?" A startled partner asked.

"Thanks to your master speech and commotion these hoodlums created," Inderjeet elaborated, "Mussalle talked about the land they parted with in the past, under fire office-bearer presumed the land being questioned is these 107 acres."

"How does he know about the eventual fate of these?" Yadav was startled to the core and frightened in equal measures to know the most kept facade had so easily given way.

"Whosoever needs to know is being made aware of, to become part of necessary planning & later execution, not much time in hand. Thus, cannot afford to keep prerequisites deferred to the last minute."

"MLA, my people now begin to doubt my ideals - I fear the truth will be out sooner or later. I need them, you need them still!" Samajwadi was pleading now.

"Then hold on to them!" Boss ordered.

"Only if you arrange for the payments." Samajwadi was defiant.

"Unless..." Inderjeet tested the water.

"I've tried to run him dry already," partner revealed.

"Has that worked?" BJP MLA was curious.

Yadav added further, "Only to an extent. Some mussalle did agree to try time and again but they are risking their lives I must tell you… he seems to be on rampage nowadays, picked fight randomly the other day, and bashed them hard – you know his ability."

"Good for us if that happens," MLA said, he had some zeal in the voice now, "Sahoo will be on his knees once and for all."

"Uh...on his knees… as if you could have him last time," Yadav taunted.

"Nah… courtesy you and that SHO's stupid heroics." MLA mocked him.

"FIR could have been filed, at the very least?" Yadav retorted angrily.

"And cost the advantage we had." MLA snapped back.

"Which advantage MLA? you lost politically...don't you get it?" Yadav almost yelled.

"Yes, lost the ground to the Congress politically but only to earn sympathy in the eyes of the public at large," MLA explained calmly, "acquisition after only that point was easy and successful and the money that you will reap off the city."

"As if, no one else." Yadav shrugged.

"So, stop fretting and press on with your actions, he must run dry now and then."

"He is one of a kind - will not yield so easily," Yadav concluded.

"Someone as well built as he is and who gets angry, certainly a true Faujji is to eventually make a mistake, surely. So be steady, wait for the right time… keep leveraging these mussalle and will turn effective someday… just a matter of time… we will net him, Yadav!"

CHAPTER 8

Gradual ascendency was the order. It was difficult to keep the feet firm as the soil beneath was slippery. The dust storm was about to fizzle out - the right time to keep pushing forward. Both were sweating. The storm was the best veil. Canal shoulders were almost 5 meters higher than the fields below. Reaching the summit took many minutes, sweating, breathless, circumspect the lean figures started an even more gradual descent; toes struggling to grip the mud and weeds; legs balancing the body and the forward movement while all along two were keeping an eye out every other second on the cot lying some 100 meters away.

"Who is in today?" asked one in a hushed tone.

"Don't know... last night Dharma was around."

Just minutes later the duo was inside the water, slowly and with a careful walk approached one of the many submerged pipes; the one leading grabbed the bulky with both hands and took it out; second on the back grabbed and started to ascend the canal angular wall; took a minute to reach the spot the pipe could have been made stationary, used thick weed to work as reinforcement and not let the pipe slid back into the canal.

Soon he was back in the water, the first had, by then, taken out another pipe.

Stabilizing his body he quickly asked, "How many should we take out?"

"These two should suffice," the other whispered, handing the second pipe to him.

Both quickly stooped the very next second and almost sat on their knees, their toes gripping the muddy slippery surface and fingers grabbing the weed to keep the body stable.

"Did you do a recce in the evening?" one asked.

"I could not much," the other closer to water surface replied, and asked in the same breath, "If you want, I am okay to take one or more out."

"Next is too far off, will take us near the cot."

They called it a day and night, of course, turned back satisfied with the desired dent effected.

The dust storm had fully settled by now. Cautiously they began scrambling the canal wall, fingers scrabbling at the grassy slope while toes grabbing weeds body scrambling upwards towards the shoulder as all along circumspect eyes keeping the cot and any possible movement around in sight. A few steps into the retreat a flurry of bricks hit them, the one ahead got struck on skull and face. The unconscious body went down into the canal like a loose straw.

The other quickly knelt low, barely holding his breaths he stayed motionless for many moments, ears picking every sound.

His chest was leaning on to canal angular wall entrenching himself as much he could, fearful he quickly ascended to the shoulder.

Once at the summit, he stopped, the whole body almost lying chest on. Darkness was giving him the guise necessary to evade potential volley in waiting.

Ears picked every subtle noise to detect the attackers' position, 'When can he attempt to cross those 10 feet?' The mind was estimating fast. Across was a set of banyan trees in line stretched until the hamlet he could flee to–his abode.

Seconds passed by, there was no sound, no voice.

A minute or two elapsed, he was now ready to sprint and be over with the ordeal.

His breaths were now settled.

Tree, canal, the water all seemed to die and no birds to chirp, he flung his body out of the large boulder's trench and put his first step out–he was just a few steps away to escape.

A boulder seemed to hit his head. But Senses felt nothing, relieved he stepped ahead, just body could not follow, struck the canal floor in no time.

Seconds later, a shadow could be seen descending into the canal, approaching the spot first pipe lied, the second pipe was reached thereafter, both were submerged back. Shadow quickly ascended the wall and walked towards the cot.

"He is in jail" Sapna Singh was standing at the cabin door.

The manager was astounded, "in Jail?!!"

"Somebody got killed"the voice was dry, emotionless. He was flabbergasted for sure, 'Ah!' he asked then, gingerly, "Personal animosity?"

"Nah!" manager looked on, "He was defending father," a voice sans emotion uttered.

"From whom?"

"The anti-protestors," she said calmly.

"So, your father was protesting... oh okay... for what?!" it was getting intriguing for Anant.

"For farmers; against the land acquisition." She replied in a dead voice.

"Hmmm..."

"My father is a Sarpanch," she stood motionless.

"Panchayat head I see…" thinking something, "You belong to which place, I mean... you seem to hail from some nearby state - right?"

"Haryana."

"Haryana... okay."

"I need some days off." She asked, eyes looking down on the floor.

"Yes… yes", Anant said without noticing the question. He was pensive, just said, "you may please take a seat."

"Protestors were demanding obviously... uh... something fair... easy to guess; but what the anti-protestors were asking?".

Young lady found that bizarre, "Who MNC manager ask such questions?" she answered in a deadpan voice, "They want the land to be taken away… some quick cash."

"I presume - a lot of farmers would, even from the protesting side - who wants to do farming nowadays?"

"More to do with politics," she answered indifferently.

While he was getting intrigued more and more, "Some might be unwilling completely... one can guess... local polity or BJP vs Congress stuff?"

"Yes," fed up, she pretended she was getting late, got up to leave, and walked toward the exit. She stopped in her tracks, turned, and said, "And religion."

He wasn't expecting that. Lady had not stopped surprising him since the time she joined the team.

"I would need two-three weeks, please." Her eyes pleaded.

The manager had gotten too lost pondering over something more compelling to notice her plea, instinctively uttered, "Should be okay, I will ask… um… will ask Chacko to assign your tasks to someone else."

Later in the day:

Anant was contemplating hard and for the majority of the day since the time lady walked out of his cabin. Hard to ignite or sustain his thoughts were not able to deduce - 'Could he be the person?'

'A wild thought Anant,' he was reminded, 'You better stay off!'

'And for how long?!' he asked, 'He seems a good option.'

'As if you had several…' inner self pounced.

'No harm in trying.'

'There is harm all along.'

'Shut…'

'And you know it!'

'What is the point then lamenting the fact all these years that I couldn't do something?' he complained.

'The nature of the task determines,' inner being retorted, whispering then as if smirking, 'I reckon.'

'What if…,' struggling to find words, 'What if…' voice up by a couple of notches.

Whispers tried to fill in, 'What if he fails to turn out to be you hope him to?'

'And if he does?'

'How about attempting something more prudent?' inner self questioned the wisdom.

'Such as?'

'Raising matters that concern strengthening the social fabric?' inner self asked.

'You sound liberal,' he thundered.

'Are you not one?'

He dropped his voice to a whisper and said chuckling, 'Trying hard not to become one eventually.'

'Signs are unhealthy!' inner self mocked him.

'So long you are around,' He tried to shrug it off.

'Only one to concert!'

At that moment Chacko and Naved entered the cabin. Faces wore a worried look.

Inner self rolled himself inside.

"All Okay?!" a surprised manager asked.

"Sapna is in dire straits," Chacko said, voice hurried, body language strained.

In ages since working with his trustee lieutenant, Anant had not ever seen Chacko in the frame he was standing in front of him, eyes pleading.

"I think we should support our team members in this time of need." Chacko had cut a sorry figure.

Words made Naved turn his face towards him - something was a-miss! It was hard to recognize the guy standing there speaking in that tone.

"Jai ho!" Anant uttered the word gazing at him, Naved gaping, pair of eyes suggesting, "Boy girl had some effect, have had some effect on this steel nerve guy - unbelievable - You in love boy?!!"

Chacko suggested unconvincingly, "We can visit her home… right?'. They wanted to laugh, deliberately let a few moments pass by while Chacko looked on, eyes almost moist.

The manager got up and walked up and down the cabin.

Work needed to be managed and diligently so if they take a day or two out, said finally "Let me call SK," number was dialled in, "Yes Anant?". The manager apprised the director quickly with the developing situation.

"Hmmm… we cannot afford three weeks' absence… when was she to fly back to the USA?" SK asked.

"She was to be there by 9th Jan," Anant answered.

"Then who will now, if you let her go to her native place ?" director queried.

"She is already gone SK… Chacko will have to go, no other option."

"Zuber should lead from off-shore then," Director said.

Chacko raised his forearm, signalling towards Anant he wanted to say something.

"Just a sec SK," Anant put mobile next to his chest so that nothing can be heard across the line, "I've spoken to David." Chacko said in a hushed voice.

"Why?!!" an irate manager asked, "You should have consulted me first."

"Sir..."

The manager cut him short and asked, "What did he say?!"

"He wants me to own the delivery, whether I work from onshore or from offshore - is immaterial," Chacko replied in a dash

He went back onto the line, "Yes SK... can be driven from offshore... David has had a word with Chacko."

"If the customer is okay - you shouldn't be bothering me in the first place, Bye Anant, need to get in another call - keep me posted though."

"Sure SK." Disconnecting the call manager asked Chacko and Naved to sit down as he began to ponder over the team makeup sans Sapna.

To keep Zuber side-lined, Chacko was thinking hard to strike a right balance proposed middle path, suggested, "Work from home can be asked for, logistics i.e. connectivity from home on VPN, internet data card, laptop, etc can be issued."

"Speak to her, if she can work from home," asked the manager.

"Sure sir."

The manager was getting worried about the quality of deliverables and their timely delivery. The customer was edgy, and the account was big. The whole management was eager to see a timely and successful completion of this first project with a new and big prestigious account.

"Zuber you know..." little realizing he was speaking in the presence of another team member.

"You wanted to visit her... can ask in person," Naved remarked, smirking. That brought smiles on all faces,.

Chacko ignored and said, "I still say - we all must go."

"I'm free on Friday," said Naved, "I can come along."

"Friday is 4th Jan. The whole of the USA will still be away..." Anant said, "I will have not much work either."

Driving back home later in the day 'Lefty-turned-Centre in teen, a Half-Baked-right-wing now shrugged looming thoughts.

The whispers had not returned since noon, vehemently 'People are needed, alone how many could have -' gushing out speaking hard with himself, 'whatsoever the cause ever was?'.

The car had accelerated as consequence, repeating to himself, 'he could come handy... he is battered and mercilessly so... in rage could see quick dividends... he must be desperate to avenge.'

The next second, 'A foolish idea... I am going crazy, I think.'

'You better stay steadfast,' inner self showed-up.

'Steadfast?'

'In your career.'

'Uh... for a moment I thought you want me to stay true to my goal and keep building the momentum to find an optimal outlet eventually,' He taunted.

'Not a bad idea!'

'Not a bad idea... uh...' he was agitated, the very next second, 'bull shit... akin to sitting on your ass doing nothing.'

'Which you have been,' inner self mocked.

'For ages now,' he gushed out.

'There could be other methods and instruments.'

'Why only us mate, that we think so much,' his centre reckoned, struggling to find right-wing conviction.

Inner self tried to complete, 'So much that we end up taking no step?'

'And look at them, they are always ready while we need to pause... take a stance... think twice to step out and to make progress.'

He stopped for a moment and then gushed out

'And yet we Hindu at large do not seem to agree even on the rival's assertiveness, its steadfast energy to the cause!'

'Bull's eye,' inner self agreed, wondered, 'They say we have been oppressor?'

'But we are not against any religion.' He was sure.

'Looks to me...' inner-being wasn't sure.

'How could it be?' he said insisting, 'if are merely attempting to undo the wrong done by a few during history.'

'Attempting- you said?' inner self queried.

'Yes, attempting - we need to.'

'So as to?'

'Be effective and bring about the change.' He uttered firmly.

'Change will be hard... correction you can say for now,' inner being sounded sure.

'Wouldn't we be attempting still... um,' he asked looking for right words, 'had these few been non-Muslims belonging to some other religion say Christianity?'

'I agree.'

'Then why so much ho-halla about Hindus oppressing Muslims, rectification doesn't imply one is communal,' he said in despair.

'Narrative mate narrative.' Inner self pounced.

'A-haan... there you go!' he felt convinced.

'A funded one.' Inner self puked.

'Yeah - a funded one!'

The home was not far away, Tejo-mahalaya had begun to fascinate him.

The news had spread - a body was being searched for. It's been a day since two young Muslim peasants had gone missing.

"One or two... that's all??!!... how can they find my Ishtiyaaq?" asked a wailing mother. The Group of women surrounding her was all chorus, "Why Muslims are targeted all the time?"

They were sitting on the dirt unpaved road of the two on either side of the canal.

"Allah will help us do not lose hope yet," said Khan.

"We have already... it's been four-five hours already... do you think you will find him under the water breathing still?" questioned mother.

"It's all in his hands... inshallah," said khan looking towards the sky, "these youngsters we will find alive."

"What about the rest of us?" asked an incoming group in chorus.

"You should have stayed put in the village?" Khan reminded.

"What for? To plead with that bastard Samajwadi?" asked one in the middle.

"Zafar soul will find it a curse Atif," Elderly Khan said in a firm voice.

"Don't dare disrespect my father anymore... You got him death!!"

The closely knitted community was shocked to hear those words, Khan was respected by all and sundry in the Muslim dominated village located adjacent to Chhattar fields.

"No one controls destiny, Atif," Khan said.

"But he does... that parasite Samajwadi," Some 25-something youngster was going berserk.

"He got us loans, money, and protection... don't act as a Kafir does.'

"Kafir?" youngster stepped closer enraged to the core, "your my-baap has done everything he could to keep us in debt and poverty."

"College, city and this English education have given us this generation," Khan said turning towards men and women present, "Yadav ji has only been our-"

"You better stop it... you have been a bland Chamchaa... keeping your interests afloat on the sweat and soul of we the ordinary,' Zafar's son was yelling at the top of his voice.

The clan leader was astounded. No one had spoken to him in that tone and manner–ever!

Youngster thundered, "Where is that five lakhs this Yadav promised due on Abba's death?"

Khan had no words.

"Why did you agree to send people when you knew Chhattar and Dharma are watchful?"

"Why could you not say a no to that mother-f*****?" hurled the next.

"And he got us deaths," added the wailing lady, "my son should have avoided you."

The whole of Ismail Khurd had gathered by this time.

"You have led us but only to appease your master," youngster concluded.

A shocked elderly stepped closer to him, "All I have done is sustain the interest of our community... we are surrounded by kafirs...", then stepping away he addressed the others, "don't you feel threatened by these Jats... how could you forget 2013 and the Muzaffarnagar tragedy?"

"And we have gotten dead bodies!" youngster declared index finger point at the dead body on the ground. He stepped up a few yards scrambling onto the summit–the highest point of the canal shoulder next to the dirt pavement, turned around and started addressing the gathering, "Ismail Khurd must decide its fate," waving a finger at Khan he said, "following this pimp has gotten us nothing but mortality... we have lost land and received dead bodies in return."

He stopped short, gaping, divers were seen emerging from the water now with another body, women folk burst into a shrill.

"Chalo kotwali... Time to seek price and restore Ismail Khurd pride," an enraged soul called upon a few of his age group, "Bring all that you have," called on the youngsters, "Bring the best of bamboo sticks... they will have to pay and pay dearly."

Many were taken aback by the sudden call, yet emotions drowned them as the second body emerged.

"See... can you continue to hold these sights... three deaths in no time and what for? We need killers to be taken to task and I'm going to kotwali... this Chhattar is there, I heard... I will seek justice for Abba's death. Come if you have some pride left... WE ARE NO SLAVES!" Youngster howled in agony.

He succeeded in enraging the young audience, "Allah-hu-Akbar," cried he as he galloped towards the far side of the village where the Police Chowki was situated at.

A large number filled tractor-trolley zipped past wails the very next minute, wheels digging furrows in soil, flipping mud slapping the gaping elderly, momentum seized now intending to avenge loss once and for all.

Anant was focussing on driving, Naved had just attended one customer call.

The car had Naved on the first seat, the rumoured couple was in the rear.

'Ma would be needing me. Would I be able to tell I need to go back in fifteen days?'

She had informed her about who is accompanying her. Discomforting looks, eyes questioning. She had not grown accustomed to still.

She lied to her manager. Or, perhaps it was her guilt conscious soul which wanted to say, 'she needs to go home because she could not go when his Bhai was in jail for killing one in protest rally and she should have been there.'

She was in ascendency those days, 'how could I?', she reminded her self. 'Onsite sojourn was too big an opportunity to let go and just like that.' She affirmed.

She was looking outside, pensive and speaking to herself, 'Two were stoned to death, and it was my brother sir…who could say that?' she argued with her conscience.

She was knocked out of her thoughts "Did they come again?!" It was Chacko panicking, speaking over the phone.

"Amma?!" His voice was trembling, "After so many months?!"

Exasperated expressions were all over his face.

"Not before Christmas," he answered in a dead voice, "um…take care!" a couple of moments later," I can come anytime you want," he added anxiously as the voice was a couple of notches higher, "I do not fear them," he almost yelled.

The call was disconnected from the other side, he was sweating, others looked on.

"Everything okay?" a startled Sapna asked him.

'They may kill… they can,' Chacko appeared lost, frightened to the core.

"What?!" Anant was shocked to hear the words, he quickly pulled over the car.

The vehicle stopped with a thump, jerking Chacko out of his thoughts.

"Who would kill… was that your Appa?' asked Sapna.

"Achan (father)," he wiped his forehead.

"All okay?" Naved asked.

"I'm fine," Chacko said calmly.

"Should we take a break?"Anant asked Chacko looking at him in the rear-view mirror.

It's been three hours since they had been travelling, traffic on Friday afternoon from Gurugram to NH-1 via Delhi can test any traveller's patience.

"No Sir… please…," Sapna said in a harried voice, "We have just gotten past the city of Sonipat, another 45 - 60 minutes max and we should be home."

"She is right, no need. I am fine," Chacko seconded her opinion, lost in his thoughts still

"Who were you talking with?" asked Anant bringing the car back into motion.

"My father."

"I hope… nothing major."

"It is, but it's been so for years now," he was speaking in a half-hearted voice, "should be fine," nerves still reeling under the thoughts.

"Christmas is still months away," Anant remarked.

"How do you know Achan and me talked about Christmas?"

"We overheard… just now."

"Oh, I was so loud." Chacko shook his head.

"We are in car dude," Naved said.

Chacko did not listen, he could not, he was somewhere else.

Anant chose to lighten the atmosphere, picked Hanuman Ji drawing - more a sticker rather on the rear of the vehicle in front, portraying only hanuman face - eyes burning and extraordinarily large than usual, they are - colours too bright and contrast heightened to emphasise the ferocity.

"Artist must have assumed he has been asked to draw a Ravan in Bajrang Bali avatar."

"Who knows - they want him to act like Ravan?" Naved remarked.

"Who they?" asked Sapna.

Naved kept mum.

"Who?!" She asked again.

"You know." Naved answered indifferently.

"No, I don't know," she said firmly.

"I understand you are a patriotic Indian," Naved said.

"Are you not?" snapped Chacko.

"Nowadays patriotic is termed synonymous with being nationalistic and being nationalistic means, you are radical," Naved said

"Radical in what sense?" asked the young lady. She was getting eager for some reason.

"Rightwingy - This is all because of the people in power and atmosphere they have created since 2014," Naved said in-dash.

"Still, to me, people form their opinion - if one does not want to become what others want him to - he will not," Chacko said.

"Easier to say than what transpires on the ground... the people to people contact in the closely knitted India," Naved said.

"You can call that Bharat," Anant interjected.

"Naved, You imply–it is a herd mentality that takes over?" Chacko questioned.

"You are making the whole topic trivial," an irritated Naved said.

Naved was generally a calm and composed person, all were a little startled to find him irate, "You can explain," Chacko said.

"BJP/RSS has gotten us an atmosphere that yields messages and incidents," Naved said, little agitated.

"You can cite examples," Chacko said.

"The message this drawing conveys... have you ever seen Hanuman drawn like this ever before?!'

"Your take is?" asked Sapna.

"Deliberate attempt to heighten the propaganda," Naved answered.

"Which propaganda and to achieve what?"

"Stop acting naive Chacko!" Naved was getting more and more rattled minute by minute.

"There is a sense of wrongdoing they have been subjected to Naved," Chacko said in an indifferent voice.

"Who they?" Naved could not understand who Chacko was referring to.

"Now YOU ARE acting Naïve!" Chacko almost yelled.

"Now you are talking mate, we did not subject anyone to anything," a firm voice disclaimed.

"Perception is the issue here Naved... no one is calling Muslims are responsible... that's you and your community fear in my view," Anant said.

"You must be joking," Naved shrugged off the very argument.

"Look closely... these people are only trying to get rid of a thousand years of humiliation," Chacko remarked.

"These people?" Anant took a notice, 'Well, he is a Christian… no surprise if we are just "these".'

"Which humiliation?" Naved asked.

"Invaders conquered-"

Naved cut Chacko short "Invaded the land! and it was the case all over in those days."

"Had it been only land, Hindus would have taken it in stride. Conversions, restricted religious practices, overt oppressions on the name of Islam inflicted a sense of slavery. It was seen, I repeat, it was seen as an attempt to dilute the very majoritarian identity," Chacko said in one breath.

"Uh… Which… Hindu Identity?" asked Naved.

"Bhartiya identity." Chacko replied in a firm voice.

"What do you mean?"

"Do not think these posters are meant to terrify you and your community?" Chacko asked.

"Which is the case," Naved had no doubt.

"Ponder over what I say. The genesis of this gesture and gestures alike are the Indignation," Chacko said.

"Of?" Naved asked.

"Indignation of a sustained effort to erase the ancient culture and heritage we all from subcontinent should be on the contrary be proud of."

"Uh… you sound like some BJP Mantri Chacko." Naved snigger at his peer.

"Especially after 1947," Chacko added in a dash.

"And what is that Chacko!?" Naved was surprised.

Chacko kept mum. He chose not to reply. He was looking out of the window. He had spoken more words in the last few minutes than he would in a week.

"Chacko…" Naved asked again, "what is this especially after 1947?"

"Inescapable sway of Left-wing ideology across intellectual life in India." Chacko gushed out.

"Wow - take that," uttered Sapna, words spoken were so strong she couldn't stop appreciating.

"Stop it... immature girl," retorted Naved.

"Mind your language guys," Manager cautioned all.

"I've studied in central university... I know and understand Left-wing ideology... their concepts," Naved said.

"I'm happy to learn that," commented Chacko.

"Yet everyone is allowed, to express and voice his or her opinion." Naved completed his point.

"Which rarely these lefties allow, they sound liberal only until you start speaking the truth in the tone and manner, they vomit themselves day-in-day-out."

"I do not buy that Chacko... the expert was dead right, our Constitution does not allow hooligans to play at whims and fancy a majoritarian society," Naved said in one breath

"Merely creating a framework does not turn people willing and act in cohesion?" Anant questioned.

"People from all walks of life converge, work together to sustain the cause - our democracy. Look at the judiciary, name any executive, talk of any elected body, pick any governmental organization, example any smallest local government body or cite any pan country organization we find in over last 70 years we have made great strides towards the common cause while not letting our personal beliefs come our way and divide us along the lines of caste, creed, and religion," Naved retorted.

"This rather implies majority has no preoccupation with its stature and prominence in public life," Anant remarked.

"It's India's characteristic, in case you have forgotten - that is being Secular and to me, most are," Naved snapped.

"That's Hinduism - Inclusiveness believed in by the majority enabling easy integration across the social fabric," Anant said in a firm voice.

"Non-sense," Naved burst in laughter, "look at Pakistan, they do not have the DNA we have - hence the consequence they face today and for years now."

"Precisely, Hindus who had in 47 or have had over the course since then or even have similar orientations today - I'm sure they do get to the groups and forum of like-minded people," Anant remarked.

"They are not many," Naved said sounding shrugging off, voice quite low.

"Yes, in fact, they could not be many - and that is being not a Majority,"

Anant added further.

"Thus, the majority believes in Idea of India," Naved tried to conclude.

"As I said - Hindus are in majority thus no qualms, no brooding on their part - integration is consistent."

"That's right-wing stuff!" Naved said in a disinterested tone.

"That's your fear mate!" Anant remarked.

"Fear?!!" Naved was flabbergasted, "they have been devastating."

"That's the perception you have, your fear has made your soul a refugee of - you needn't be in the first place." Anant said in a dead voice.

"Right-wing Hindutva has had the most serious implications and has advanced under the Modi regime." Naved remarked in a low voice.

"I cannot fight your perception, nor I am an RSS follower. Still, much of the attribution qualify merely in the category of stray and fringe incidents-," Anant was cut short.

"Merely?! that's laughable," Naved said, chuckling.

"You can list the instances of RSS vandalism and rioting," Anant countered, "and I will of instances of other radicals."

"To?"

"To show..."

"To show RSS has not committed as many as the others have?" Naved countered.

"No," Anant said firmly, paused for a moment or two looking on intently and then said,

"To show both have been responsible and involved yet form the minority."

"Minority?!" Naved was surprised.

"Radicals and extremists have been a minority - takes us to the primary belief I stated - Indians in the majority are not extremists." Anant said.

Naved was thinking, said promptly, "Doesn't conclude..."

"It does."

"I have my doubts. This needs to be conclusive, logical so to convince," Naved said shrugging off.

"It is." Anant emphasized again.

"How?" Naved asked, hands making gestures mocking him.

"Had extremists been in Majority - You wouldn't be quoting Pakistan today."

Anant focussed on driving. They all kept quiet thereafter.

Chapter 9

Chhattar was at the Kotwali, Dharma in the company.

"You should have brought the mussalle here, the law would have punished the guilty." MLA Inderjeet was preaching.

The absence of Samajwadi Yadav surprised the friends.

"I could have... had I been there." Chhattar mumbled.

"Denial won't work Faujji," MLA said smirking.

"None of us was there," Chhattar said in a low voice, eyes gauging the floor.

"Cot... someone there... must have heard something, right?" MLA whispered.

"We sleep on the cot and that's all," Chhattar adjusting his posture. He was cautious to speak the right words.

"Of course, and the very reason why I'm asking," MLA said in a dash, leaning back on the chair.

"You are so sure about whatever caused the death - happened in the night?" Dharma asked.

"Could be the case, no harm to investigate from all angles," MLA Inderjeet, hands clutched together holding the head from the rear.

"Has the BJP mandated MLAs to assist in police work?" an agitated Dharma asked.

"Could well be the case looking at their withered fortunes," Chhattar commented.

"Do you have any objection if we have so?" MLA asked with a grin.

"Nope, quite innovative though we must say," Dharma said.

"So, since we all know who did it..."

MLA paused, some citizens had appeared on the gallery, Chhattar turned around.

Eyes met. He found her exasperated, a soul, which was shaken to the core, yet firm as ever she would be, on the outskirts.

'Facade is necessary Laado?' inner being yelled, pleading. Brother would call her sister with deep love, 'Laado'. Ages seemed to pass by in seconds, 'When did the list time you call her Laado? Nah, not even in your thoughts, Chhattar.'

His Laado was in a traditional salwar kurta attire, he was relieved, could not say which one was satiating him more with her being in attire or a long rope from MLA.

'He has grown weaker,' she said to herself.

Brother kept a steely facade on, was feeling the nerves inside though - it had been three months since they met, he felt emotions overwhelming his senses, about to slash the brim - and may fall over, he pulled them back – it was harder than sturdy would usually find.

The very next moment, senses spotted the entourage.

"He is my sir," the young lady had spotted the indignation on brother's face straight away.

Chhattar folded his hands, Dharma got up, extended his chair towards Anant.

"Namaste... No please," folding his hands Anant requested them—"no formalities necessary."

"These are my colleagues," said she pointed towards Naved and Chacko.

"You can go home. They are our guests. They must stay tonight," Chhattar said.

"We are here... uh... to do the legal formalities," Anant gingerly said.

"Yes, he looks to be in a greater need now," MLA commented, smirking.

"If we could be of any help... that's the whole intent...," nervous Naved tried to pitch in, looked at Chacko, who appeared extraordinarily calm and composed, "Do we need any papers?"

Villagers could not decipher any word, MLA pulled his chair close to Chhattar, "So, since we all know who did it..."

"The way, all know who draw the pipes out every other night, right?" Dharma snapped.

"Yes ... yes, Hindu and Muslim farmers rivalry go a long way back in history."

It was Yadav arriving, flanked by a few aides.

"First time I'm hearing that," Chhattar shrugged.

"But people believe in if said so," MLA stepped even closer, "from a pedestal."

"Pedestal that you have, right?" Chhattar countered.

"That polity has," grin widened, "politicians have."

"Make merry then," Chattar said in an indifferent voice.

"Community has named you," It was Yadav, "you are the prime suspect".

None commented duo balked at the very idea.

"It is the second case in less than three months." MLA said.

"FIR is yet to be lodged," Dharma countered.

"Mussalle are eager, what option do you have?" MLA said, little agitated now.

"You can lodge ours, let's battle this out in court," Dharma retorted.

"And until that happens, you could remain in where you were." MLA said smirking.

Emotions overwhelmed Chhattar that very moment, he felt the pain, he was there lodged, captive, helpless just a few weeks ago.

"You couldn't care less, did you?" Inderjeet's face meant every word, "hardly anything we received during the time you have been out."

"That's absurd!" Chattar almost yelled.

Dharma, Sapna, and the citizens feared worst at Chhatrapal's snub.

"Had you needed this, Yadav would have called; You never needed to," Chhattar was not merely uttering the words, he was shouting, "all you needed was an excuse to get rid of the blunder your chamchaas committed and-'

Politician cut accused short: "And we wrest the initiative, took advantage of the situation and rest you know."

"So, stop speaking start acting now," Chhattar challenged.

"Precisely the reason you are here Faujji." Yadav said calmly.

Words left all surprised.

"They may attempt again," Yadav continued, "rather they will."

Chhattar wasn't sure what he meant.

"To cut the water?" Dharma asked.

"Besides attempting other ways to keep you off the farming, what is the option you have?" MLA said.

"You know us," Chhattar said.

"The first salvo has landed you here," smirking, "how long will you keep going?"

"So long as necessary," Chattar said in a defiant voice.

"And so long you are free," MLA concluded leaning back on the chair, smirking.

"Dharma time to go I guess," Chhattar said.

"Only," said the MLA as friends got up, "as if to come back soon."

Smirk and grin were mimicking each other, wicked face was traumatic.

Chhattar felt smashing his face.

Every minute Anant, Chacko, Naved were being overwhelmed, the ambience, the words, the roughness, the arid dialect; the burning eyes and without fear; faces yearning to get over the line this second, that minute - numbed them.

Dharma wanted to get away, his friend had just come out of a very hard time courtesy the very person standing next to them.

"I lent a helping hand to and be part of the mob that brought down the recently erected darawaja by the local authorities at Taj Mahal courtyard," Suddenly Chhattar uttered. Out of the context words and body language quite contrary to his defiant posture until that minute, surprised all.

"We are proud of what have you done... Keep defending your fields... We never shy away from teaching lessons to Anti-nationals." MLA Inderjeet said, grinning.

"And a lot of them... right?' Chhattar had begun to dissect now.

MLA kept grinning.

"We will keep you informed MLA," Chhattar said standing up from the chair.

"MLA SAAAHABBB," politician asserted, sound and waving index finger made meaning amply clear.

"They will," Tyagi appeared, bearing a fake smile, entourage in tow.

Every villager present was shocked.

"Chhattar hope you are okay?" asked a concerned chief.

"Ji... was about to leave... they have nothing to prove."

Chief asked MLA with a perturbed tone, "Where I need to sign?" right arm stretched out to an aide, "bail amount is ready," a 2000 Rupee stack was stamped on the desk, "2 lakhs must suffice... or should I get more?"

"Arrey Tyagi ji... You are my elder... Do not embarrass me, " Inderjeet said, signalling to one constable to bring something fast, "Please take a seat."

Lifting one he was sitting on a short while back and brought next to the old man.

"We all know who miscreants are," putting his arm around Chhattar old man said, "yet I see our boys big punished."

"Same I said to them," said the MLA, "they have done us proud."

"Proud?!" Tyagi and Bishnoi community leader was surprised.

"Mussalle... you know much better than me," MLA Inderjeet said grinning.

"Ah... if could have gotten rid of them long back," Tyagi remarked.

"47?" MLA asked.

"47...71," Tyagi replied.

Naved could not believe someone could utter those sentiments so blatantly, Chacko put his warm palm on his shoulder, "First timer?"

"Not at a Police Chowki but..."

"But to words and the language?"

MLA got up and held the old man's hand warmly. Picked the notes' stack and placed it on his hand, "Please do not embarrass us... they had been set free already."

Tyagi looked at the duo's eyes to confirm. They nodded.

"Shukriyaa MLA ji," elderly body language, facial expressions suggested a big relief, "Sahoo, and I have been together since ages."

"Who doesn't know?" MLA said wearing a broad smile, "he he."

"Chhattar has been the best in Army... look at him now... what farming does to a human being." Tyagi said in a disappointed tone.

"Only in India, sir," MLA remarked.

"Perhaps if Yudhvinder could survive the tragic incident." Tyagi continued.

"He is doing just fine now," pride could not keep Chhattar silent, his family was being discussed.

Tyagi realized his mistake and quickly said, "We all are a big family... do not discount us," Old man sounded pleading and advising at the same time.

"I am indebted by your gesture," Chhattar said.

"You need not... no one needs to..." Tyagi said in an emphatic voice, "it is a family that has come for you... gone are the days when the entire village used to be one family."

"Ram Rajya our government is trying to bring about," a beaming BJP MLA declared, "Vasudhaiva Kumtumbkam... not far in future we shall have the old values being practiced."

"36 Biradari need to work in tandem if they could," Old man wished.

"They will, BJP is the way forward... look at the work we have done," MLA added.

"If you could have helped farmers, Agriculture economy would have strengthened, the community at large would have benefitted." Chatttar commented.

BJP MLA countered, "Look at our work - Kissan Fasal Bima Yojna, Advice to farmers just an SMS away-"

Dharma interjected and said mockingly, "Doordarshan Kissan Channel... Kissan Helpline... Wonderful... certainly they get us good prices in mandi, no longer dallal (middleman) harass us... MSP payments arrive in time... and what not - Awesome!"

MLA sliced aside, "And much more... Increase in MSP... Loan waiver to come."

"Loan waiver only when the elections arrive," Chhattar commented, "and elections only 8 months away," added Dharma, "Awesome, should we not go and get one loan now," "the friend asked looking at Chhattar, the expression made up, a smirking moment later, "And get that waived a year down the line," friend complemented, both chuckling.

"Chhattar," Tyagi got up, stepped closer to him, put a warm hand on

Chhattar's shoulder, said aloud, "Sahoo told me about your eagerness to let you land go and be acquired by the agency."

"Sane advice," MLA seconded from behind, "We have already begun disbursing the compensation...15% have been handed over already."

"Only the near and dear ones, "Tyagi turned around and retorted and then said further turning back towards Chhattar, "Beta... you let your fields be acquired."

All present were astounded, Chhattar the most, he said, "Agency will probably take years to compensate all."

Pointing the index finger at the MLA, the old man said, "And if Agency will take years to pay you, I'm ready to buy."

Chhattar was startled at the offer made to him, looked at his friend, gaping, asked in a hushed tone, "Probably for years you will have to bear the loss."

"Land is never a loss for me my mother. I will find a way to deal with it you know, but you cannot..." Tyagi said, and then continued in an encouraging tone, "you have a family to steer, a sister to marry off, an old father and an ill brother to support... do not get me wrong... just be realistic."

MLA interjected to complement, "And public welfare will be benefitted too... acquired land will get us corridor... economic activities will come to our village... boost to the local economy and what not."

A large crowd had begun to gather outside.

SHO left the ensuing conversation and came out with a few havildars in tow, "What the hell are you doing here? Get lost..." in a hushed tone, "Mussalle saale."

"Ask Yadav to come out," Someone in the crows said seething in anger. It was Zafar's son Atif.

SHO did not reply, asked havildars to stay put and keep a vigil as he briskly walked back.

Tyagi, MLA, Samajwadi all were stunned to see SHO face.

"Kaun mar gaya saale?" thundered the enraged MLA.

"MLA sahib I've not seen these mussalle as rattled as they are today." SHO replied

As MLA Inderjeet walked towards the gallery, accompanied by Yadav, to see it first-hand, an alarmed SHO warned, "At all costs, you must be out of their sight sahib."

An already frustrated by the ongoing family Melodrama inside, MLA turned back, retorted Yadav, "You go… handle your people."

"I will you know..." assured a complacent Samajwadi, "But I need compensation and now in full." Politicians wanted to make a killing of the situation.

"If I say no?" MLA wanted to test the water.

"I will not be able to stop them.," said Yadav, locking the forearms with each other and resting them against his chest.

"To your peril, Samajwadi," MLA thundered in utter rage.

"Choice is yours... If you cannot... I will simply walk leaving them to deal with you directly," threatened Yadav.

MLA looked at the entourage, asked, "How many of them?"

"Some fifty-odd," one replied.

"Can you all handle... uh..." MLA asked them, and then mumbled, "I do not foresee see they dare to take on us... merely here to frighten us... but…."

"We can handle for a few minutes while sahib you could drive off in the meantime," some suggested.

"Don't worry... they are just farmers," MLA said.

"Okay Mr. MLA, I take your leave then," Yadav said grinning.

MLA only smirked. Signalled SHO to trail Samajwadi, who readily followed.

The very next minute Samajwadi was outside, in front of a raging crowd.

"Where is Khan?" Khan's absence straight away filled him with anxiety, "I've never dealt with them without Khan," his senses reminded him of urgency.

"Where is that Chhattar, Yadav?" asked the youngster firmly.

Indignation was all over his face. No one had dared to address Yadav in the tone and in the manner youngster just did.

"Zafar didn't teach you I think-"

Yadav was cut short as youngster snapped "Both Chhattar and Muaavjaa (compensation) and right now."

"Ha ha ha," addressing his aide Samajwadi said, "look who is talking... saale Atif your baap massaged my legs... asshole should I remind you the class that you and your mother belong to?"

Enraged to the core, ignited youngster ascended onto the veranda the very next second Yadav was standing on, aide and two havildars were a few steps behind.

Atif attempted a horizontal strike, sideways from the right with the bamboo stick. Yadav made an evasive action to avoid the strike, succeeded in half as stick struck him on the thigh. A stroke of pain paralysed it for a moment. Strike and the swiftness frightened Yadav. He limped back towards the gallery, aide, and havildar scrambled to hold youngster but were met with a barrage of bamboo strikes - the whole group had by now ascended on the veranda. They were surrounded. One havildar fired one shot with his service revolver in air to frighten and disperse the herd, got a couple of sticks on his forearm in return. He fell on the floor.

All ran inside, while youngster yelled calling on the rest on the ground to join them, "Murderers are inside... we can get them today or never."

Many responded, 30-35 men ran inside trailing the havildars.

Havildars, joined by a few from inside, shut the gallery door, "one in the rear too," reminded one, two ran in the back to close the door situated in the rear of the building.

"Should we try from the back?" asked a struggling Atif.

"No, we can easily get in from here itself," said one, "a matter of time," said a few.

Clan pride had submerged them. The first time downtrodden found themselves dominating, dictating terms, "Come on, this is the time," youthfulness egged on, a sudden windfall had cast aside nudging thoughts of the aftermath.

A few threw petrol bombs from the broken windows.

"Allah-hu-Akbar," youngster called on raining bamboo blows on the rickety wooden door.

Immediate ascendency looked more rewarding than the worrying thoughts of ramifications; the sweetness of dominance every minute was eroding the bitter memory of years of unending agony of class, caste, creed, and slavery.

Inside, MLA had grown fearful by then, 'if Yadav was treated the way he had been, no one was going to be spared.'

Samajwadi scarcely made his way back ... in much pain ... lied down on one bench. An aid started to make desperate calls.

"Tyagi ji, you can come with me," Inderjeet signalled towards the old man.

"I have done them no harm... they will not hurt me... you take cover." Tyagi took a seat in a corner.

"They will not spare anyone... come with me... larger the group brighter are chances to survive.'

"If sighted with you, they will surely kill me," Tyagi declined the offer.

"As you wish old man," said MLA as ran towards the rear side of the building.

Youngsters had by then broken the rickety door, were now outside the hall, doors were newer, "should survive a few minutes, "Chhattar said to Dharma.

Fear was writ large all over them - Chacko, Naved, Anant...

"You all stay here," cautioned Chhattar," Laado!"

Looks in the eyes were enough to rush sister in the shelter of the elder brother.

"Stay calm and composed," Chhattar addressed the three citizens, "do not engage in dialogue and stay quiet... remember they are not here for you."

Looks and body language convinced the three, they huddled themselves in a corner.

A staircase was leading towards the first floor which housed multiple rooms and some cells. One of them housed Chhattar, how could he ever forget.

All three swiftly reached the first floor.

"Cell will be safer," said Dharma.

"Safest... room doors are wooden... will give way eventually," said the sister.

"Only if they run out of petrol bombs," cautioned Chhattar. Bottles with petrol and ignited could easily be sneaked in between the iron bars.

Chhattar spotted the cell doors were locked, "Keys are downstairs in the cloak room," and rushed back, "I bring in a few."

"Nah Bhai...," sister screamed, "They could have broken in by now."

"We have no other option," said bother. His eyes were confident, she relented.

He ran downstairs, found everyone at the same place. Incessant blows were being attempted with screams of kafir–the door to the central hall was about to come apart any minute.

MLA, his aides, and SHO were not there, 'must have left from the rear,' Chhattar said to himself scrabbling through a large trunk full of keys and locks. He tried to decipher one that must look relatively newer than others and must appear in the use of late. Anxiety was getting on his nerves, the head could not gather much, every other second someone inside reminded him of a waiting sister. Frightened of losing time he stopped decoding, picked 2-3 keys and locks randomly, and rushed out, running back towards the staircase he for a moment slowed down to check the other occupants.

Tyagi, his aide, and three citizens stood still.

Suddenly table was deemed best shield - 'will avoid direct hits of petrol bombs,' he turned back, descending multiple steps in one plunge.

"Stay calm... and..." breathing heavily, "and you will be okay," he tried to sound reassuring to the citizens as he lifted two tables.

"We could be with you... probably safer," pleaded Naved.

"Nah, they will attack us, if you get along, any attempted swipe will hit you equally," staring eyes denoted consequences.

"Remember ... just stay calm... Okay?!"

Frightened, they could only node.

He rushed and back on to the first floor and in the cell in no time. Swiftly he and Dharma started to flip through keys, trying one after another. The looming voices they could overhear. The door had given way downstairs. They were closing in.

Downstairs:

"Tyagi... MLA and Samajwadi?" asked the angry mob leader.

Tyagi signalled towards the backside of the building. The night had fallen and with power cut off by fleeing havildars, it was going to be pitch dark inside Kotwali.

Group noticed the citizens but did not bother much about them. They gunned for the kill, quickly scrambled towards the long dark alley.

MLA, Samajwadi, SHO, and entourage had taken refuge in one big room at the very end on the righthand side of the alley. There was no rear entry, alone door had been sealed off long back citing no use and owing to trespassing.

A hand brought a lunging youngster to halt, "They are inside."

"Yes, I can see Rustam."

"Chhattar is upstairs?"

"Yadav… today or never… he cannot call Ammi names," Atif shrieked

"Don't be naive, killing him cannot get us anything standing here."

"Let's see if it does?" An enraged soul laughed off the sane advice.

"Bhai… we must do only much that can get us out of-no-man's-land.'

"We will," assured the burning eyes, pride blinding senses - a leader must not let momentum recede, he turned around and ran towards the group raining blows on the door, he joined in egged on - "Allah-hu-Akbar!"

Inside spines felt the nerve; a few had drawn the eventuality on them. Samajwadi was calling on his enacting skills to attempt and stay steady with his pleas. Group barged in. It was dark, but they could figure MLA out easily white Kurta pajama attire and saffron jacket. Mob leader struck first, a full-body blow - MLA crumpled to the floor in a dead faint, an incessant flurry of strikes massaged him from head to toe.

It was over in minutes. Enraged young minds felt relieved. They had paid some price. And some pride was restored.

"You there?" suggested his eyes, the leader could read in the darkness his friends' quandary.

A sense of victory relieved the senses. Now they could think and began to reason as emotions settled back in the normal routine stride.

"Samajwadi?!" leader recalled, started feeling the other parts of the big hall - it was dark.

"Light the sticks!" he called on.

"I have none left - all used!" the friend answered, "We must get out now, and fast!"

"But many of these policemen have seen us," asked now a nervous leader.

"You could have avoided it, not now… time to rush out." His friend said in a dead voice.

"Perhaps darkness will shield us." fatigued and exhausted emotionally, he failed to drive his body.

"Chal Bhai, we must get out of here." Two held him from sides and scurried out of the Kotwali.

CHAPTER 10

Much of the Kotwali had been put on fire.

Huddled together, they felt each other's breath. Anant, Naved, Chacko - none stirred for minutes as they waited for voices to fade away.

An eternity seemingly passed by before they could muster the courage, stepped out gingerly, one following the other. The group headed for the first floor. Shivers in their nerves, their ascent was slow and took much time.

Many of the cells and rooms were intact, on the first floor.

"They must be inside one of the cells," Anant whispered to Chacko.

"Should we not just yell? If he is there, he will shout back... simple... right?" Naved mumbled.

Chacko cautioned, "We can check all of them in no time, and yet be safe."

Checking cell one after another, they moved down the alley. It took some minutes before they arrived in front of a cell.

Eyes met, Sapna felt relieved to see Chacko unharmed.

Dharma quickly unlocked the cell, and they all were inside. Dharma locked the cell again.

Two tables had been placed in a standing angled position at an arm's distance from the iron bars while all inside had taken refuge between the wall and the standing tables.

"Should we stay here?" asked Anant.

"It will be safe until Police enforcement comes over," said Chhattar.

"How are you so sure?" asked Chacko, leaning his back on the wall next to the iron grill.

"We have informed them over 100," Dharma replied.

"We could ride out, they may not have set vehicles on fire," suggested Naved.

"Anyone can intercept us on our way back," Chhattar said, "Let the police come over... we will be safer."

To stay any longer panicked Naved, he retorted, "You cannot trust them... they are always late."

"How many times have you dealt with them?" Chacko said with a half-smile.

"I read the newspapers!"

"Wow-" Chacko was in splits.

"And you? must have done some Ph.D. mate?"

"Stop it now, you both," Anant said.

For the next many minutes' silence prevailed over; The relief to be together, and being a greater force now began to settle their nerves.

Anant, Chacko, and Naved were now sitting with backs on the wall which was on the left-hand side from the iron bars. On the opposite wall, Sapna was standing beside his big brother who was sitting on the floor. Dharma was standing close to the cell door to keep an eye on the gallery for any incoming threat, attempting some desperate calls every other second.

"We wanted to come last time... um," Anant broke the crushing silence.

"We felt the pain. The worst time perhaps you and your family have gone through in these recent months," Chacko complemented.

"I must say, I am astonished to find you all here," Chhattar said.

"You are not the only one sandwiched between right and wrong," said Chacko.

Anant noted it with curiosity, mumbled, 'Certainly not in the context Chhattar made his remarks'.

Naved was surprised too, 'How could an inland issue be an occurrence with someone half the time living outside the country?'

"Time is all-powerful, we keep walking into either side," Chhattar said with a deep breath stretching his legs, "No Hindu is right or a Muslim always wrong."

"It is terrible to undergo that experience, I fully understand," said Chacko.

Chhattar did not say anything. He was utterly exhausted and in deep thoughts, wiping his head now and then. That evening he had a close shave.

For the next few minutes, silence took over an already heavy atmosphere. All were pensive, grappling with the turn of events in that fateful night, and what lied ahead.

After many minutes passed, Chhattar's voice broke the monotony, "My actions to demand builder the top-ups were to keep the kitchen running."

A confession seemed on its way out.

"Righteous in my view. Lending a helping hand to and be part of the mob that brought down the then recently erected Darwaja at Taj Mahal courtyard was..." tongue ceased, he had to try hard a few times over before some words he could finally utter and with pain, "to evade arrest and prolonged confinement."

Sister could barely hold her tears.

"My family needs me at home while baapu is away..." Chattar carried on confessing turning his head towards the visitors with a slight grin trying to keep up a brave façade, "... as always and younger bedridden," all could sense, the strains of this responsibility etched on his face as he concluded, "it was a conscious decision - I'm no right-wing activist, Mr. Chacko."

"Not all of them are, some are for power and gradual elevation in the corridor, most are sincere towards the cause though," Chacko was talking in a tone some seasoned cadre would, Anant was all agog, "Killing someone is an agony which causes a pang of overwhelming guilt and is too powerful that one could hardly lift himself to take care of the rest of his, what would now be, an already trodden life."

"This side of killing may not qualify too," replied Chhattar, "this is to just stay afloat."

"Both communities have had issues but only a few such incidents across many decades," added Dharma.

"Who can forget Muzaffarnagar?" commented Naved, eyes straight and staring.

"Muzaffarnagar was not a religious problem," countered Dharma.

"Ratcheted up to sound and to be seen so," added Chhattar.

"Yet I lost Yudhvinder," sister uttered with a sigh.

"He will be fine soon!!" an elevated voice warned, eyes pleading to some greater God, the lesser one hadn't bothered to grant any concession years on - an elder brother was a pitying figure.

"Taau will take 2-3 hours to reach here," Dharma decided to alter the context. Chhattar couldn't care less as Dharma said further "but the police will be in soon." All noted the positive news, "What was the need for you to come here?" an angry brother asked.

"It was our brainchild," Anant replied.

"What an excellent timing!" commented Dharma.

"Farming needs a steady course to harvest in the end, and get home something to eat...," Chhattar was attempting to clear Chacko's doubts, "so when someone gets in the way... whether a weed or a religion... situation is unto the farmer to devise a way out."

"Yet killing two isn't justified," lamented Naved.

"In the farmers' world–yes!" replied the sister.

"And Laado is right," added elder brother.

"Killing is necessary sometimes," observed Chacko.

"Wow - we have an expert with us," a pissed off Naved said.

"I could be one killed," turning his face towards Naved, Chacko countered.

"And why so?" asked Anant who was following every word and intriguing facial expression since the time Chacko had that strange aborted telephonic conversation. It was a Chacko he was not acquainted with.

"A long story," Chacko said in a low voice.

"I'm surprised at your openness to share," Anant nudged Chacko.

"Blame the atmosphere. I asked this gentleman downstairs," tapping at Naved's shoulder, "Are you in police chowki for the first time?"

"And what could be other's story," Naved uttered disappointedly, "a Muslim-Hindu ages-old hatred filled atmosphere could prompt a Christian to narrate?"

"Are you a Christian?" a surprised Chhattar asked.

"B. Jay. Chacko," replied the Christian, "Bhaskar Jay Chacko."

"Bhaskar?!" all uttered in chorus.

"My mother was a Hindu, father a Baptist."

"Oh…" again in chorus. No one ever knew his initials and were surprised.

"Mere a cross religion marriage could not be the enigma I've seen in the last few hours," Anant noted.

"I was affiliated with the Communist party's student federation back in my student days in Kannur," Chacko said.

"I see," Anant said.

"I had to flee."

"Flee from?!" Anant was turning curious.

"BJP or RSS?" quipped Chhattar.

"Must be RSS hooligans," Naved concluded.

"Nah," Chacko retorted.

Visibly in pain, he closed his eyes. A few moments passed by.

"From those Leftists," said he, lifting the eyelids.

None could decipher much, wondered the reason.

"There are cadres in every steam of the federation," Chacko resumed.

"Stream?" asked many in chorus.

"You can think of groups or divisions."

"Okay."

"One division contributes through content in academics, print," Chacko said further, "the other one contributes with the boots on the ground; Others in representation at social strata–all to keep the leftist sway intact on the public."

"Doesn't RSS have similar designs?" Naved questioned.

"I found them not as violent," Chacko said calmly.

"You must be joking." Naved grimaced.

"In fact, there is no comparison," Checko remarked.

"As it is obvious that your student life is over, so why does your life seem affected still?" asked Chhattar.

"I left them, that is why," Chacko replied in a dead voice.

"So, doesn't seem an extraordinary event," said Naved indifferently.

"I opposed them and left!" Chacko elaborated in a dash.

"And they came after you?" asked Anant.

"It happens with all that leave and opposing them is inviting big trouble," Chacko answered.

"You could have without getting noticed," said Chhattar, "I would have done the same."

"I," Chaco stopped, some commotion outside was heard.

"Must be the Police force," Dharma said optimistically.

"Excellent! Let's open this cell please," An excited Naved stood up and got close to the door.

Dharma hurried, scrabbled through the keys, and pushed one in the lock, "No!!" yelled Chhattar stopping Dharma in his strides, "Whosoever it is, let them appear first. Let it remain locked."

"Makes sense," Anant seconded.

They all waited in silence and it was not long before a group of policemen with an SP ranked office in lead appeared in front of the cell.

"Half of the Police chowki has been gutted," Officer said.

"I called you up SP sahib," said Dharma, "This is my friend Chhatrapal, Sarpanch Sahoo Singh's son."

Chhatrapal and Dharma recognised the officer at the very first glance. He was the one leading the police contingent during the protests at the SDM office.

Officer was surprised to see the number and the obvious different social segments and demography they all appeared to hail from.

Chhattar noticed the curiosity, narrated the whole sequence of events.

"Still, procedures need to be followed," Superintendent of Police said, "We cannot let anyone go until individual statements are recorded. the FIR is being registered."

"Can we go home afterwards?" asked a still nervous Naved.

The question was naive, a scared mind would ask officer reckoned, "Of course," the officer said with a smile.

"We will need escort Moudgil sahib," demanded Chhattar.

"You may not," said the officer.

"And why not?!!" asked Anant.

"One we do not have the number," the officer replied, "The police reinforcement has been sent to Ismail Khurd."

"Ismail Khurd!" curious to the hilt, Dharma was up in a dash and asked,

"To arrest the rioters?!"

SP did not pay any heed, continued, "Second, a large number belonging to minority farming community have begun to gather at Ismail Khurd from the nearby villages. Samajwadi party cadres are also out."

"So, they want to deter arrests?" asked Dharma.

"And to garner a political stir from the whole saga," replied Chhattar.

"Someone has been killed downstairs. Anyone of you if witnessed then let me request not to be fearful and come forward to testify," asked a very expectant SP.

"Who else?" Chhattar presumed more casualties, "They all were in a group... Yadav, MLA, SHO, and a few others."

"Not sure. The dead body has the clothes normally politicians wear," the officer replied thinking," I am not too sure whether our MLA or Yadav survived."

"Yadav has," said Dharma disconnecting the call. Sahoo Singh was on the other end.

Officer looked at him perplexed.

"He is there in Ismail Khurd with his Samajwadi cadres," Dharma answered.

"Some farmers are going to be slaughtered shortly SP sahib," said Chhattar in a cold voice.

Officer took out his cell phone. His subdued expressions suggested another social upheaval in making. The next moment, he retreated to downstairs, guards in tow.

"What's the matter? Can someone tell me something?" Naved heartbeats had begun to peak again.

"You remember the group who attacked?" asked Chhattar.

"Yes... almost all were youngsters... uh... one over-the-top... um... in the lead."

"They are getting lynched anytime now," Dharma added.

"Really?!" Naved was stunned.

"By Samajwadi cadres," Dharma elaborated, "while police will be busy controlling the gathering force of Muslim peasants."

"And you term it as caused by Hindu-Muslim hatred?" questioned Chhattar.

"Sitting miles away in cities," remarked Anant.

"Fed by leftist dominated media," commented Chacko, "Portraying, in the Hindu dominated area Muslim farmers are being lynched alive for the reason they are not responsible for, yet the socially outcast minority in this country has always been subjected to."

"Scourged by the majority in the region," added Chhattar.

"You get it now?" retorted Chacko.

"All I can see is one Muslim's viewpoint is being dominated by all Hindus and a Christian," Naved said calmly, "even that one is half Hindu."

None said anything. Some were startled, others not even a bit. Rejection in popular opinion had always been the case in matters questioning the minority appeasement.

The cell had walls on three sides with a fourth side completely made of iron bars. One standing at the extreme left corner, which housed cell entry door, could see the whole passage up to the staircase.

Chhattar asked Dharma to lower his guard. "Nothing is prying on us any longer. Take some rest, still a few hours before it is dawn."

A shawl Sapna was carrying had just been laid. She sat down.

Anant took his cell phone to check the strength of the signal. The presence of the police force had a soothing effect, their senses were no longer on tenterhook.

Little later: "You said... you cannot go back?" asked Naved.

"Unless I want to get chopped," Chacko replied in a dead voice.

"That's extreme!" Naved shrugged off.

"They deal in extremes," Chacko's voice was deep, without emotions.

"Were you successful in your endeavour that rattled your ex-mates at the federation?" queried Anant.

Chacko did not reply immediately, he thought hard and said a few moments later, "You are making me recall the most terrorising days of my life."

"You are free not to share," Anant said, raising his forearms, palms straightened facing outward.

Chacko pondered on as a few minutes passed by. There was silence. Dharma was duly focussed on sending and receiving messages—communication with the outer world was key to determine an optimal time to step out.

"University was big," and not long before Chacko began narrating the events, "A few hundred teachers; 2-3 thousand students; the Federation used to organize events, talk shows, seminars, nukkad natak, etc."

"You participated?" asked a curious and rather quiet lady that far.

"I was more into logistics..." replied Chacko, "a computer science student... humanities dominated the number and were the front runners."

"Yup... Art and Literature matter" commented Anant.

"Things went smooth until 26/11 happened," Chacko described further, "A flurry of sessions on Kashmir were organized. The theme was to justify to a great extent the causes. The content camouflaged with terms like non-state actors; these actors' social trauma; historical backdrop used to be laid out at the start of the sessions. I was overwhelmed with twists and turns."

"Discontented you raised your voice?" curious again, she asked.

"They smartly compose the content," Chacko answered, "You do not feel it, least leave confused. And best-"

"Brainwashed," interjected Anant.

"Yes, you can say," Chacko stopped momentarily, "It was the first time I felt at odds with the rest of us. Later we were asked if anyone wanted to be in the field. I volunteered. We were taken to Baster."

"Baster? Naxal heartland? Wow, which year?" Naved enacted, the expression mocking Chacko's narrative.

"Yes, 2009 and believe it Naved." Chacko said gnashing his teeth.

He was asked to ignore, "Go on," urged Chhattar.

"An ex-army office is interested," quipped Anant.

"Ji," Chhattar nodded," I spent a few months there in 2007. Later, the army units were completely withdrawn. The CRPF and the guerrilla para-military forces took over."

"It was an eye-opening experience," Chacko resumed.

"You survived I'm surprised while being at odds. The gestures, expressions, body language do give away what's cooking inside," remarked Chhattar.

"You are right, Sir."

"So, you had to flee?" asked the young lady.

"They organise Sabha in the hinterland. Initially, the content was for the Tribal something like Your land and forest in which you have been living in harmony with 'Jal-Jangle-Zamin' are under threat. So do not give in. Oppose the multi-nationals… come out… protest. Later, Command would alter the content to the tyrant Sarkari system. That it identifies protestors and captures. You have every right to defend yourself. The tribals are thence pursued to get armed by the Federation Command, and in the last comes the final nudge: Some of you the most effective protestors the Sarkari system is about to zero on. You will be arrested if you stay in the village… better-become part of the strength… so come, retreat and join ranks in the forest and stay free."

"Never mind… I have also read Urban Naxals," Naved commented with a wry smile.

"Naved, you find it amusing?" Chacko was rattled.

"Never mind, as he said," Anant urged him to ignore, "please continue."

"The leadership lives in the cities. Their families are habitats of mainland India. The mainstream India they live in. Their lives go on and are hardly affected. The poor tribal does the hardship - fighting, the bullets, bearing the stigma of being a social outcast, or the System's apathy. And when away from these he is subjected to chores. He must arrange food, water, and other essential supplies to aid forest sojourn of these city dwellers."

"When you got into the fight?" asked Chhattar.

"When the session… um… we were back on campus after spending some two months. I missed my internship while the final semester was about to begin. So, when the session on the Babri Masjid demolition anniversary was being planned, I questioned the narrative. They asked me to stay put. I resisted. I was elbowed to fall in line."

Chacko adjusted his posture, thinking hard.

"Session was planned with an aggressive narrative. I was okay with the content criticising the Ram Mandir movement and demolition of 6th Dec, but-" he stopped abruptly.

"But?!" asked many in chorus.

Dharma was disinterested all along. He was busy gathering information from the outside world. There were quite a few hours still left before the Sun rises.

Chacko resumed, "But not the last part which demeaned Hindu mythology; questioned the practices; gave it a fervour to suppress the minority and in carefully chosen words stitch that with there is no-justification to hold states together in a hurriedly assembled area consisting of heterogenous ethnicity, language, and cultures. And all this amidst sloganeering of Ek dhakka aur do…"

"Ek dhakka aur do Babri Masjid tod do," Naved took over, "Kar sevaks chanted all the time leading up to the demolition, Bastards!"

"Your point was?" Sapna asked Chacko.

"Well… I read the underlying hatred for us, the Hindus, "Chacko said in a deep breath, "And you know, most of them are Hindus themselves - this is the irony. They look down upon themselves. Our Heritage, Identity, historical events are laughed at. We are deemed as ill-educated-rustic heard."

"You took some action? I guess you must have?" an eager Anant asked.

Chacko said, "In one session, I could not hold myself any longer and uttered something like - 'Any ancient civilization be it ours, Greek or say Persian must be allowed to be pursued from an academic standpoint at least.' - just one time and the slide began."

"I find it to be a perfectly neutral statement," said Chhattar.

"I said–be it ours–that 'ours' raised eyebrows," Chacko said and stopped for a moment or two before resuming, "had I said, 'Hindus' instead, I reckon it wouldn't have been a crime as offensive as 'ours' did to them."

A knock at the cell gate distracted all agog. A policeman was standing with a few bottles of water.

Dharma took all of them and thanked the policemen.

Chacko grabbed one and gulped it fully.

All looked on as he resumed, "Middle into the year local municipality elections were held. The same set of cadres who went to Bastar was requisitioned. My indignation found an avenue - opposed intimidation as a tool to beg the votes."

"You must be stupid to have not been aware of–intimidation is the sole modus operandi to get most of the votes left to hold on to, election after election," Anant remarked.

"I had to flee to my hometown, but their cadre followed," Chacko stopped as a smirk appeared on his face, then said," I was the rebel... and a rebel must not be spared. Federation allows hardly a whisper of discontent to pass unpunished and there I was… one… who had screamed on their faces."

A havildar appeared, surveying those inside the cell, said moments later, "Chhatrapal?"

"Yes," said Dharma.

"Are you the one?" havildar asked.

His question was not answered, instead, Chhattar remarked, "Haven't seen you in recent time - must be newly posted.I'm Chhattar, yes," Dharma added, winking at Chhattar.

"You need to come down"

"We all are witnesses. Are we not being called downstairs?" Chhattar asked gently, getting up.

"I do not know. You will be called if needed," Havildar snapped.

All were surprised.

"Should I come with you?" asked the sister, and it was a spontaneous gesture. Brother felt it. He would have turned a stern face on other occasions deeming she was little and will always be. He did not, nodded in affection. Dharma accompanied, all quickly stepped out.

Chacko dialled a number with worry widely etched on his face. "Perhaps his father," Anant tried to guess, "hope they are safe."

"They seem to be in a situation," Naved remarked, "we can only wish them luck."

Three were back minutes later, surprising the citizens. "Not sure if they called you to ask a riddle," remarked Naved.

"Can you stop your American English, will you?" manager sniggered.

"I feel so safe," pointing finger at farmers Naved admitted, "with you around."

"SP wanted us to sign a few papers, routine paperwork," said Dharma.

"It is still three hours to dawn…" Chacko observed.

Dharma, by then, had lied down. Havildar had sent over a few sheets. Naved and Chacko were now sitting in opposite with their backs leaning on the wall facing brother and sister. Dharma slept while others chose to stay awake. Chhattar was pensive, pondering on.

"Taj Mahal was a small-scale palace built in centuries before Shahjahan. Believed by many a Hindu Raja constructed it. Some westerners conducted research and found evidence to this effect."

It was Anant speaking in a manner, reciting some poem, all along eyes fixed on Chhattar. None could make much out of this sudden burst, "Manager needs some sleep," Naved whispered to Chacko.

"Evidence such as?" asked Chhattar smiling, he had now sat down next to her sister, warm shawl comforting the aching bones.

"Carbon dating." Anant answered.

"Never heard of this," Chhattar shrugged.

"Government after government kept the business as usual," Anant said.

"What else?" Chattaar asked.

"I have just started," Anant said with half-smile.

"Keep it brief." Chhattar said in an indifferent note.

"Shehanjehan acquired the palace from the Rajput ruler in 17th Century-" Anant said.

"To build the Taj Mahal?" Naved chipped in.

Anant ignored and continued, "And Mumtaz Mahal body was brought later from..."

"Behrampur," Chhattar completed the sentence.

"So, you know some of it?" Anant was intrigued.

"Have been making rounds since eternity" Chhattar smiled.

"Matter of discretion I suppose, so-"

Chhattar interjected, "I reckon-"

Anant cut short him short, "Let me finish then you can decide. It is the minimum and the very least one in us must accomplish."

It was quite startling for the citizens to find the manager to behave and speak in the manner he did in those last few minutes.

"Who us?" snapped Chhattar, little agitated

"Us–the Hindus!" said Anant.

"Wallah, I become an outsider in no time," Naved sneered.

"Accomplish... yes... but only when you first start to endeavour," remarked Chhattar.

"Ain't we?" asked Anant, shoulders up, palms turned up.

"Count yourself and," pointing at Chacko said Chhattar, "...him so far."

"I am sure I will not return disappointed," Anant said in a firm voice, beaming.

"What you have said is way too far unimaginable," ex-army man was certainly taken aback.

"Hence you want to take time?" Anant's countered.

"Everyone would!" Chhattar had stopped looking at Anant.

"Do we have time?" Anant egged on and it was bizarre for many who were present there.

Chhattar pondered for seconds, "Yes we do have."

"I guess not!"

"We cannot be at the mercy of guesses while determining the course as significant as this one," Chhattar said in a firm voice.

Naved scratched his head. He was not getting even an iota of what was being talked about between the two gentlemen.

"I am aggrieved. Relieved," Anant said smiling, "At least you understand and underscore it as something significant."

Chhattar did not say a word.

"Think as much for as long as you want, but," Anant stopped momentarily gathering his thoughts, "But do not fret," looking intently in his eyes he said, "there is no fear, no need to fret."

"I'm thinking about the ramifications," Chhattar remarked.

"We have had many, time to step forward," Anant said.

"Taj Mahal is a symbol," Chhattar said firmly.

"For liberals and leftists," snapped Chacko. Naved could not believe Chacko jumping in and yet again.

"Even for me!" Chhattar said in a dash.

"You?!" Chacko was surprised.

"And you know…" addressing Chacko farmer said, 'I'm neither a liberal nor a leftist.'

"Words are similar to-"

Anant was cut short by Chhattar, "And many more like me, perhaps the majority."

"I do not have data to disprove or counter that," for a moment Anant seemed to concede the argument.

"It is not about who and how many, perhaps-".

Chhattar was cut short as Anant quipped, "In quick succession, you have used the words–perhaps! if in doubt open up and let me lend a helping hand."

"Perhaps the country comes first," he said in a low voice.

"Of course, and for all of us," Anant complemented.

"Perhaps should be deemed wrong," Chhattar was pensive now.

"Oh, I see. The reason I find my friend pondering over since the time I uttered sane advice?" Anant egged on.

"Could lead to insanity!" Chhattar snapped.

"Just as a thousand others have led to in 1000 years?" Chacko said in a hoarse voice.

"No one knows what must have conspired on the ground. All the details to deduce and infer the reality of times gone by is hard," Chhattar said in an unsettling voice. It was quite unlike him. Anant noticed the underbelly nerves.

Emboldened now, Anant tried to emphasize, "We have anecdotes; recordings on print; observations documented; they all must suffice to yield the inference."

"I will not reject altogether what you are saying, Manager," Chhattar said.

"You must be crazy," hands tied, one forearm stretched out flung wide, "Is it for real?" said Naved looking at Chacko, "Can you decipher this for me man?"

"Do you see any difference between what one keeps in his head and the one that is vomited?" remarked Chacko.

"Are you suggesting - a thought and a conversation potentially planning the crime must be looked up as equal?" Naved asked, surprised at the nudge.

A sister present uttered ever so hesitantly, a big brother was all ears, "570 years passed before we could illuminate the Sarovar at Ayodhya."

"Sapna, history is past now, we are in the 21st century," Naved almost yelled.

"Then why the agony still?" she asked vehemently.

"Which agony?!"

"Identity Crisis!" It was Chacko who answered Naved's question

"Certainly not an Identity crisis. Propaganda to remain in power. The more they yell, the more they will be heard," Naved rejected the very idea.

"That's your fear Naved and that of your community at large," Anant disagreed.

"Would you be reaching to every Naved?" Chhattar asked Anant.

"To?"

"To tell what you have so conveniently said to one Muslim just now," Chhattar replied.

"How would you control all the Hindus? in other words," Naved snapped.

"In other words–Mob violence," Chhattar gushed out emphasising the gravity of the issue.

"Mob will as it has, part and parcel of this whole saga," Anant said.

"I am convinced. I am with the people who are no less tyrant than who burnt father and his sons alive," Naved muttered.

"He was a missionary," corrected Sapna.

"You are brainwashed!" thundered Naved.

"If we are then do not discount yourself either. You and the generations have been brainwashed by the leftists' crafted textbooks," Chacko countered.

"And the symbol of oppressions must be corrected," Anant added.

"We will have the consequences," Naved yelled.

"Who doesn't foresee that?" said Anant calmly, eyes fixed.

Chhattar was startled, "You are sure of the communal consequences, yet I find you in conviction to carry this Tajo Mahal audacity."

"Course corrections involving millions will not have any consequence is implausible," Anant was dead sure of what he was planning to do and the aftermath.

Chhattar could not believe it, asked pointedly, "I'm questioning your ability to convince your conscience while quite aware of the ill-effects?"

"On the contrary, I am sure consequences will turn out to be." Anant said intently.

A liberal was flabbergasted. An event with the potential to engulf the country has its visionary calm and composed.

Looking at the gutted facial expressions, Anant remarked, "Do think of the words and remind yourself of the narration Islamist jihadists the world over have always accorded of?"

Chhattar was still lost, 'Is he for real?!'

While Anant continued, "But do not curse yourself by losing your way in these words carefully chosen to serve several purposes: From earning a livelihood, to doing a duty, or elevating oneself to next level calling successful."

"And doing the holy duty in the name of God," Chhattar tried to complete.

"There is no god but Allah," Anant winked.

"You hail from beautiful world people dream to be part of and yet, here you are bent upon destroying all," Chhattar commented.

"Destroying all to attain and recover the lost and much more significant," Anant said, beaming.

"Reminds me of Munich 2005 - Ali in the staircase?" Chhatar said smiling.

"You watched?" Chacko was surprised.

"Yes, don't typecast, a villager can understand English." Chhattar said.

"And watch a Hollywood movie... not bad," added Anant little excitedly and then addressing Chacko, "and how could we forget we are speaking to an ex-army officer."

"The irony," commented Chhattar with a lamenting voice, "Indian Army, like any other army, has far more soldiers than officers. Popular perception has no place for soldiers hailing from rural India forming the backbone of our country's muscle."

"I did not mean to discredit them," Anant quickly clarified.

"I know - you are just as a victim of the perception the way common people are."

"I will not disagree, yet it is not common to find rural India watching Hollywood classics or those which are off mainstream," Anant said with a half-smile.

"Um... a modern Indian?" Chacko said

"And what is that?" Anant was a little surprised.

"Be a Bhartiya and you will realize," Chhattar winked.

"What you meant when you said - don't typecast?" Anant asked.

"Yes, that is I meant," thinking hard Chhattar let a few seconds pass by, said, "Mingling these two, gel and come together to form one society with access to all amenities with equal distribution of resources."

"Some parts of Europe, have reached the stage at?" Anant tried to supplement.

"Will take some time," Chacko remarked.

"Perhaps years and decades," Naved said smirkingly.

"I must say, I am astonished to find you here with the cause that you embarked upon this short odyssey." The ex-army man was in some shock.

"I will not debate. I have shared my intent, I have been hesitant to share with anyone so far," Anant said frankly.

"I assumed your family must have?" Chhattar was quite eager to know.

"They have the same thoughts as you have," Anant admitted.

Chhattar did not say anything. The dawn had just beaconed.

"I can wait," Anant said, eyes fixed, gauging.

<h1 style="text-align:center">CHAPTER 11</h1>

C hhattar arrived home in wee hours with the younger sister in tow.

"How could you murder two when you are even not out of the first mess?" It was Ma, tears about to strike her wrinkled, aged skin.

He perhaps did not hear, ambled towards the centre.

Smoking hukkah in the centre of the courtyard, Sahoo Singh was pensive, worried. The youngest quietly strode towards veranda and sneaked into her room.

"Where have you been, Baapu?", he asked.

"Jind rally."

"Really? And what about us that you have conveniently forgotten about?" Son asked little agitated.

"It wasn't the time to take those lives Chhattar," Sahoo lamented.

"They were eating into our staple," Chhattar said gnashing his teeth in rage, "The pension cannot provide this family with thirty days of sustenance if you do not remember."

"You should have avoided; your strikes have raised a storm." Sahoo said in a low yet heavy voice.

Chhattar did not answer. He quietly laid on a cot at some distance from where Sahoo Singh was sitting.

Father warned, "They will make the most of you being my son."

"Celebrate then!" son exploded, hands stretched out, "your party will have then a minority card to play and shore up its meagre fortunes."

"Had you not been the prime accused," father snapped.

"Do not worry I can take care," enraged Chhattar yelled, "and stop acting now!"

"Bodies next to our fields; Lynching in your presence in the Kotwali," a fearful father was going berserk now, "the first episode was still to die down that you added another?"

"We could have been attacked..." Chhattar clarified, "they were after me too... we were just lucky to survive."

"Uh... Who will vouch for you," father shook his head in disbelief, "and this merely a story?"

"Tyagi," snapped an angry son, "he was there... he has been helpful... you two have been close, right?"

Father startled, he was taken aback, looked lost for a moment or two.

Inside:

Ma barged in and gave youngest a full swipe, "Dare not bring any chhad (young lads) again," slapped her twice more, "that too in Kotwali?" crying all along, "how could you?!!"

"She is no longer your Laado... Umaricca returned if you can see," mocked a smirking Bhabhi, "27th year kicked in already... high time you get her a groom."

Submerged in tears, mother scorned, "Baap and beta earn hardly, and you are a curse." As the raised voices outside made her anxious, Ma hurried herself out, stepping out a shaken mother gushed out, "Never a day passes by when we are not ridiculed... stop all this now Laado, otherwise..."

She felt nothing, wiping tears she deemed an insult to injury, her self-esteem objected, 'Why should I?' whispered to herself, 'Baap-beta hardly earn... educated and an earning hand mauled...'

"He is in merchant navy... tall and good-" said the onlooker. She caught her breath and stared at her Bhabhi, "You went too... so much interested?!"

"Ma wanted me to come with her," Bhabhi defended enacting expressions the next moment, "at least someone will not be staying in a village...," relenting the next moment, "He lives in Mumbai," sparkle in eyes.

"Uh... he could be married already...," Sapna said shrugging off, "a mistress perhaps?" Defiant, she couldn't care less.

"Inside a marriage who gets Mrs," remarked a crumpled soul, "or who becomes Mistress - God knows," the married lass sighed.

And just moments later, Bhabhi said at the top of her voice, "We are Jats, not mussalle." Some pride was speaking.

"Before 1955, all well-to-do Hindus in Delhi had mistresses," Sapna said calmly, her mind was elsewhere.

"What?" Bhabhi could not understand any of the words spoken.

She had the adjective 'Feudal' to utter the agony and an urge unto herself to strive - someday to finally unshackle. She had come much far, the marriage she must overcome - the last barrier. And she is determined to pass. Income has provided her with independence, and in turn, a self-confidence pivotal - herself now plotting her strides on—no Ma was deemed necessary.

Outside:

"I doubt... unless," and veteran added gingerly, "and until we are sure of Tyagi's political affiliation."

Chhattar termed hardly a reason worth discussing, "He has always been seen with you... your favourite Ekta Manch."

"Of late, he has grown interested in Paintees Biradari (35 castes)," stopped momentarily, "elections are merely a few months away you should remind yourself Chhattar."

"If he needs my land," Chhattar said, "he will have to slide with me," a flooded confused mind flicked the very idea.

"Tyagi wants to purchase our land?" The veteran did not appear surprised.

"He said so in Chowki, Baapu," Chhattar answered

"And would he in return become your prime witness," Sahoo asked going back to puffing hukkah very calm and composed, "that it was not you who lynched SHO?"

"Me?!!" he got up from the cot, startled to the core, "SHO was lynched?!!...." eyes widened, "Nah Baapu... it was MLA... SP told us a body with white kurta-pajama and saffron koti-"

"What do you think?", Old man snapped, "An MLA of the ruling party gets canned to death, and the accused would roam free debating with father."

"Still, how could SP get it wrong?" Chhattar shook his head.

"MLA men forced SHO to change clothes with that of MLA... and mussalle mistook him being the politician and massaged him to death." Sahoo said in a dash.

Chhattar could for a moment feel the sheer pain by the incessant blows which the innocent was subjected to, "he just obeyed his masters," he mumbled, collapsing on the cot he held his forehead.

"Nah," Sahoo remarked, "he paid the price of wrong choices he made willingly."

Chhattar jerked himself out of looming despair, "So…" getting up, left hand clenching eyes right hand holding waist from the side he couched in anguish, "is it my time to struggle with the wrong timing Baapu?!"

"Irony is… even our land cannot fetch us a leeway," Sahoo Singh said in a dead voice.

Chhattar taunted dejectedly, "You can still find cheer in your political upward momentum this episode has guaranteed."

Their relation had grown arid emotions, yet some respect for steering the course—but until when? Chhattar did not want to know.

Wiping the sweat from the forehead, Chhatttar said, "I will speak to Tyagi."

"And he will speak to MLA Inderjeet," an experienced politician observed. Words rushed the breath of the young farmer already in tatters; the veteran carried on, "and to Yadav."

"Yadav…?" senses assured Chhattar of dire straits.

"And don't know who all in the Imperial city?" the old man concluded a hoarse voice.

"What that never-ending city project has to do with our land?" anxious to the core, young farmer shrieked.

"Nah…," the old man said gingerly, "they want our land… this is what they are after and for a long time now."

"How do you know?" he sighed, eyes widened.

"The way you would never come to know." The old man replied calmly.

"You never told me?" A Son was angry.

An agitated father complained, "You ever wanted to pay heed?"

Despair struck the eventuality to pieces - "Unless we are ready to sell… how could one?" Chhattar mumbled, called on senses to convince a desperate will.

"Words of a man not in control and trying in vain," father noticed his desperation.

"I am yet to respond to his offer," shouted a rattled soul.

"Land has been notified Chhattar if you have forgotten... we are just supposed to receive the compensation," Sahoo Singh retorted.

"I will continue to hold on..." Chhattar yelled, voice searching for some defiance within, "Ekta Manch will continue to hold on,"

"Farmland elsewhere will not be touched Chhattar... ruling party is not stupid... will take a decision only once the elections are over... but our land and Muslims' land will be taken out at all cost."

The first time in years, father and son were speaking to each other willingly. They understood they must collaborate now to fight an opponent and damage looming imminently.

"Why?"

The veteran did not answer, continued, "This stretch was never intended to be acquired for freight corridor, the all-powerful know; Rest ever mattered? No – Never! Mussalle have agreed a lot earlier. It is just our land they need. And once acquired, the entire stretch will be available for the city they had been vying for since the time city project came into being."

"I fail to understand all these ugly manoeuvres Baapu," broken he held his head in agony.

"Freight corridor, if you look closely Chhattar, was never designed to be spread as far as Imperial city is. They just made 107 acres part of the whole freight project only to snap it easily through red tape - a notification!"

"Notified land can only be taken over for the project it has been notified under?" Chhattar asked.

"Only If not all the land is deemed necessary. Some parts of the land can, and there are numerous examples of Chhattar, be returned to farmers."

He stepped closer, "But shall we not be that lucky?" asked gingerly, holding Baapu in his strong forearms.

"Nah," father said in a dead voice,"they will keep that under notification forcing our hand as stipulated under the law not to plough to arm-twist and until we agree."

Sahoo then looked away, thinking hard.

"We agree to what?" son stepped near, sat on knees, hands holding father's forearms.

"To accept a meagre compensation!" Sahoo answered.

"But land... a notified land once paid for requisition..." little agitated yet expectant at the same time, Chhattar asked, "can only be utilized for the goal it was to be acquired and hence notified?"

"To be disbursed later," Sahoo answered calmly, "to an interested party, though auction declaring not fit for use. The project goal, design, spread change with evolving needs of Sarkar and its welfare schemes." Experienced politician Sahoo cited one example: "Tata Steel had been allotted land post the acquisition by Chhattisgarh government. Tata, two years later, said no to project citing difficulties. The BJP government put the acquired land into the NDMC pool rather than returning to the original owners - the farmers. Now, this newly-elected Congress government is returning the same land to farmers."

He was distraught. The old man sounded so sure and speaking in such an undulating single tone as if he was reading some script.

Sahoo Singh carried on elaborating the contours of the power structure, "Twists and turns in the power centre have no limit and when it comes to land... ordinary must count itself out."

"Any way out Baapu?" despair laden mind let the body lose, he was off the knees to the ground.

Father did not reply, he was pensive, thinking hard.

"Any way out Bapu?!!" he yelled in desperation.

"Perhaps...," pondering over, the seasoned campaigner muttered, "some form of agitation."

"What? Will it get our land?" he sprang back on his knees.

"It should let us retain our land Chhattar, and something more probably."

"Ekta manch?!" Chhattar asked.

"Nah," Sahoo shook his head, "politically it has lived beyond its sell-off date. BJP is not touching these lands until new government formation and is back in the seat."

"What else then?"

"Time to revive Jat Aarakshan Andolan!" Sahoo Singh said in a low voice.

That very moment, the main door was thumped multiple times in no time. Chhattar rushed, lifting the latch he pushed open the door.

"Mudgil Saab has summoned Chhatrapal Singh." It was a lanky lad, appeared to be a DSP, flanked by a gunman and few constables.

The summons did not surprise Sahoo Singh.

CHAPTER 12

❧

The corner was vacant, he said to his senses or perhaps senses spotted - something was there installed - uprooted afterward. The wooden reinforcements hanging from the wall suggested so. And also the floor at the corner decayed now more than the rest.

"Chhatrapal...?!"

He was awakened, turned senses on their head to roll himself back in the world – worldly-wise was he - uttered indifferently "Ji."

He had just carried the lacklustre body into the accused box.

It was the Sessions Court.

The judge was busy with something and was casual - body and senses on the other side were equally worldly-wise, accused noticed.

"Charge?!" asked the lord, eyes still wandering about searching something in the drawers.

Prosecutor Sangwan was already standing. He had to rush to the next hearing in the adjacent hall – so only a little time on hand.

District court campus was a sprawling building, housing many courts chaired by SDMs, District Judge, and Sessions Court judges.

SHO Saini lynching case was being heard in one of these lower courts.

The witness box stood opposite to the accused box. Both were next to the judge's cubicle, him sitting on an elevated chair. Two tables, with chairs surrounding from three sides facing the judge, were accommodating lawyers, one standing replied, "Chhatrapal Singh son of Sahoo Singh killed SHO Ramesh Saini in cold blood, prosecution demands the death penalty. FIR copy is with the lord."

"Who wise pressed Death Penalty?" Tyagi was bemused.

"Sangwan," replied MLA.

Constables scrambled for chairs and benches from adjacent rooms to comfort MLA's entourage, which had just and almost barged in. They sat behind prosecution and defence lawyers.

The courtroom was small. Its sole entry and exit door was half-jammed, half-opened. People could be seen strolling in the passageway and they were many onlookers in them, just curious enough to peek inside for a minute or two before strolling back into the passage. Accused and Witness boxes were carved out of an extended Judge's cubicle. Hall hardly had a seating capacity of ten audiences in the two rows of rickety wooden benches.

Dharma was the sole in attendance from the other side.

"Defence will field witness to prove the contrary. Accused himself was captive and locked inside cell number 47 on the first floor while the lynching took place in the storeroom at the ground floor," countered Sarkari vakil.

"Police file charges… not the lawyer," Tyagi corrected MLA.

"Really…?" MLA's facial expression suggested ignorance.

"Get them turned to life imprisonment in the next hearing, I suggest," added Tyagi.

"Why have the others present not charged?" asked Yadav, "We can nail them in one shot now."

"Our politics has strict no-no to bait on fairer gender… Yadav," veteran reminded the fellow politician.

"I want Zafar's son, by hook or crook," countered a fuming MLA.

"You don't need courts to punish mussalle… we can get them at any time… relax," said Tyagi and then added in the same breath, "We got to get this Jat on his knee. Father-son are trapped can't you see, we need to play our manoeuvre smartly and play hard."

"And in defence… who… has now been accorded this responsibility?" The judge stopped as he looked up, free now from the drawers, towards the lawyers' benches, "Oh… Dhankhad… Okay," addressed prosecution, "Any witness? Cross-examination can take place today," Judge seemed in a hurry.

Prosecution lawyer raised his forearm towards the backbenchers. MLA hurried in the witness box, took the customary oath, said. "I was there. Chhattar was in the group that attacked us in the storeroom. It-"

But was cut short, "how many were in the group MLA Sahib?" asked the

Judge.

"Two… um… three."

"Two or three?" Judge prodded.

"um… three" uttered Sahib.

"You want to question the MLA?" Judge asked defence lawyer.

"Three or just two?" moving swiftly, defence lawyer Dhankhad asked the MLA.

"Three!!" witness rattled, gushed out.

"Or more?"

MLA stood motionless. He felt pulling his hair out.

"Could be more… no?" defence pressed, "Yes?" looking to unsettle.

"Three" said MLA and calmly so.

"Sure?"

"Yes!"

"And who were those three?" The defence lawyer prodded again.

As MLA scrabbled his head, defence lawyer quickly added, "1–accused, 2–could be his friend… Dharma… right MLA sahib?"

"Um… right," said a lost witness.

"Then why Dharma is not co-accused?" thundered a young lawyer.

MLA looked at prosecution lawyer bewildered, eyes nudging to cover. Yadav whispered to Tyagi chuckling, "Your vakil is an a**hole!" Sangwan was picked basis strong recommendation by Tyagi.

Before prosecution could utter, defence threw in the supplementary, "And who is the 3rd you have been so confident about?"

Witness stood speechless looking at prosecution as judge complemented defence, "Who is the 3rd?" Trapped MLA jerked his head slightly up nudging prosecution lawyer to step in.

Judge spotted, addresses the prosecution lawyer, "So you know the answer?"

Sangwan said, "Ji 3rd is… um…"

"um… baap Sahoo Singh?" The judge suggested, smirking.

"Ji Sahoo Singh," nodding his head, lawyer signalled to MLA to repeat.

"Arrey O cartoon!" judge thundered at the prosecution lawyer.

MLA felt disgraced, took his mobile out to hide behind.

"Why mobile was not taken away and in custody?" The judge yelled at the policemen flanking the witness.

"There is no case, lord," Defence lawyer snapped, "Chhatrapal was not part of any group. All is a figment of the prosecution's imagination. The case is deliberately filed to coerce the accused in giving up his land."

"Land stand acquired already lord," prosecution lawyer pitched in, "so my lord-.'

Cut short, "Only notified so far," yelled a vociferous Chhatrapal.

"O Indian Army," judge snapped, "dare you to speak again out of turn."

The defence lawyer strolled back to his chair.

MLA was asked to step out. He returned to his seat fuming, "Who the hell recommended him," asked him as seating next to Tyagi, "He is a donkey, I tell you we are to lose and lose fast!"

"Any more?" questioned the Judge.

"None for today... um... we... I mean–I request for next date," said a floored individual.

"Monday, after three days."

Outside:

Sahoo Singh was with the Congress district chief and state election committee convenor.

"Your son will not be handcuffed, I have spoken to SSP."

"Shukriyaa Janab."

"You have single-handedly revolutionised congress worker with your marvellous Kissan Andolan," Convenor patted Sahoo Singh's back.

"Shurkiyaa janaab..." Sahoo thanked and then said gingerly, "wanted to meet for that cause."

Convenor could not understand, said ignorantly "But I guess ruling establishment has ceased all acquisition until general elections."

"I am concerned with Jind by-election results." Sahoo corrected.

"Of course, we all are..." Convenor agreed, "consolidation of non-Jat votes has let BJP score a major score. 35-biradari morcha dented our prospects severely."

"And on a seat never won by a non-Jat candidate belonging to any party," Sahoo remarked.

"True Sahoo, very true."

"I guess sahib, the time has come to consolidate Jat electorate," Sahoo said intently.

"And how Sahoo?"

"Perhaps time to revive Jat Aarakshan Andolan," Sahoo said in a low voice.

"Hmmm," Convenor thought for a few moments, and then agreed, "Not a bad idea. And since we seem to be trailing our rivals, in any case, Congress is poised to try all tricks."

Convenor then let a few moments pass by, pondering over the situation. He said a little later, "A few khaap panchayats have staged a peaceful gathering in the last few weeks."

"Ji," Sahoo nodded, "I've organized one on the Maharaja Surajmal birth anniversary."

"That's good," Convenor liked the initiative taken by Sarpanch and asked, "So, do you find the people willing? Would they come out on the streets and protest? "

"Fear of consequences," Sahoo answered in a disappointing note, "as witnessed after 2016 protests are still intact."

"Precisely the reason state chief and party strategists are keeping this option on the back burner," Convenor shared with the Sarpanch.

"But if revived, we can have major emotions flowing for us during the elections," Sahoo stressed the idea.

"Sahoo I commend your thoughts. And the zeal to attempt this rather a deadpan," Convenor wasn't fully convinced, "But be pragmatic. We do not have time on our side. Hardly any time before Lok Sabha elections and thereafter, in 3-4 months, state elections will be held."

Despite the disinterest shown by an important state party stakeholder, Sahoo Singh egged him on, "A trigger is needed janaab. Perhaps an episode to hammer our community out of their slumber sleep."

Convenor ignored the plea, "Party and opposition have done tremendously well in securing farmers' anger–party workers need to sustain mood for a few weeks more."

"What about stakes in the state?" Sahoo Singh was curious.

"Only after we do well in General Election 2019, we need to focus on State Election," Convenor said in an indifferent note.

"How about attempting this force - a dry run - to ascertain the gains? To reap during the latter rather than deferring until the finals for us here?" Sahoo attempted to rationalise his argument.

"Some khaaps have thus come out as early as last December," Convenor nodded, "you can attempt in your area. Rest assured of leadership support."

"Shukriyaa Sahib Ji." A relieved Sahoo Singh said.

"Ram Ram Sahoo."

Convenor was up and walked to the waiting Scorpio car, in last strides stepped closer to Sahoo and said in hushed tone, "so long as your son Chhattar is entangling in land dispute we can secure last negotiations. Ask him to resist if he must in falling for other avenues, winning and retaining power can push BJP folks to any extent - keep him alarmed. Party has a stake in him since he is an accused in a case involving our political opponent."

A few minutes later, Chhattar, policemen, and Dharma stepped out of the court premises while SSP Mudgli addressed local media journos.

"Maintaining Law and order is our primary concern. Therefore, DC sahib has appointed Tehsildar Arun Kumar as Duty Magistrate to supervise all the administration with assistance from my department with a DSP and required number of constables."

"How long will it take to nab the other alleged culprits?" asked one press reporter.

"That is for the court to decide," SSP clarified, "we have had so far been satisfied with our probe and have apprehended and produced the person with charges."

Chhatrapal noticed policemen were busy attending to the media person and their questions.

"Call up that manager, say I am interested," Chhattar shouted to Dharma as he walked towards the police van.

"Manager who?"

"Laado can get you his number," he said in a hushed tone as police whisked him past a waiting Dharma.

"Hmmm… Okay."

"Vakil sahib must meet me tomorrow at the jail, alright?" Chhattar reminded

"I will also be there!" Dharma said.

"Of course, you will always have to dost," said a hurried Chhattar as he was bundled inside the police van.

"Bail is a distant possibility."

"Why?!" exclaimed Chhattar.

Defence lawyer Dhankhad was calling on Chhattrapal in the district jail, accompanied by Dharma.

"It's a murder case, Faujji," the defence lawyer said, "Secondly, a policeman on duty was lynched. And to aggravate, the local polity is a stakeholder with elections around the corner–nope you can't get bail."

Chhattar turned pensive, "Makes sense."

The defence lawyer said further, "I fully understand. Anyone will be desperate to get rid of animals inside and the suffocation."

"Nah – animal insides are least of my discomfort, I just need three-four days outside." Chhattar clarified.

Lawyer Dhankhad was surprised, "Only three… four days?"

"Even two would work if that makes your task any easier?" Chhattar proposed expectedly.

"Not even a bit," Dhankhad shook his head, "You can at most be hospitalized for a day or two in the pretext of some check-up, you know."

"Good, that can be attempted," Chhattar was thinking hard now. Faking illness seemed much probable scenario, asked, "But then how to convince the Jailer?"

"Right," the lawyer said," You cannot bribe him since your rivals have turned hawk eyes round the clock."

"What if a family elder is admitted to hospital with severe illness?" asked Dharma.

"Awesome, there you go…" lawyer said with a smile, "definitely easier."

"Dharma, of late looks like you have grown fond of Bollywood…

Kashyap… Bhardwaj products," said Chhattar grinning cheerfully.

Friend whipped the newspaper, both arms stretched, "Your Bollywood is living here," pointing to one news report of a Gurugram property dealer jumping the parole after cooking up family exigency story.

"What is the procedure? Will I be accompanied by policemen?" Chhattar asked.

"Yes, the law has no provision to do away with unless one is in power to meddle," said the lawyer smirking, "and Congress is not."

Chhattar could only smile, "Least of my worries Vakil," turning towards Dharma, "Manager will be in today?"

"Saturday–tomorrow." Dharma said while still glued to the newspaper.

"I hope you turn out to be one?" Chhatrapal welcomed Anant, "please take a seat."

Meeting time was restricted to ten minutes to every visitor except family members.

"I was pleasantly surprised to hear from," looking at Dharma manager said.

"But you will turn out to be the one you claim to be?" Chhatrapal sounded insistent.

"Yes."

Chhattrapla carried on, "I would need three days for us to do what you had been vociferously orating about the other day."

"The other night? And what you need me from beside, of course leading you and the men?" Anant asked expectedly.

"Dharma will take you to our defence lawyer Dhankhad. You will assist him with some paperwork… affidavit… few thousand in security money if needed etc and…" a broke Accused murderer paused.

"And?!" Anant nudged, curious.

"A car is needed from now until we are back from chambers," Chhattar said in a low voice.

"Chambers?!!" both Anant and Dharma uttered at the same time, jaws dropping open.

"There are chambers in the basements. There are at least two," winked

Chhattar smiling. Anant smacked his lips.

He was in for something he always thought would always remain just wishful thinking.

"You never sounded the other day-"

"The other night," murder accused corrected Anant.

"Yes… the other night you were almost ridiculing me," Anant said with a smile.

"Your thoughts, your beliefs, you are a likable person," Chhattar got up, "I may not get out any time soon manager or perhaps forever be inside… you never know how ugly political manoeuvres could eventually be–never rule out the worst."

"Is it the way to prepare for the worst?" asked, now a deeply concerned friend.

Murder accused, trapped and an in debt farmer could not notice, carried on, "Muslims have been responsible for my grief… younger bedridden, elder framed, family in tatters," he paused, appeared lost as several moments passed by, tears welling up eyes gradually, he uttered finally, "this could be my vengeance!"

Other modalities were quickly discussed and shortly after both left with Dharma bewildered to the hilt. He surely didn't know the person who was there - for a few minutes - certainly not his friend. 'Perhaps a changed man… and why not - a desperate soul in testing time has his options cut out.'

Both lawyers, presenting the prosecution and the defence, were sitting in front of the judge in his chamber.

"Who is ailing?" asked the judge.

"Accused's mother," Defence lawyer Dhankhad said.

"Anything you could present?" thee judge asked further.

Defence lawyer stood up, "These are the hospital records…" pushed gently one file towards the judge, "some bills… prescriptions…" and he started flipping through the papers, "the ongoing consultation records etcetera."

"Agra?" the judge was surprised to note the accused mother was hospitalized as far as Agra, "Is that a hospital in Agra?"

"Ji."

The judge thought for a few moments and then asked, "How many days?"

"Ji," the defence lawyer said gingerly, "Five days!'

"Five days are too many Sir," prosecution lawyer Sangwan objected.

"Traveling alone will take a day," clarified the defence lawyer, "and he is not in the best of shapes we all know."

"Never mind. He is not an army man posted at the border either," said the judge.

"Two days maximum my lord if really someone is hospitalized," pleaded prosecution lawyer Sangwan.

"Add traveling time Mr. prosecution lawyer?" asked the Judge as he began writing down the order, and then proclaimed it very next minute, "Three days are granted! One policeman will accompany him all the time," Judge pulled the head up, snapping out his right forearm, has said to defence lawyer Dhankhad who was looking on, "nothing can be admitted against this if you are planning to," Judge said firmly.

The defence lawyer did not utter any word.

"Next hearing will be right the very next day–the fourth day," Judge announced, signing the parole order.

"We will be on time and present Sir!" A jubilant defence lawyer said.

"You better be!"

Both the judge and prosecution lawyer Sangwan stood up and left the chamber. Following them, Defence lawyer Dhankhad quickly typed the text, "Granted, just a constable to bear with."

"A luxury rather…" murder accused replied, "and days?"

"As many you had hoped for," Dhankhad typed back uttering the words simultaneously as he was joined by a IT manager who was waiting and a friend Dharna who was in the passageway.

"Awesome!" both quipped as they drove out towards the district jail.

CHAPTER 13

"**M**unshi?!"

"Ji faujji."

Accused out on parole monitored by a police constable was surprised at being addressed with respect, "I thought you are dealing with a murder accused?" he asked.

"Patience faujji, the truth will prevail," Constable Munshi said puffing bidi (weed).

"Policewala and Philosophy… waah kya baat Munshi!'

"Any reason you are yet to visit the hospital?" constable Munshi asked.

Chhattar winked, "Maata ji is doing just fine Munshi."

"I did not step out for days while ma was going through her last strides.," Munshi was nostalgic.

"I will," Chhattar patted constable's back, smiling, "I can promise Munshi."

Trio–the friends and the manager were in Agra. On the first day of parole, the threesome had taken shelter in a hotel near to the destination. The third, Anant, would let a private sigh out every time eyes would dangle out of the window, reaching for the horizon and Shivaalay in ruins on the foreground.

"So, the Chambers?" Chhattar asked Anant, stepping inside the room.

"You can think of rooms," paused for a second…took a deep breath and said, "and a Shivaalay."

"Shivaalay?!'

"By all accounts."

182

Premchand, popularly called Munshi because of a famous writer whose name was Munshi Premchand, was the head constable escorting the accused.

"Accounts?" Chhattar could not understand much.

"Two books have been written," Anant replied turning away from the window.

"And some westerner, right?"

"Yes," Anant nodded, "two of them."

"Book could be a quick and cheap way to publicity," commented Chhattar, collapsing on the sofa chair.

Anant was startled to see him questioning the narrative still, "We have passed that stage, right?"

Chhatter sidestepped, "You were talking about Shivaalaya."

Anant thought for a few moments, perhaps trying to collect his thoughts, and then resumed, "There are two staircases situated behind the main building on the marble plinth–closed for ages now. Via these, one can reach the 22 rooms in a secret level immediately below the marble platform of the Taj Mahal."

Chhattar asked, "And if we succeed to-"

Anant cut him short and carried on describing, "On the inner flank of the 22 locked rooms, in the secret level in red stone below the marble platform, is a corridor about 12 ft. wide and some 300 ft. long."

"For sure will not be as easy as you describe,"

Anant ignored Chhattar's comment and continued, "Hidden inside could be valuable evidence such as Sanskrit inscriptions, gods'/goddesses' idols, the original Hindu model of the Taj, perhaps the desecrated Shiva Linga!" The excitement carried on cutting the other short.

Anant shut his eyes, moist in no time, folding his hands as he murmured holy words.

"For sure will not be as easy as you describe," Ex-army man repeated with a thump.

"Of course, not," Anant let a few moments pass by, and then said, "they are closed and that's the challenge."

Dharma got up, "Chal Munshi, we get some Agra petha... it's been years," walked to the door, constable following, Dharma stopped at the exit, turned, friends' eyes met, both smiled.

"Any other way in?" asked Chhattar, turning to IT Manager.

"From the riverbed, there are windows walled up by Shah Jahan," Anant replied.

"Breaking in will be a massive challenge altogether," Chhattar remarked.

"Had that been easy, Taj Mahal wouldn't have stood to this day," Anant eyes sparkled at the mere thought of achievement if they succeeded, "And that is why we are here in the first place–right?"

"So, what has been your plan?" Chhattar asked, adjusted his posture.

"My plan?'

"Yup…"

"Either way," Anant said in a firm voice, "we must reach the story underneath the marble platform."

Chhattar nodded, thought something for a moment or two, and then asked, "How many stories you think this building has?"

"Almost 7, including 1 basement." Anant answered.

"And your Shivaalaya?"

Anant gnashed his teeth, "As if you do not worship,"

"Jats have hardly much to do with festivities.," Chhattar said, leaning back on the sofa chair.

"Worship... Worship," Anant emphasised what he meant.

Chhattar quipped, "Jai Bajrang Bali."

Anant retorted, "Devo ke Dev Mahadev is worshiped by everyone."

"Chalo, jaisi bam bam bhole kee ichchha (As God Shiv desires)," Chhattar said smiling, "So once in what shall we be up to?"

The Hindu objected, "If you can stop smirking, it will be easier for me to remain convinced of your intent."

"Don't you find it all childish?" Chhattar almost burst into laughter managed to tone that down to a chuckle spotting burning eyes on the other side, revised the very next moment, "I mean the eventuality in all the circumstances must be planned for."

"Contingency plan will be the last one," Anant replied calmly, "first we must know what we are up to and what we must achieve."

"Make sense," Chhattar nodded.

Anant continued, "22 rooms level has a wide gallery with rooms on both sides - all walled up with brick and lime."

"Where we shall end up once we break-in from the riverside?" Chhattar asked.

"No idea Chhattar, we could well be in one of the rooms adjacent to this gallery."

"Or?"

"No idea." Anant shrugged his shoulders.

"That's poor know-how on your part," so far indifferent to the whole conversation, Chhattar lunged his upper body forward in utter surprise, "we must not end up stranded one floor below or above the point of destination."

"I do not disagree," said Anant began to think for a moment or two before bending on his knees. Knelt he started scribbling few words, followed by a bizarre map Chhattar could hardly make anything out of.

"Better if you describe simultaneous to your progressive artwork," Chhattar asked, right forearm stretched.

"Must say, you have a zeal for life," Anant said, kept drawing, "Hardly a step out of the gruesome shadow of 3rd degree, yet beaming at the top of Haryanvi wit."

"Say thanks to your brilliant artwork," disinterested now Chhattar stretched himself back in the very comfortable sofa chair,"and out of the world idea.

Anant ignored and moved on, "There must be a staircase to move to upper floors."

"Remember we are only two," Chhattar cautioned, "with little time in hand presumably, we cannot think of engaging in dismantling walled up doors and windows one after another."

"I always thought one or two sojourns will not suffice," Anant shared his idea.

"Rather visits," Chhattar cautioned further, "we cannot spend more than three-four hours in one go."

"Only if luck stands on our side all that time..."

"How many visits you foresee? you must have done some recce?" asked

Chhattar, putting his elbows-on-knees and looking intently at Anant

"None thus far, we all together will." Anant said in a low voice.

"You must be kidding!!" Chhattar was startled to the core, jaw dropped open, "All this has just been floating in your head and with no information gathered from the ground?" he shook his head in utter disbelief, "and there you are embarked upon finding partners?!" He almost yelled at the top of his voice.

"Calm down," Anant held his forehand straight, "Always thought of reaping most in each recce visits once one is with me."

Chhattar jerked his forearm in anger freeing from the grip, "First thing first," he said gasping, "We must do a recce, zero on potential entry points, gather concrete information of building layout and structure and finalize the plan."

"In unison dost!" Anant snapped.

"You a Manager…" Chhattar stopped for a moment and with grin gradually appearing extended to the widest points in no time, he quipped, "or Munshi?"

The manager snapped, "So we have one more hand–always welcome–chalo chalo time is short!"

The next morning - Day Two.

Foursome reached the western entrance of the Taj Mahal. While tourists can enter from the opposite side through the eastern gate, western gate registers most footfalls.

"Two elephant cut-outs used to flank both sides of this huge gate," remarked Anant as the group stood in the long serpentine queue, "it was a Hindu temple built by Hindu Raja almost thousand years ago, plundered by invaders for years, finally snatched by Shah Jahan. Thomas Twining in 1794 noted the Court of the Elephants of the Taj."

"Is it not a Mumtaz Mahal mausoleum?" asked a bewildered Munshi, the police constable.

"I do not…" Anant drew himself close to Chhattar, murmured, "find it the greatest idea to have a policeman around giving us company."

Chhattar stepped away, eyelids fully drawn, jaw dropped open–lunged forward the very next moment and whispered in a hushed tone, "Munshi accepts bribe!"

A fuming manager resumed, "Mumtaz Mahal was buried in Behrampur. This beautiful gigantic place was taken over by the Mughaliya force while some piece of land was given in lieu to the Rajput ruler who owned this place at that time. And later the dead body was brought here."

"To?" asked a puzzled Munshi as foursome cleared the security check and stepped inside the monument.

All were flabbergasted. "To make it," replied Dharma putting on a serious face, "Mumtaz Mahal mausoleum."

Chhattar stopped almost midway in his stride, "Munshi Manager Mausoleum," then turning to Manager said, "How does that sound? Since you are about to unearth a phenomenon."

Anant termed that ugly, ignored, and resumed, "The marble plinth supporting the four-storey edifice–first two housing the artificial Jehangir and Mumtaz graves–while plinth itself is one story with all its sides walled up with white marble."

"How many stories are we looking at then?" asked Dharma.

"The main attraction is the white marble structure. This four-storied white marble structure has under it two stories in red stone, reaching down to the river level. And one basement."

"7 stories?!"

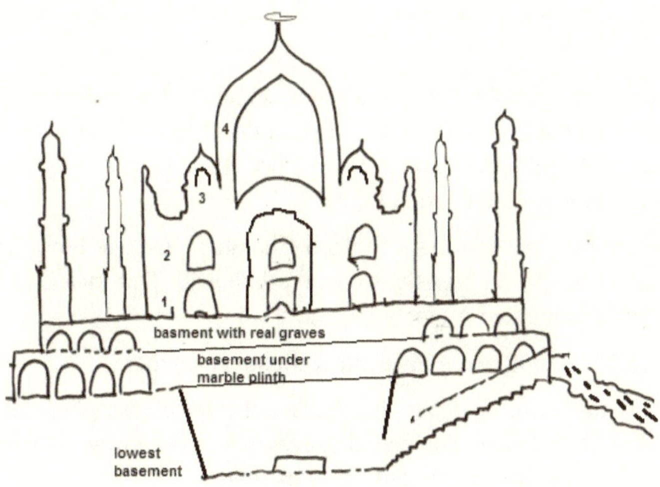

Image inspired by images available on the internet on this subject.

<u>https://johnnicholsonofindia.wordpress.com/illustrations/the-mystery-and-real-tragedy-of-the-taj-mahal/</u>

"Yes," replied Anant and swiftly strode towards the monument's main attraction. All followed him. As they walked towards the edifice, Anant pointed at the many rooms located on either side of the Road between Western Gate to Eastern Gate with many rooms on either side, "these provided shelters to devotees and pilgrims."

"So, it's a Pilgrim spot now?" a surprised Chhattar could not stop taunting.

Much angered at the disrespect and the mocking tongue, Anant replied dejectedly, "Agra has had 5 Shivalayas, much venerated since ancient times; four are visited and worshiped to this day; 5th isn't traceable-"

"And the Taj Mahal is the 5th."

"Tejo-Mahalaya, if you don't mind," Anant snapped.

Just as they were about to reach the edifice Anant subtly drew Chhattar's attention towards a little passage near the staircase which was leading to the marble edifice, "One could earlier enter the sealed chambers below, but they were sealed a decade ago," said Anant pointing at the brick wall.

There is a strict tradition to take off one's footwear before stepping on to the 19 feet high marble plinth of the Cenotaph. Dharma, as well as constable, found that odd, Anant snapped, "Only before one enters temple footwear is taken off... right?"

An otherwise simple outing to a historical place was turning out to be utter amazement to the head constable. Dharma drove him to the river end of the plinth while Anant and Chhattar approached the staircase to ascend into the cenotaph chamber on the ground floor.

"We are now outside the Cenotaph Chamber. Just see how the steps in plain marble break up the designs on the plinth wall. This means that they are not original," remarked Anant with zeal.

Seconds later both were inside the cenotaph chamber.

This is the main chamber that houses the false sarcophagi of Mumtaz Mahal and Shah Jahan. The actual graves are at the lower chamber, where tourists' entry has been restricted for years now.

Anant was particularly interested in showing two aspects to Chhattar.

First was breaking up of floor artwork and design by the graves' placement, points to an afterthought. Second, the octagonal marble screen around both graves. "Every Shivalay has Octagonal perimeter. Quite possibly, Shiv linga was uprooted and graves placed, explaining the breaking up of floor design."

Anant then pointed at the rooms around the cenotaph chamber, "These are areas where other forms of worship were held around this central shrine."

Chhattar was all agog by now and getting serious. The Haryanvi wit had taken a back seat. He was pensive and thinking hard–something was troubling him.

"Let's move to the back," said Anant in a hushed, hurried tongue.

While coming out, they spotted Munshi stepping inside, with Dharma in tow, cajoling.

Anant took the muscular, six-footer-heavily built-imposing-figure down to the red stone platform which shoulders white marble plinth.

"So, are we standing above the 2nd storey, Manager?"

"No on the ground. The 1st is the white marble plinth," answered Anant and started explaining again the palace's structure, '4 stories is the white marble structure–right?"

"Hmmm…" Chhattar nodded.

"2 stories are–the red stone and the white marble plinth–ground and the 1st, and we're right above the ground floor now."

"And the 7th? You said a while back, " Chhattar was much puzzled.

"The basement," Anant answered with a smile.

"All you have learned from those two historians if my memory serves me correctly?" Chhattar asked looking towards the red stone building on the far right.

"Yes, and some westerns too, one is quite laborious. He is an American. A Christian-turned-Hindu hosts a website with invaluable information, you can say an expansive peep into hidden truth of Taj."

"Once we get back, I would like to have a look," said a pensive Chhattar dialling Dharma's number, "Can you come now?"

"Now, let's move to a place we are here for," said Anant with arm stretched towards the river end of the platform arousing Chhattar's curiosity. His head was up as a spontaneous reaction with eyes surveying the riverside platform end. Chhattar straightaway spotted an opening on the floor surrounded by short walls on three sides, "is that not a staircase?" he remarked.

"Yes," said Anant as he strode across the platform, Chhattar in tow.

"To your 22 rooms?!" Chhattar asked

"There you are!" an excited voice commented on the swift internalising on his part.

Reaching the opening, Anant stopped momentarily to look around. It was closing at noon, not many visitors were visiting the wonder at the part of the day and whatever number was in most of them were glued to the main attraction.

There is an iron grill frame, which is horizontally placed all over the staircase and covers the opening entirely. To his utter surprise, the small iron door carved out of the iron grill was not locked.

Anant said to Chhattar in a low voice, "Perhaps opened for regular cleaning and the sweeper must have forgotten to lock it back."

Anant swiftly descended. There were some 20-25 steps. At the bottom, there was an iron gate locked. No sooner did he reach the gate, he tried to peep inside, pushing his head towards the space between the bars.

Foul smell greeted his nostrils with eyes spotting what looked like bricked walls on either end of the alley, the darkness inside hiding the hideous work.

The smell, the darkness, the dark alley clouded his senses. He felt enraged, ready to barge in and tear open with bare hands. Hinduism, he felt buried there, seething in anger through chambers in silence he could hear still the shriek of enormous agony, of the weight of Islam profound by graves above.

Suddenly he felt a palm on his right shoulder. He was jerked out of his slumber, subconscious mind frightened. He turned around, fearing the worst. It was Chhattar. He let a sigh.

"Let's move out," said Chhattar.

As they stepped out, Munshi and Dharma could be seen walking towards them.

"Who are you? It is not allowed to go in." It was some complex official pointing at the board next to the staircase.

Anant had clearly trespassed.

Chhattar spotted a frightened soul yet to escape from the first-time tangible insult a Haryana born brought up in a society sans Muslim for years, worked in a cosmopolitan ambience since grown up had experienced. The ex-army man intervened, "We are from Haryana, on some governmental task," pointing at the incoming the head constable - Munshi.

The official took note of police uniform, said, "Okay, but you should have first taken permission at the office."

"We are to visit the office; some paperwork needs to be done. Could you please direct us, in which part of the office is located?" asked Chhattar with a perfectly made-up naïve look.

"Next to the main gate," said official, "And beware of the consequences next time," glaring the manager before walking away.

"Riverside now manager?" asked Chhattar.

"Yes."

"Let's break for lunch first. Aur Munshi... Agra ka petha khaayega? (Munshi would you like to taste the famous Agra delicacy?)" said Chhattar putting an arm around him as the group strolled out.

Anant in the tow breathing heavily still.

CHAPTER 14

T hat night–the second night in the hotel room.

Dharma was chatting with vakil on WhatsApp, lying on a chair.

Chhatrapal and Anant were sitting on sofas facing each other.

Both were glued to laptops, Anant had brought two, the ex-army man was surfing the internet for all the Taj related material.

Suddenly, Chhattar started reading out emphatically, "Peter Mundy, English, noted in 1632 (a year of the death of Mumtaz) that the Taj was a most famous building for any tourist to see."

"How could the Taj Mahal be built in one year? Historians say construction started in 31 and took 22 years," remarked Anant, "Mundy refers to the fact the Taj was famous before the Shah Jahan seized it."

Chhattar was eager to learn more, resumed, "De Laet, Dutch, likewise noted the same and called the Taj The Mansingh Mahal i.e. Palace. Albert Mandelslo in 1638 (7 years after the death of Mumtaz) likewise referred to the Taj as predating Shah Jahan but seized."

Anant added quickly, "Thereafter someone at some point turned the Taj into a tomb and the body of that 'much-decayed corpse' was now INSIDE instead of buried on the grounds as Tavernier recorded."

Ex-army man read out further, "E. B. Havell, Mrs. Kenoyer, and Sir W. W. Hunter have all confirmed the Taj was seized by Shah Jahan and looted."

A rejuvenated Hindu now pounced, "Tombs of saints are Sufi and ornate tombs are illegal according to strict Islam. And if the Taj was originally a holy place of Shiv ji and Mata Parvati, then what happened to that aspect?"

Anant stooped and looked towards Chhattar, who was gaping, startled to know aspects, claims, reports hitherto not ever talked about by mains stream media or even for that matter, in the academic circles.

Anant carried on, "A locality in, nearly 4 km away from Taj Mahal, is called Bateswar and in 1900 A.D., General Cuningham, the then Director of the Archaeological Survey of India (ASI), conducted an excavation at Bateswar and discovered an edict, now known as the Munj Bateswar Edict and kept at the Lucknow Museum. The epigraph contains 34 verses written in Sanskrit, out of which 25th, 26th, and 34th verses are important in the present context.

"An English translation of the above verses reads as"

Anant stooped momentarily and resumed reading emphatically.

"He built a marble temple which is the abode of Lord Vishnu and the King bows down to touch His feet. (25)"

"The King has built another marble temple which has been dedicated to the Lord Who has the moon as is ornament on His forehead. (26)"

"Today, the 5th day of the bright half in the month of Ashwin, the Sunday, in the year 1212 of the Vikram Samvat, the edict is being laid. (34)"

"The Munj Bateswar Edict was laid by King Paramardi Dev of the Chandratreya dynasty on Sukla Panchami in the month of Ashwin, in the year 1212 Vikram Samvat (or A.D. 1156)."

Quite curious by then, Chhattar got up and took a seat next to Anant, called Dharma who quickly joined them. Chhattar had spotted something interesting on one of the many sites he was surfing on the internet and wanted to show them, "Look at this door on the wall at the riverside." The photograph was quite old. It showed a riverside view of the entire red stone plinth. Chhattar said further, "Looks most vulnerable, parts of it have decayed... we could easily break in from here."

Dharma said, "This photo looks quite dated, I do not recall seeing this today when we did a recce of the river sidewall."

"This is not a wall, this is 2 storey red stone building," Anant corrected them, "look at the arches," pointing at the part of the photo where arches horizontally placed above the basement where there was this door Chhattar was talking about, "these are rooms... all walled up with bricks and lime."

"Correct, can we break in with most primitive tools?" asked Chhattar.

"Primitive... you mean just a couple of hammers and... and..."

"Let's say two-three spades," added Chhattar.

"But that will take us too much time to break in?" Anant wondered.

"Yes, but then we cannot haul a drilling machine there... talk sense Manager."

"Right," excitement had taken over Anant, overwhelming his senses.

"So, what's the plan now... we have done the recce..." Dharma asked.

"And only a day left with us," Anant reminded.

Chhattar stood up–"Plan is, we shall wait until midnight and will reach the river end from Bhairon mandir rear end."

Bhairon Mandir is situated at Yamuna bank next to the Taj Mahal on its western side.

"Good," said Dharma.

"So that means we have two nights with us to get in?" asked the manager.

"Do we have spades and hammers ready?" Chhattar asked Dharma.

"We will have to buy, I'm afraid," replied the friend.

"And it's too late now, shops must be closed by now Dharma."

"That's utter casualness on your part, Dharma and Chhattar..."

"You could have thought... you are not a Taj tourists' guide. Or are you one?" Dharma snapped.

"We are letting time pass by..." Anant retorted, "we could have easily leveraged tonight."

"Stop commenting manager," Dharma said in a firm voice, "the bricks won't stand strikes for more than a couple of hours... you must rather think about what we are supposed to do once we have broken in."

"Strikes will cause loud sound... will attract security personnel... I'm assuming there must be some,' Anant cautioned.

'If someone comes... we will flee.... no other option," replied Dharma.

"Just like that..." Anant mocked the very idea and was stunned too, "so easily we are ready to give up instead of drafting a better plan, place, and time."

"If you can stop daydreaming manager," retorted Chhattar, "think about the size and gravity of the task, significance of the place. It is straight work– get in as fast as we can, hope thumps do not reach anyone."

"And the security in place?" Anant asked.

"We will leverage Munshi… police presence will help us get some cover."

Anant was intrigued by the suggestion, asked, "How exactly?"

"Munshi… um… will break into a conversation with the nearest around. I will brief him on which topic to pick… thanks to you guys," winking at Dharma referring to right-wing renewed fervour and volunteers, "Munshi will get to talk about many subjects, Taj itself is a controversial subject."

"As if we have just learned and gotten enriched with hitherto unknown facts," winked Dharma.

Anant was fuming all that time, "And who will hold back this policeman if he decides to unleash his duty once he is back?"

"I will bribe him," said Chhattar calmly.

Anant exploded,"You are repeating yourself… that's just a probability… okay even if after accepting he turns hostile?"

"You will also bribe."

"Are you serious?" Anant was surprised, "Even with two bribes if he still feels compelled to serve his oath?".

"I will bribe him too," said Dharma.

"Thrice will be the burden, not many in the history this fraternity would get out of—he will be mum forever," said Chattar.

Anant did not say anything, he was getting flooded with multiple emotions simultaneously. On one hand, he was just a step away from achieving the grandest individual goal, on the other, the enormity of the task was trembling him to the core and third nervy stunning anticipated feeling of being inside once broken in and what he does to make that public?

"Let's call it a day," said Chhattar lying on the bed, Dharma walked out to accompany Munshi who was waiting outside. Anant stepped out to the balcony. He wanted to rather grapple with the moment and enjoy the excitement and edginess of task cut-out to the fullest.

Struggle long over, Opportunity Seized,

In Shelter now—Up I go, March I forward,

Whither to conquer, that 'Desire' to fulfil,

Will he be? Quandary a still!

Four shadows.

It was 1 past midnight.

All found stranded on the rear door of Bhairon mandir. The door was locked from ages, though a relic, albeit rickety.

"It will make much sound if you force yourself out," cautioned the manager in a hushed tone.

"Let it," replied Chhattar, "nobody will care to follow us all the way up to Taj river end," as he put hammer to the rusted lock. Relic couldn't put up much resistance, once more proved enough. None in the mandir heard perhaps or two sounds were too low a number to make inspection necessary.

The relieved group quickly descended from the mandir concrete structure onto the pavement and began moving towards the destination walking between the Yamuna and the river end wall of Taj. Any beacon was not being used to avoid detection.

The pavement was bushy, Anant deemed it a good camouflage.

It was a mere five minutes careful walk that took them at the edge of the grassy area between the Yamuna and the marble structure of Taj and was quite similar to some municipal corporation park sans any benches or anything concrete. The area had a perimeter established with barbed wire all around it.

"A wrench can us get over it, don't fret," said Chhattar.

"That everyone knows, I am thinking whether it has electricity running by any chance," remarked Anant.

"No," said Dharna.

"Why not… it is a possibility," said Anant.

"No," said Munshi as Chhattar opened the carry bag with fingers thumped inside scrabbling for a wrench.

"Why a no?" Anant almost said in regular volume.

"Shh….," said Dharma reminding the manager of the order, "Because you are not at Pakistan border."

"We are through," said Chhattar as he cut down and made an opening swiftly.

All swiftly moved to the other end. Chhattar wanted to explore the area around the bricked-up wall. Soon the group was standing in front of a doorway, walled up with brick and lime, presumably.

"You have served the nation Faujji," It was Munshi, "Now, you are serving your Dharma."

"What?!" was the expression on Chhattar's face, "Serving Dharma...," then pointing at Dharma, "Dharma?"

"Nah, you are serving your Dharma, Yudhishter's Dharma."

"Munshi... can you lend us a helping hand, we need to break this door open," asked Chhattar handing him a hammer.

"Will always remember this day," said Munshi, voice gutted, hands folded, looking towards the heaven every other second.

"This is night," Dharma said.

Munshi continued, "Om-Namah-Shivaay... Jai-Shiv-Shankar." Each chant a note higher than the previous, "Har-har-Mahadev-har-har-Mahadev.... Jai-Shiv-Shambhu."

"Munshi!!" Chhattar yelled, "have you gone mad... what are you doing?!!" Chhattar had dropped hammer by now. Anant was startled to see him reacting the way he had just now.

Munshi stopped utterances and stopped looking at heaven, turned to Chhattar, "I'm with you whatever you will do will remain buried in my chest forever... Let's do it now... you have given me a chance of a lifetime..."

Chhattar and Dharma could not believe their eyes, stood speechless. Munshi picked the hammer, stepped closer to the wall, and said, "Tell me, brother, where I must strike...," then closing his eyes he uttered one more time, "Jai-Shiv-Shankar-Jai-shiv-Shambhu."

Chhattar held constable's forearm and jerked him out of his slumber, unabated chants came to a halt, "Bol Faujji..."

"Let's go... will come some other night," said Chhattar pulling him all the way back to the perimeter. Anant was flabbergasted, said, "Can you explain to me what is going on... why are we not doing we had come here for."

Chhattar kept walking.

"I'm speaking to you!" Anant almost yelled.

"We are returning to Panipat..."

"Why?!!" he was stunned.

"Parole is ending in a few hours and I do not want to jump my parole," Chhattar said calmly.

"But then only you had fixed the last night?" Anant grabbed his arm from behind and stopped him.

They had reached the perimeter by now. Some security personnel's torch faded light could be spotted pointed towards them, "Please do it fast," said Chhattar holding manager's hand.

"But Chhattar…"

"Shhh… we will fix another time… right now let's get out of here."

Chapter 15

“We have sought approval from the central leadership to give you a ticket from Panipat Rural in the Assembly election.” Party convenor was meeting Sahoo Singh and his supporters.

“Ji meharbaani.”

“Kissan Ekta Manch’s success was much talked about when central leadership met with our state leaders,” Convenor continued emphatically, “Your work has been pivotal in underscoring Gandhi scion’s pet pan-India General Election 2019 project aimed at raising the plight of the farmers to a level, farmers, and their continuing distress and everyday struggle become the main agenda for these elections.”

“Shukriyaa janab to mention my name in the meeting. Your patronage has led us to the best of our abilities. I will work hard to secure the seat,” a beaming face said.

“Yes, that is paramount Sahoo,” Convenor said standing up, “You don’t know how much I had convinced the state leaders to get you the one you have with you secure. You need to secure this seat for me and support me in during state president elections.”

“Everyone wants to work under your leadership,” Sahoo Singh said in a reassuring tone, “Our state president has been of minimal effect.”

“He is a novice still,” said the party convenor with a smirk on his face.

“By the way,” Convenor stepped closer to Sahoo Singh and dropped his voice to whisper, “Samajwadi Yadav is about to change camps, will join Janta party.”

The news did not take Sarpanch by surprise, he had expected something on that line around the time elections would get held. The veteran was rather worried now, remarked. “Yadav votes will only strengthen our rivals’ position–

they are surely moving towards 35 biradari votes consolidation Sahib."

Lok Sabha elections had been announced.

Votes were to be cast in 7 phases from 11th April until 23rd May 2019.

Haryana has 10 seats.

Four parties were on fray; Ruling BJP, the predecessor Congress, Indian National Lok Dal of O.P. Chautala, and its splinter group's - Jan Nayak Janta Party.

"35 biradari vs Jat is a larger state-wide narrative. You can't do much Sahoo nor I can… just focus on securing your seat… that's all we need!" Party convenor said little dejectedly.

Party high command had fielded Convenor to fight the General Election from the Karnal parliamentary seat.

Votes were to be cast on 12th May 2019, all over Haryana.

Sahoo Singh folded his hands, "Singh Sahib…" aide quickly followed that up with, "Zindabad!" And one more round, "Singh Sahib… Zindabad (long live)!"

Convenor ascended on shiny mammoth SUV, folded his hands as the very next second convoy zipped off.

It was a two-room haphazardly built home, one of the many or rather all with Punjabis the whole occupants in that alley. Everyday struggle though long over as was the case until the turn of the century when Punjabis firmly believed each day was to survive and to hope for the best for the next, the community was now wary of dwindling BJP political capital. 2014 massive victory infused confidence to get to power in a state whose politics had always been dominated by the Jat community. Jind By-Polls had boosted their confidence by going in a cutthroat triangular fight–BJP, Jats votes, and Congress.

BJP fielded its candidates from all 10 seats, including Karnal. In 2014, BJP contested on 7 out of 10 Haryana Lok Sabha seats.

"Compensation is yet to be distributed," one complained, the daily wager was in a dirty white pajama.

"Don't worry, I'm working to release them as early as they can….be patient," said Gopal Middha. Wager noted gold chain peeping out of politician's sparkling white politician's kurta.

"BJP is your party… BJP has the government," fumed the aged man.

"We need to show our strength brothers and sisters," Aide moved Middha to the pedestal, a makeshift one, to let the leader address all. "Can we forget the 2016 riots and arson enacted by 1 biradari?"

The crowd began to gather; a mike was quickly scrambled for and handed over.

"This election is all about Paintees Biradari vs 1 biradari. And the majority must remain the majority. You can see the way we all have seen since 1966 when our state was founded… that these people from 1 biradari they dominate us… you find them in more numbers than any other biradari folks in all Mahakama (government departments)… they have dominated power corridors… they rule municipal councils… time has come for Paintees Biradari to stand up…"

Mike got punctured that very moment, aide scrambled some thumps.

Among the gathered, most were shopkeepers. Their shops were not gutted in 2016 by Jat Aarakshan Andolan. They were just lucky to have gotten away.

"Who knows?" was the fear of many writs large on anxious faces, "with elections on the anvil, Jats are mobilising strength…" said one.

"We will get back in power….no need to fret… we have law and order with us… a Punjabi is a chief minister, not a jat!" retorted one hyper bullish

"Wasn't he in 2016?" asked the one realistic in long kurta similar to the common attire of the elderly found on the other side of the border.

The aspiring lawmaker resumed in the meantime, "If we do not come together 35 biradari will be defeated. 35 biradari defeated now will surrender our rights - rights enshrined in the constitution. We will lose dignity and 1 biradari will enslave us. Can you let the memories of 2016 fade? You were targeted; hoodlums we are fighting against so come together; we cannot let 2016 be repeated and in any form."

Shopkeepers and small-time businessmen were investing hope in to see Manohar Lal Khattar, who was the BJP Chief Minister since 2014, retaining power. A rich standing in corner supervising this 'Chai pe Charcha' had invested money to sustain his ascendency in political corridors.

"Bhai Middhaa–zindabad… Vote for Gopal Middha…"

"What about the promised compensation?" another hand-to-mouth survivor yelled, waiting for the money Manohar Lala Khattar promised years back.

"Every affected will get the riots compensation…" Middha answered.

"When?!" complainant asked, waving his forearms in frustration.

"Be patient… let me get you your compensation," Middha said and then turning to one aide, "Can you note down his details… remind me when I meet our Party President."

That very moment Supporters broke into sloganeering to prevent any more pointed questions to spoil the grand outing, "Bhai Middhaa–zindabad… Bhai Middhaa ko vote do… Vote for Gopal Middha…"

A few took the complainer aside, almost pulling him out of the crowd, "Dare you now interrupt the speech… you can speak to me later… chal number likh mera (note down my number) ."

It was Monday, the fourth day from the parole day, and he was standing there motionless. Dharma had taken a seat behind the defence lawyer. And to his right, parked horizontally and haphazardly, was the rival camp. Laal topi had kesariya donned and gleaming all over, giving his pale teeth a run for the money. Tyagi looked pensive while MLA was furious to find a trivial entourage.

The prosecution had filed after the last hearing a list of people whom they want to question in the present hearing. The goal was to frame the duo–Chhattar and his friend Dharma for the murder of SHO Kalia.

"Can we hear some words about the presence of the listed witness?"

Voice was low today. The judicious throat was struggling to open up.

"Yes Sir… Dharma is present," Sangwan answered, the prosecution lawyer.

"That's remarkable," commented the chair, "let's see how much he vomits on the face of his friend," said he, smirking.

Dharma strolled to the witness stand, a little circumspect, eyeballs frantically searching for the avenue.

"Were you there that night, Mr. Dharma," the prosecution asked.

"Where?"

"In the police chowki." Prosecution lawyer Sangwan specified.

"Which chowki?" Dharma asked, shrugging his shoulders while face wore a look of ignorance.

"Sir… accused is acting naïve," Sangwan complained.

"If so… ask some relevant questions," the judge said without looking up.

Vakil adjusted himself and the tone, "Police Chowki Panipat Rural!"

"When Sir?" Dharma carried on.

"4th January," Sangwan snapped.

Witness turned his body towards the Judge and said, "Yes Sir I was there with my friend who is standing there," pointing an index finger at Chhatrapal.

"Chhatrapal Singh is a retired decorated Army Man. We were there because SHO Saini had ordered us to be present in connection with some incident at the canal next to our fields," uttering unabatedly Dharma turned his body towards the frontbenchers, "And there we found MLA and Samajwadi Yadav who were later joined by Tyagi-"

"So, wait a minute," prosecution interjected attempting to stop his monologue.

Witness ignored and carried on, "And suddenly some mussalle appeared... shouting Allah-hu-Akbar. Yadav went out, and he was attacked, next minute they barged in."

"What you were doing there and where were you both inside the building?" Sangwan interrupted and asked pointedly

Dharam did not answer, continued his narration, "So once they were inside, we went up locked ourselves in one cell and that's it!"

"Who killed who?" asked the prosecution.

"Who is who here?" asked the witness.

"Who was killed by the mob?" prosecution lawyer shouted.

"I do not know... I heard SHO was killed... by the way, do you know who killed who?" asked mimicking prosecution lawyer Sangwan's body posture, a burst of laughter went out in the courtroom.

Vakil was pissed off, appealed to the chair, "Sir..."

"Lord!" snapped the judge.

"Yes Sir... Lord... My lord..." Sangwan said sheepishly.

"As they say in movies," remarked Dharma winking.

"Can you shut up?" retorted prosecution.

"This vakil is Monkey or donkey?" Yadav whispered into MLA Inderjeet's ear.

"Both," answered MLA.

Prosecution lawyer stepped closer to the enclosure housing the Chair, "My lord," said he left hand adjusting black tie, "in the witness list you can see," index finger now pointing towards a pile of papers lying on the right side of the judge's desk, "we have people who can vouch both friends were part of the mob that killed SHO."

"Oh…" the judge asked enacting a foolish tone, "and they will be called to testify?"

"Ji?" asked lawyer, body leaning towards the chair, arms resting on sides.

"Who asked you to become a vakil?" Chair thundered.

Sangwan could not understand any of it, asked naively, "Ji?"

Disgusted, the judge dropped his voice, "Call them please."

"Who Sir… my father?"

"Nah… turn around."

He did so exactly as was told, body turned, neck at 180 degrees trying to capture judge's instructions, who said, "Them…," pointing at the bench housing the politicians.

"All three Sir?"

"Lord… lord," corrected Dharma.

"All three lord?" Sangwan repeated.

"Do we have three boxes?" The judge was furious.

"No Sir… matlab… My Lord, sir."

"Only My lord," Dharma poked in.

"Shut up," Judge thundered quietening the witness, and then said to prosecution, "Call them one by one…," eyeballs glaring, "and first is?"

"Ji… Mr. Inderjeet, our respected MLA Sahib," answered Sangwan adjusting his posture.

MLA strolled into the second witness box. Dharma looked on from the adjacent box.

Accused Chhattar threw in some words abruptly and in haste, "Sir… this is not acceptable?"

"What is not acceptable?!!" an irritated judge asked.

"That prosecution has 2 vakils and I have only 1… not acceptable,"

A bewildered judge asked, "Who is the 2nd one?!"

"You My-lord … not only today you have aided this guy… you in the first hearing as well," Chhattar said in a dash.

It was a bombshell - A fury hit the assembly, "This is CONTEMPT of the court… you…" Judge yelled, index finger waving, a glare in the company in the backdrop, "You will be charged with CONTEMPT-"

Faujji bisected the thundering voice, retorted, "Nah… Contempt of court? Nah… that happens for Supreme Court… you know… High Court," enacting some faces towards the prosecution vakil, arms stretched out casually, "Uh… not for this session… yes… sessions court."

All the hell broke loose, "You can be charged with an attempt to-"

The old man was cut short once again, "Sir…" It was Dharma.

Friend Chhattar corrected, "Nah… My Lord."

"Yes, My Lord," pointing at Chhatrapal, "This person is a serial offender… he has carried out another contempt."

An exasperated judge stopped midway through his manoeuvre, and yelled, "which contempt?"

"Contempt of Tejo Mahalaya–the high and most beautiful marble courtyard." Dharma said emphatically with a wide grin, teeth gleaming, arms stretched out towards the audience.

"What?!!" the old man was certainly about to faint.

"Asked Munshi Premchand," said Dharma, arm stretched to the full towards head constable Munshi who was standing next to the accused box. Infuriated and much confused now, the judge turned towards Munshi and so did a hundred eyeballs present in the courtroom. Not even once Munshi had seen, so many eyeballs locked at him, thousands of cases he was part of. So, there he stood nervous yet elated and ecstatic to be the centre of attraction, he gushed that very second, "Ji Huzoor… Faujji cut the wires… spade in hand there he rushed to break in… the entrance to the basement and the divine dwar of Mahadev… you know… Jai Shiv Shankar has its linga established there… ages-ago."

"Shut up constable… and you all-" Judge stood up from his chair and yelled at the top of his voice.

Dharma took no note of the Chair, and said to prosecution, "You can press charges–this is indeed contempt of court," both arms stretched urging. Prosecution eyes sparkled and bounced on the opportunity, "My-lord we press charges," rushed back to prosecution desk, lifted on and read out IPC clause,

"IPC… xxx and we are permitted, landlord… I mean Me, Lord, to press these charges formally in next hearing."

Dharma yelled, "Press the sedition charges… he has tried to break into Taj Mahal-NIA must be called in… which IPC for Sedition vakil sahib?"

Prosecution flipped through the pages and said, "Yes… there you go–"

Witness number 2 MLA yelled, "Nah… we are not going to press any charges."

Startled in fury, chair retorted collapsing back on the chair, "Who 'WE' here?"

Inderjeet's hand was out, index finger out and wrist turned inside, indicated himself, "I am WE!"

Judge thundered, "Stop this…" up from his seat again, "You all have behaved in a most untoward manner…"

"Contempt of the court… sedition?!" both vakil and Dharma asked on the chorus.

"Shut you up…" he yelled at the top of his voice almost out of breath now, "The only court has the right, and the court will decide… DISMISSED."

And there he walked away… a learned judge.

CHAPTER 16

"Seva medal... unprecedented heroics in Kashmir... participation in strategic operations in the northeast... and the Naxals... your son Chhattar has fought for the motherland and people of this country."

It was Sahoo Singh speaking at Maharaj Soorajmal (the Jat warrior who fought in the 3rd battle of Panipat) Jayanti samaroh. He was addressing prominent Jat leaders of the region.

"Yet... BJP government has pressed sedition charges!" cried a crestfallen, hands in the air, "Can some believe this?"

The crowd burst into a murmur.

"Can you believe this?!!" politician repeated, murmurs turned steadier.

"And don't we all know why sedition charges have been pressed," the veteran added.

"Why so Sarpanch?" asked one ignorant.

"Because he belongs to us and they..." index finger stretched out of the fist, right arm in the air, "they are after us.... they want us to yield.... they want Jat to kneel... Jat Aarakshan Andolan is the target... not my son... not your son... Jat unity is the target... our future is at stake... they are telling us to forget our rights or bear the cost!" He stopped abruptly, let a few moments pass by, and then yelled, "Jats need to stand up and get counted," the candidate standing in the upcoming assemble election on a Congress ticket from Panipat Rural called on Jat fellow leaders.

"Jat leadership working hard in the whole of Haryana calling on every Jat household to come forward and become part of Jat Aarakshan Andolan!"

Many agreed writ large on their faces was the agony of the aftermath of Jat Aarakshan Andolan in March 2016 though. Thousands of cases were filed by state government charging Jats and rightly so. A stern law and order can only bring the order necessary to curb plunder, loot, and abject discriminatory targeting of Punjabi community who are routinely called 'Sanaarthi' in local dialect to denote refugees, or even Pakistani to dent a permanent psychological stain. Other castes have only been accomplice - a craven abdication of social duty necessary to maintain social cohesiveness to strengthen the demographic vitality of our democratic nation.

"Panipat cannot remain a bystander," Sahoo Singh thundered, "We must unite, our leaders need each of us, every Jat must pledge—one for all and all for the cause!"

All agreed in chorus.

A few demanded a careful thought first, to decide the way forward without having to face the last experience.

"In-fact this is the only method we can adopt - a show of strength," Sahoo Singh cautioned the fence-sitters, "otherwise, our political rivals will keep filing the cases…"

"You mentioned political rival," an elderly stood up, "Even if a Jat dedicates himself for the cause… Congress will still not win the majority."

"How?" Sahoo asked.

Elderly answered, "Consolidated Jat votes will get polled to all the Jat candidates of Congress INLD and JJP, what is the gain you are looking for?"

Elderly's question seemed to resonate with many who were present, "What is the end goal of this strife if only BJP to eventually nudge us out and retain the power in the state?"

"It's a number game," said the elderly turning towards the gathering, "We must not decide in a hurry," then turning around towards Sahoo, "Only once we are sure of getting a majority and power, we must risk lives of thousands."

Sahoo retorted, "It is a sign of weakness." The elderly person was taken aback and many others. "It would prove we do not have the courage to take the adversary head-on." Sarpanch turned towards the assembly, "Jat votes consolidation will get us Jat majority in the Vidhan Sabha. A Jat majority will get us the rights we have been fighting for and haven't been accorded since 2014 Modi wave." Stretching his arms outward veteran pleaded, "This is the time… and… This is the only time. Earlier we start the agitation, more will be the consolidation and better the Jat numbers in the assembly. The second phase of Agitation can begin only the first achieved."

"And what will that be, Sahoo?" asked the elderly.

"Once we have the number, and in the seat, the central government will have to concede to an elected State Government demand." He stopped for a second, looked around, resumed, "There are two issues and our demands, therefore: first: Jats must be given reservation under the central government."

"But Sarpanch, OBC status has been granted to Jats since 2016," asked one.

"Which of course is of no use since that grants us jobs and admission just only in the state," Sahoo replied, "And any state, we all know, have a lesser number of jobs and educational institutions than the departments and institutions under the central government. We need a reservation in central government jobs and institutions."

Many agreed.

"Second: Cases filed in the 2016 riots against our youths must be withdrawn."

"And how do you intend to drive the Andolan, what should be our strategy?" asked another.

Sahoo continued, "Strategy is simple and straight forward. Each one of us will educate his friends, relatives, acquaintances about the alarming situation."

"Hmmm" many nodded as Sahoo carried on elaborating.

"Periodically, an assembly will be organized like this one. And youth in good numbers must join and hear us."

"Make sense," remarked many as all listened to Sahoo Singh attentively.

"Jat leaders of Jat Aarakshan Andolan will address these gatherings and will spell out tactics. With consolidated Jat number, we can stop the BJP works from entering the villages to ask for votes–this will help us consolidate Jat votes and at the same time, will leave a dent on BJP votes. Our leaders have planned for huge 'Chakka-Jam' day to force the hands of the central government. Now on only the united force of Jat can bring us the reservation."

"We agree Sahoo," said one leader, "and a case-in-point is Delhi March in 2017. Remember how half of the national capital had come to a standstill."

"The agenda that time was to force state government in coming to an agreeable point and start withdrawing cases.," added another.

"So, do all agree?" asked an anxious Sahoo, whose face wore calmness to look a composed leader.

"Nah…" said one standing up, "until we are convinced that we can force their hands as we could last time."

"We can…" Sahoo said emphatically

He was cut short, "Nah… we need to discuss now and in detail…. do we have the people ready to march… a large number can only be the force… don't forget many of that 2017 march are reeling under the oppressive sedition charges and thousand other cases."

"Sahoo if you don't know…" one more stood up, "Government has constituted four groups headed by IG rank officer to look into and resume work on hundreds of cases."

"All the more reason to deter," said the veteran.

"And the end goal?" one shouted, "Even if we succeed to secure a large gathering and force a day or two?"

He was complemented by another, "At most 2 days and then assembled man, women, children our force will start to disperse while the government machinery will continue unabated to frame us."

"Please do not forget that Lok Sabha elections are around the corner and will be followed by assembly elections… BJP cannot afford to lose Jat votes," Sahoo tried to convince.

"How could you say so Sahoo… do they need to?" objected many in a chorus, "Do you remember the Jind by-elections… Jat candidates lost and they have smelled our weakness… non-Jat votes consolidation won them a seat that had never been won by a non-Jat until now."

"Friends," politician said calmly, "Don't you think for Jats to survive, our total strength must speak and act in one voice and for that to happen an overwhelming networking drive must take place?"

Many agreed but argued, "That's the challenge Sarpanch… what could be the motivation and of what nature to get the community to agree and votes get polled in one direction?"

Sahoo Singh did not immediately answer the dilemma. He let a few moments pass by and then said the carefully chosen words, "Shrinking livelihood, fear of losing land rights, no reservation in government jobs will eventually force each one of us out of our slumber. All we need to drum up our fears, go spread the message, the community is going to be shamed and none could prevent the abject slavery–an eventuality if Jats are not united."

Words did the desired impact - all in attendance began to fret. They were beginning to come together, at least in discourse.

"Why to give up just now?" Sahoo Singh egged on the fellow Jat leaders.

A resolution was later passed unanimously condemning no progress on Jat Arakshan and filling cases basis unsubstantiated facts. Many khap leaders were shown as present and onboard. Multiple khap panchayats would be organized to revive the cause, followed by a grand 'Chakka-Jaam' day on Jat leaders' choice.

23rd May 2019, General Elections 2019 results were announced.

Congress party convenor lost Karnal Lok Sabha election. The entire state unit was at the Party convenor house. Sahoo Singh was distraught. 35 biradari versus 1 had the desired effect. Ruling party secured 10 out of the 10 Lok Sabha seats, three more than the last elections while the vote share had increased from 31% to 34%.

Modi magic sustained the BJP quest one more time. It was a clean sweep in Haryana and many states like Gujrat and Rajasthan.

Congress President lost its bastion Amethi while winning only 1 seat of his mother Sonia Gandhi in the whole of Uttar Pradesh

Congress party high commands, party workers, Working Committee, and its supporters at large were completely overwhelmed by drastic elapse in Political Fortunes of the grand old party. 12 crore votes were cast for Congress while the incumbent the BJP polled 30 crores riding on aggressive Modi centric campaign.

"I'm not much surprised," said the losing man. It was quite startling for Sarpanch to find the convenor of his usual self. A loss being termed as a political heavyweight defeat in the political circles had no apparent effect on the looser.

"It is not the end of the road," said he, "And neither an end to our prospects in upcoming Assembly Election. Party Workers have lost momentum, though," admitted the party convenor disappointedly.

Haryana Assembly Elections were to take place in October 2019, to form the 14th State

Assembly.

"Sahib," lieutenant Sahoo Singh spoke, "let me assure you-" but was cut short.

"Nah–it is the moment and time we all must shun our usual rhetoric. A defeat like this has a demoralizing effect on party workers. We must devise a way out of this 35 versus 1 narrative Sahoo. Otherwise, we are staring at another defect in the Assembly Election."

"Ji."

"Any way out?" Convenor yelled in agony.

"Farmers have overwhelmingly voted for us. Our strategy to consolidate farmers and Jat votes did work but…" Sahoo tried to convince his master.

"These two segments of voters were expected to vote for us, and they did," convenor said and then stopped for a moment, "My candidature was to check these segments voting strength. High command knew the political implications of getting its next president defeated. 35 versus 1 will dent our chances once more if we fail to add votes to loyal segments"

"Farmers and Jats form almost 25% vote, Sahib."

"Which of course of no use unless the rest of the castes get divided" soon to be State President snapped.

"In the current politically charged atmosphere and-"

Sahoo Singh was cut short.

"And with rival's tail up, only a deft tactic could get us any electoral currency," convenor affirmed.

"Whipping up sentiments to cement farmers and Jats votes in this general election sahib," Sahoo said gingerly, "… implied other castes were made sure of our political commitment to return to a Jat patriarchal social structure of the 90s and that means political isolation for all the rest."

"Thence, getting a turnaround in three months is impossible Sahoo," Convenor said in a dead voice.

"Ji," Sahoo felt losing hope all of a sudden, results were far too dramatic than anticipated by most of the exit polls.

"So, time to learn from our rival," said the convenor getting up and patting the back of his trusted lieutenant.

Sarpanch could not make much of that.

"Can we not speak to all farmers?" convenor asked.

"Ji?" Sahoo could not fathom because all the farmers had voted to Congress, who 'all' that president in waiting was hinting at?

"Sabka Saath Sabka Vikas, you know I know and even they know is a political jumla," convenor stopped for a moment pondering and then said,

"Speak to Muslim peasants, they hardly voted."

"Ji–zaroor."

'But Muslim votes will only bridge the vote share marginally–you can think of the others, I learnt you have had friends," convenor said to Saho with a sparkle in his eyes, smirking, "now going gung-ho in the opposite camp?'

Sahoo smiled back.

"Well,… that's the spirit Sahoo." Master winked.

"One of them has had a political aspiration for long," Sahoo Singh smile widened, pausing momentarily he said, "Shukriyaa Sahib."

Sarpanch quickly took leave, flanked by two aides. Several ideas crossed his mind in a matter of seconds. "Where would Tyagi be at this moment? Let's congratulate him in person," handing the phone over to his aide he said, "I am sure he can spare a few minutes for his old friend on a busy festivity day."

An hour later:

"Welcome Sahoo."

"Badhai ho Tyagi. You are victorious. We have been defeated."

"Nah… cannot use such words as I am not associated with any political ideology. I'm an ordinary man. You can say BJP has won… Inderjeet just happens to by my friend and a BJP MLA."

"Your modesty inspires many. You are a leader, and no one can deny that," Sahoo said taking a seat.

Tyagi chose to step aside, "How can I help you my friend?" said he offered the visitor a glass of milk.

"Shukriya," said Sahoo. Pondering over the right words he let a few moments pass by before breaking into a whisper, "Chhattar is in jail".

For a few moments, friends' eyes were locked with each other's.

"I own a piece of land which can be taken over at any time," Sahoo said further.

Tyagi's face wore ignorance while no comments were uttered.

"My party has just lost the Parliamentary Election." Sahoo added leaning back on the chair.

"And massively so. My wishes are with you and your family as they have always been," Tyagi said in a dead voice.

"Yes, I know and that's why I'm here," remarked Sahoo wearing a half-grin.

"If you are here asking me to withdraw the case then you know, I did not file the case." Tyagi looked away.

"Nah Tyagi," Sahoo lunged his upper body forward, and said in a low voice, "I'm here to ask you to contest the Assembly election."

"Contest?!…" Chief of Bishnoi and Tyagi communities was flabbergasted.

"Assembly Election?!!" grappling with words and hundreds of thoughts he could utter hardly, "A gamble at best to get someone in the fray who can only vouch for his biradari votes."

"Tyagi, the party wants you to fight election from Panipat rural," Sahoo said looking intently towards Tyagi.

"Um… on a Congress ticket…" Tyagi adjusted his posture, "You must be crazy… to lose in the end?!"

"Nope, as an independent." Sahoo replied in a dash.

"Ha-ha-ha," Tyagi broke into long laughter. His senses were little sure now though but of the opposite, "to go bankrupt for nothing in return and to lose izzat (the stature)?"

"My party will fund the campaign and yes you are likely to lose," Sarpanch Sahoo Singh said firmly, eyes fixed.

"Sahoo Singh," Tyagi thundered and then the very next moment dropping his voice to a mumble, "I think few more sips and you will be on your way."

"What you in turn secure, will be," Sahoo said cautiously relishing another set of sips of delicious hot milk.

An angry Tyagi could only murmur, "Go on I'm listening… you are getting older and an insane too."

"What you will secure…" Sahoo said in a low voice but firm voice, "… will be the Next Sarpanchi Chunaav!"

The leaders of Bishnoi and Tyagi communities were startled to the core. He had not expected and imagined in his wildest thoughts that will be in offing. Sahoo Singh had won two consecutive Panchayat elections. Although BJP had made inroads in the last election, Kissan Ekta Manch's success had provided this veteran with an overwhelming edge over his rivals. With just a few months to go before the next and possibly to be scheduled right after the assembly election, Congress rivals may not have funds and slogan to take on this heavyweight. His win was a foregone conclusion. Even in his worst case, BJP and others will find it toughest to win over the rural hinterland hearts and minds.

Tyagi quickly calculated all the possibilities and asked gingerly, "What if you lose the Assembly Election?"

Sahoo Singh's reply was instant, "I will not stand for Sarpanchi.'

Still unsure, Tyagi asked another question, "Congress has just lost the Lok Sabha election. It may lose the Assembly seat. Yet, it will not field one who is going to win next Sarpanchi hands down… right?"

"Right Tyagi." Sahoo affirmed.

But the chief of Bishnoi and Tyagi community was not convinced, said smirkingly, "Just because one fine day in May 2019 Sahoo Singh said so… right?"

"Right, because Congress has nothing to gain from Panchayat elections and even BJP will not be unleashing all its horses."

"Right?" Tyagi mimicked Sahoo Singh's tongue and manner.

Sahoo Singh put the glass down, wiping the greyed moustache as he said, "Sarpanchi will not get us what party needs. You will not get this chance for the next five years because your vote bank will not be needed by any party until the 2024 elections. Bishnoi and Tyagi communities to vote for Congress is what we need right now," and then he stopped for a moment before he gushed out looking straight into Tyagi's eyes, "and you will continue to crave Sarpanchi until you breathe your last."

"Sahoo!!" chief thundered.

Sahoo Singh carried on with his caustic comments, "Your following is well known, but would it ever translate into votes? Votes that can secure any win for you? Nah… at least I do not expect that to happen unless…"

"Unless…" Tyagi was getting tempted now. Sahoo Singh smelled a kill for an easy guess as that was becoming a question.

The veteran threw in to seize the moment and secure the prize he was there for, "Unless you grab this once in a lifetime chance," dropping his voice the very next moment to a whisper, "It is NOW or NEVER."

Tyagi asked one in attendance to arrange for hukkah. The offer had made him ponder over many-a-things.

A few minutes later, "Sahoo… case…," a pensive Chief began slowly, "will not be withdrawn–that's one."

"Yes, I heard what you said a few minutes ago and I know it is not in your hands." Sahoo nodded collapsing back in the chair.

"51 Acres will be ours," Tyagi said.

"Hmmm… let me hear first what all you have in your mind." Sahoo said leaning back

"Inderjeet must get to know all of it."

Sahoo deflected that demand away, "Hardly matters if I agree to forfeit acres."

Tyagi did not like that and objected, "I will have a lot at stake, you may decide to walk away and will lose nothing."

"You support us in Assembly Elections. My vote bank will vote you in the Sarpanchi chunaav." Sahoo said in a calm voice.

Tyagi retorted, "Nah–your needs are urgent, not mine. Your party is in dire straits, not my friends. So, you are not on an equal pedestal."

"So?" Sahoo Singh, the astute politician, prodded.

"What if… you decide…" the chief was thinking hard before uttering every word, "… not to honour your words, once the Assembly election is over?"

Sahoo Singh spotted the genesis of the question, "You just want an answer to convey ditto to your friends... right?"

"I know you Sahoo," Tyagi said sincerely, "you will keep your promise but I'm wary of your leadership. Your convenor if decide to turn his back on you, will you still have the strength to keep your promise and support my candidature?"

"Sarpnachi chunaav is to be held just after Assembly elections," Sahoo Singh brought his body forward and held Tyagi's hand, "These two parties have just completed a marathon. Another litmus test will only be sucking their resources. Don't worry, no one will have energy left to think about one sarpanchi chunaav."

"Can I trust you?" Tyagi asked looking intently in his eyes.

"I'm here because I can trust someone." Sahoo Singh affirmed without shifting his eyes

Tyagi did not say anything. His head was down, eyes now staring at the floor, mind in oblivion.

"Let's get land out of our way… " said Sahoo drawing his chair forward, "and… now."

"Chhattar will not like it." Tyagi reminded Sahoo important that land was for Chhattar.

Sahoo nipped that argument straight away, "My son will like compensation and a handsome one."

"That Inderjeet can only guarantee," Tyagi said in a cautioning tone.

Sahoo snapped, "You don't understand… or do you? BJP has won 2019. Railways report to the central government. Notified land, of all the farmers, will be acquired now. The state government is not the decision-maker."

"Social Impact Analysis is only halfway through Sahoo if you have forgotten," Tyagi retorted.

"I remember and I will get it to 70% mark," Sahoo said firmly.

"How? Something hitherto very hard to accomplish, how would you?" Tyagi questioned the reason for him being so confident.

"Compensation… money is what every farmer is looking for. They will give consent." Sahoo answered calmly.

"So… will you not protest now?" Tyagi asked the subject had turned him very curious.

"Good that you are not in politics. Only until the assembly elections are held." Sahoo said.

"Which are not far off anyway," Tyagi said, and then thinking hard for a moment or two he asked, "What is the definition of this 'handsome compensation?"

"The regular compensation and a villa in your Imperial City and a constructed one." Sahoo said emphatically.

"Imperial city belongs to three, Inderjeet will have to agree." Tyagi shrugged his shoulders.

"He will, I'm sure." Saho said with a wide smile.

"I find this all ridiculous Sahoo," by now a very confused Tyagi exploded, "Inderjeet the sitting MLA you aspire to defeat. You will leverage his partner's vote bank to vote against him and yet you are sure of him agreeing to all of this?!"

"Think through the need and greed, you will have answers." Sahoo replied. He was smiling. An ooze of confidence had begun to appear on his face thinking about the possibilities.

"No, I get none," Tyagi was getting irritated now.

"Okay, I tell you. Listen carefully once and for all." Sahoo requested Tyagi to sit calmly and hear his words attentively.

"Go on," said the Chief, running his fingers through his hair in despair, emotionally he was on a tenterhook.

"Fifty-one acres are not part of the land Railways wants to acquire."

"True. And so is the case with Muslims' land." Tyagi seconded his opinion.

Sahoo carried on, "Almost all farmers want money, and the party needs farmers."

"I know… so?"

"So, sooner I get them the money, easier to switch over to the next agenda. Politics is a career every politician needs to sustain… do you get it?"

Chief could not utter anything. His face had rather begun to gape now.

Sahoo drew his chair closer to Tyagi and said in a low voice, "Your MLA Inderjeet could not get 70% consent to impress his party."

"Thanks to Jatwaad." Tyagi said dejectedly.

and added in a whisper, "Neither he has those fifty-one acres."

"Perhaps I'm understanding your game now, Sahoo." Tyagi said leaning back on his chair.

"This is how I arrived at the offer, an offer you may not get ever again," Sahoo added in a firm voice.

"What about you, son? He is brutally caught in that sedition case."

"He will come out, you needn't worry." Sahoo Singh did not want to elaborate on the way out.

"Uh…" Tyagi taunted, "As if you are the judge."

But Sahoo could afford to drop a hint, smiling he said "All about witnesses Tyagi."

CHAPTER 17

A few weeks later.

July 2019, five months since the time agitation on the Aarakshan agenda was 're'-launched to drive home votes, Jat Aarkhshan Andolan morcha was meeting to renew its pledge to an 'Unabated-Ferocious' agitation, now on.

"Backward class commission report did not find Jat caste economically, socially, and not even in Education backward."

A speaker among many listed for the day mentioned quoting commission appointed by the UPA government.

One rising from the first row yelled, "It said…" and disappointedly so, "we dominate government jobs also."

"This is the reason why our case has no legal base…" shouted another.

Sahoo Singh found the majority of the leaders present there to be in despair and frustrated. It was a direct impact of massive Modi 2019 win. The astute politician had refused to accept Not-A-Widespread- Participation-by-An-Ordinary-Jat as the reason for a struggling campaign as many would say.

"Modi gave 10% to upper caste. No one, even the Supreme Court could stop it. It is because he is Modi and he accomplishes what he intends to," complained one…

"Khattar (the BJP Chief Minister in Haryana) is against us, will not give us the reservation," someone at the back, shouted.

"It was constitutionally valid ordinance hence has survived till the day," yelled the Sarpanch rising from his seat.

Rebuke failed to restore any order. "How?!" asked many in one raging thundering chorus

It made Sahoo Singh roar with rage, - "Section (15) (6) allows reservation

219

over and above 50% of the limit to the weaker section. Modi issued the reservation under that section."

Not many could understand the legal words and the implications for the community. Faces were left gaping, grappling for words, and a counter-argument.

"Jats must be included in the Backward Classes category which gets 27% reservation!" declared the leader, "That is the only way."

"How is that different Sahoo from our ongoing and earlier demand of getting quota or reservation in education, jobs, and other sectors," asked one elderly sitting in the last.

"16 percent reservation from the total 27 percent is being given to BC-A categories, which are more backward, and 11 percent to BC-B, which includes Sainis, Yadavs, Gujjars, Kurmis, and Ahirs. All these are farming communities like the Jats. We, the Jats can be included in BC-B by bringing the total quota to 14 percent instead of 11 percent as the central government still has 3 percent at its disposal."

The sincere meaningful argument from the leader who had stature impressed many, a murmur followed.

But it was the leader himself most disappointed at the turn out in the last months. The average public stayed away from the stir, flooring the hype Andolan had secured at its fresh launch in January.

A few more questions from the gathering followed as a fiery exchange of ideas and counter-ideas started to play counter-productive to the usually present jat comradery. Sahoo Singh was pensive and grew a little lost by that time.

It was a trump card he played to his boss and was the most convinced soul to defy Modi wave, and yet they were defeated in the General Election. He had begun to have second thoughts.

"It is too late," he confided in his inner being, "abandoning the agitation at this juncture will be suicidal to his political credibility." Aspirant Member of Legislative Assembly was looking down the barrel–blank and out!

His mobile rang. Aide informed him of sitting BJP MLA Inderjeet being on the other side. He thought for a second before putting it next to his ear and said calmly, "I am in a meeting. Will speak to you Inderjeet later and –"

"Hear me out you old man…" Sahoo was cut short by a thundering shout from the other end, "let the last day of withdrawing nomination arrive, I will withdraw my nomination. Then, it will be Congress vs the rest and my builder partner will win hands down from Panipat Rural."

And the telephone cradle was smashed.

Sahoo Singh immediately stood up and walked out into the courtyard dialling his party convenor. The next moment, soon to be Party President was assured of his grip on the matters and would not let the newfound support (of Tyagi to garner Bishnoi and Tyagi votes) slip. Boss was politely pointed out the urgent need to release some funds to Tyagi, the independent candidate, to prove the Congress' commitment.

The message received from the opponent was not disclosed. 'Not yet Sahoo…' he murmured to himself walking back to attend to the commotion inside pondering fast over the elaborate arrangement necessary for Tyagi's planned massive campaign.

He stopped at the doorstep, turned around, and walked back to the courtyard, reminding himself of a pending talk.

Sahoo tried to soothe his nerves down as he dialled Tyagi's number. Moments later, "I am arranging funds for the same. Shortly you will receive the first chunk."

"I need to get my head around all of this Sahoo. There has been a delay in releasing the funds. I am not sure how convinced is your boss with your nascent idea. I do not want to be stranded, defeated." Tyagi said in frustration.

"That you can leave to me you do need to bother on that and rather focus on your campaign," Sahoo said calmly.

"You know you need your convenor to believe in your calculations too?"

"President… He is State President and he is convinced… do not worry." Sahoo replied.

Tyagi did not say anything. His mind diverted towards the urgency. Funds were needed and needed immediately. Not that the mighty landlord had no money to afford the massive campaign and canvassing. On the contrary, the fund's release he had been anticipating would just prove the Congress leadership commitment to his candidature Sahoo Singh has been so vocal and sure about.

The silence on Tyagi's end had by then prevailed for far too long. Sahoo Singh perhaps read his mind. The seasoned politician tried to break this monotony. He broke into a speech without a context,

"It will not just be Tyagi and Bishnoi communities you are to approach chief. Nope–that is not our campaign aimed at. 35 biradari versus 1 is BJP's campaign motto. Tyagi your campaign will be - neither for BJP nor for Congress. You just need to approach all. While Tyagi and Bishnoi will vote for you, the implicit effect will be some of those 35 biradari casting their votes to you too."

Words confused more an already scrambling Tyagi with all kinds of doubts and scary thoughts.

"But how much will that be?" asked a baffled Tyagi.

"Incumbency does result in some voters getting disillusioned, many turn sceptical at the end of the tenure end, many promises remain unfulfilled - all these will slide towards you," Sarpanch eyes were fixed and voice was firm.

"But these will hurt you equally Sahoo!"

"Nah–any reduction in BJP vote share will benefit me since my vote bank–Jats and Farmers - will not break away."

"Hmmm."

The penultimate day of nomination arrives. It was 5 p.m. when Sahoo Singh called on his Party Convenor at the latter's home.

Panipat has 4 assembly constituencies, in 3 Congress came second in the previous 2014 Assembly Election.

In Congress versus BJ fight in that election, the castes% votes secured were as follows:

Panipat Rural (Jat BJP-40.08% |Non-Jat–Congress - 9.8% 4thposition)

Israna (BJP-32.58% | Congress-31.1%)

Samalkha (Jat- Independent–34.6 | Jat–Congress–20.6%)

Panipat City. (Non-Jat BJP-66.49% | Non-Jat Congress-27.98%)

"One of them Israna is reserved for Schedule Caste candidate," Sahoo Singh was apprising convenor the boss of his ensuing strategy.

"Okay, one in every Parliament Constituency is reserved," said the Convenor.

"So Israna is out of the equation…"

"That goes without saying… move on Sahoo… we have 3 places," glued to his mobile convenor said, checking quickly the time, "… to choose 1 from and file you and your old pal from."

"Panipat city witnessed a non-Jat candidate polling 40% votes in 2014 Sahib."

"Understand, no point… but that's not even a factor here… the city will have the middle class… won't vote you in… target farmers and non-city dwellers Sahoo." Convenor nipped the idea.

"So, let me file from Panipat Rural sahib and Tyagi will too file his nomination but not from Rural."

Convenor head was up in a flash, eyebrows tilted, startled he shouted, "You must be kidding, where are we heading Sahoo?!! Have you considered the fallout?"

"Inderjeet has got a good tactic in place and surely we will be hit," Sahoo Singh stated the reason, "He is going withdraw his nomination if Tyagi contests from rural. Tyagi will have a high chance of winning if all those votes meant for BJP come to his ballot."

"How would we know…" convenor countered the argument. Suspecting something happening quietly without his knowledge man-in-charge asked, "When did you get to speak to him?"

"MLA only called on me, a few days back," Sahoo replied.

"Hmmm…" thinking hard for a few seconds, boss a few moments later said, "Okay, go on… which constituency?"

"Either Panipat city or Samalkha."

"Which one Sahoo?" both arms spread out wide, short of time boss demanded an urgent call.

"The one which has all the Muslim votes," Sahoo said in a low voice.

Convenor could not get much of the tactic Sahoo was adopting, "Now what these Muslim votes have to do in your calculation? Panipat district has hardly 2% Muslim population."

"There are 2 reasons Sahib," Sahoo Singh began stating the rationale gingerly, "Why not leverage this 2% who are sure shot will not vote for a saffron party."

"Okay, and second?"

"They are farmers and peasants–may come handy after the elections," Sahoo said calmly.

Sarpanch had cunningly and smartly too, pitched in his agenda. He had formulated the plan weeks back.

"After the election scenario, I am not interested in Sahoo," getting up and impatient, "I immediately need to leave for Delhi, you inform me once your Tyagi kaafila reaches Election office," cutting short and to conclude fast, the boss asked - "So you will contest from rural?"

Sahoo Singh got up in dash and said, "Ji Panipat rural."

"I am not sure if you even remember that Congress candidate polled only 9% votes in 2014 chunaav and he stood 4th," Convenor said little dejectedly getting onto the waiting Scorpio.

"Sahib…," in a low voice, "candidate wasn't a Jat," Sarpanch snapped.

Convenor could only smile. He was wary for Lok Sabha defeat had shred established political demographics, caste, religious and regional equations.

Next day: A startled Tyagi camp headed towards the District Collector office. The nomination was filed from Samalkha.

It was 5 in the morning and Chhattar was already up. Panipat rural was voting that day to elect lawmakers for the 14th State Assembly. Section 144 was in force and was effective in most parts of Haryana.

Dharna joined him soon as both set out to lead one group of 15-20 Jat andolankari. The task was to put up stiff resistance allowing no vehicle to pass on the outskirts of Panipat rural.

Sahoo had secured a day's parole for Chhattar on the ground of bad health and the younger son is bedridden. The aspiring lawmaker was old and would need someone from the family to complete the modalities needed through the election day.

"BJP voters, traders, middle class, non-Jats have livelihoods outside the region. If we deter them on the name of Jat Andolan, perhaps the numbers cut will propel Tau chances by some margin," Dharma said.

"Let's hope for the best bhai." Chhattar remarked.

The spot they reached was a 20-fee-wide unobtrusive road connecting a cluster of villages to the national highway. With many arriving from far-flung places of livelihood in the last minutes to vote, cutting the road off will fetch the necessary upper hand.

Small pockets like the one under seize by Chhattar and his men, were seemingly free from any law and order agencies coverage and thus witnessing the most intensified agitation and incidents of arson.

BJP had cadres to ferry from every nook and corner besides banking on Punjabi community social engineering skills in getting all the non-Jat votes cast and be counted for.

Jats had in this triangular fight had fallen back to the last resort and the method they were most convinced with if not the most trusted one–raw strength deployment on the ground to intimidate and see through the utter consolidation.

25% of votes had been cast since morning; it was about to be noon. Faujji was keeping a close watch voting percentage on his cell phone juggling between the live news reporting sites to know the latest updates. "More the vote cast worse for us," he mumbled to Dharma.

"Perhaps not more than 50%," Dharma did not agree, "it's already noon, 4 hours are past, just double the current number and still we shall have fewer votes cast than the average in the last 10 years."

"Let's see, fingers crossed bhai, you never know, last hour is always the game-changer."

"We can only hold onto this stretch Chhattar and just hope for the best elsewhere."

Some news channels' broadcasting vans had begun to arrive, suddenly.

"This road connects the rural Panipat with national highway 1..." uttered one harried news reporter stepping out of the van, camera crew in tow. "Here we see Jat- Andolankaari..." said one other pointing towards the tractor-trolley parked in the middle of the road and across, with few vehicles wanting to get through, "and you can see how people are desperate to vote and yet finding it difficult to get to the other side and reach home..."

"Let's talk to some of these people," One from the prominent national broadcaster was seen approaching the point of vehicles blockade. All villagers in presence were curious to note its presence. "Usually, they stick to the mainland, do not venture into the inner land," said Dharna. "That's right," said Faujji who was standing on the trolley.

"Where you need to go?" the young reporter asked one car driver.

"Ji, Samalkha."

"What is the reason you travelled out of your place when you knew today is the day of voting?" asked the lady.

"I work in Delhi, couldn't get leave hence..."

"Okay..." she turned around. A small crowd had gathered around her peeping into the camera lens. Faujji noticed she was uncomfortable to find a mob though small being more interested in her than the camera, he off-boarded himself, "Hey," calling the young reporter.

She turned around, "So, here we have the local leader who is not letting people vote," commented she, nudging the crew to start rolling the camera pointed towards his direction.

"You can wear this," said Chhattar offering her his jacket.

"What?'!" said she startled, straightaway waved at the cameraman, who immediately stopped recording. "I've... um.." she was not too sure, "no need... there is no cold," said she adjusting her top at the waistline to block off the sight of any flesh peeping eyes and glares which were following her the very moment she stepped out of van constantly adjusting her body-fitting wardrobe.

"Wrap around the waist," advised Dharma.

"Ma'am," said the camera crew, "Producer wants to head towards the highway..."

"What happened?" She asked tying the jacket sleeves around her belly with jacket now hanging securing her waistline. She felt relieved. No need to adjust the top any longer every other second. Onlookers were still interested though, eyeballs prying on other parts.

"Highway has been jammed... incredible scenes to capture..." replied an excited cameraman.

TV reporters had begun to pack and bundle themselves inside their vans with all hell seemed to have broken loose somewhere in the vicinity. Jat-Andolankari, after stopping the traffic to curb the movement and secure the margin necessary to win without letting non-Jat votes to consolidate, had allegedly put many vehicles on fire on the Delhi – Ambala – Chandigarh highway.

The young reporter opted to stay back, said to herself, 'Could be some moment worth capturing and prove more important to the producer than the routine news of vehicles put on fire by miscreants.'

Within seconds a din had given way to silence, all the vans had disappeared. The scene was back to where it was a few minutes back. One peeper held the jacket and lifted it, others in the group laughed, with reporter turning around and holding the jacket firm, "Leave it... idiots," she shouted.

They all looked in their teenage. "Perhaps college students," Chhattar said to Dharma.

The teenager was egged on by the group, Emboldened, he jerked, and the jacket came off, another round of laughter followed. Many in the crowd found this objectionable yet no one intervened fearing the worse.

Faujji patted at Dharma, who strode in fast and slapped one while shoving the other one down on the road, snatching the cloth in the meantime. The group charged at Dharma who immediately broke into a sprint. "Bhatta thaa le (pick some boulder)," screamed faujji. The phrase made friend recall the trick of years gone spent in fighting the rival groups in Sonepat college days. Dharma quickly grabbed two big ones without breaking the pace and soon positioned himself on a vantage point across the other end of the road. College students split themselves into two groups: 3 were in pursuit of Dharma, while rest were ready to take on his friend – Chhattar - the six-footer. All 6 could have gotten hold of the main threat however the boulders had a promise of unleashing jeopardy thus three had to get as close as they could to a waiting Dharma. Dharma sent one-off, missing the intended recipient, hitting the third, and halting the pursuit temporarily. The second boulder changed hand and now was ready for launch at an ominous trajectory at any moment. At the far end near the tractor-trolley, the leader of the first group had the bamboo nicely cut to come handy in the expected situation like the one he expected to relish. "Saale Faujji..." cursed he as he attempted a big swipe from the right, onto his left, hitting brutally just above his elbow. Two in tow stopped in their charge concluding the brutal strike was sufficient, yielded pivotal few seconds to a trained army man. Faujji assessed his bearings, grabbed the cane with his right, and seized it next moment with an emphatic jerk followed that with a heavy blow on the teenager's neck to floor him motionless. 'Stay away from head,' he reminded himself, enough number of murder cases. "Aa jaa bhai (come on lad)," he called on the one in the two. The one in front strengthening his grip on cane watchfully stepped forward. While second in the tow retreated, picked boulder, and ran back to the two standing at a distance from Dharma. Faujji termed that a good move unleashed a flurry of strikes. He had no time, Dharma could be in trouble any passing moment. With second tumbling, Faujii sprinted in the direction of the other group, Dharma finding faujji breaking into a charge, sent off a couple of boulders, first missing completely second hitting but without much impact. Charging in Faujji engaged the first two, cane coming in much handy. The rest two moved closer to Faujji while keeping an eye out towards Dharna and his boulders. Dharma strode in boulders in hands, enacting the launch in every second stride threatening the damage and keeping the two off an active engagement with Faujji, who by now, had surmounted the challenge. Teenagers, the last two, still on feet chose to flee than to get vanquished.

Lady reporter had been offered a jacket in the meantime.

"Ma'am?" it was the cameraman.

"Yes," she had been shaken to the core. Yet felt safe, with some females now solacing her.

"Producer Ma'am wants this be broadcast as a sexual assault..." the cameraman, still excited, said, "she wants you to enact a weep... with clothes little ruffled... I will set the camera rolling and um.... and probably the right sleeve... uh... be torn apart to make it appear... um... the way it should be?"

"Shut up?!!" lady shrieked.

"Why not she yelled that emphatically little while ago Dharma, chad (lads) would have vanished without putting up a fight you know."

Both chuckled on, one wondering the result of this hard-fought battle, the other called on a few to ferry the injured scoundrels to hospital.

Chhattar cell phone rang, Bapu was on the other end.

"It's already 1 and I find you still there..." father sounded little panicking.

"Had to handle a difficult situation here Bapu," Chhattar replied looking towards Dharma who was taking stock of the situation and issuing renewed instructions to their men hold on until the day ends.

"Okay... it impacted our prospects then you can tell and if not... then I do not have time really..." stopping momentarily, "Make sure, you carry some..." father could not utter the word, stopped.

"Carry what?" asked Chhattar as he waved at Dharma, asking him to hurry up.

"Carry... um... bottles."

Son stopped, his hand holding the phone was down that very moment thumping the thigh. He pulled it back and shouted, "I'm not going to bribe anyone Baapu."

"You are not. They are expecting it and we are just following the tradition," father said firmly.

"And if I do not?"

"This is not the time-" Sahoo said and stopped abruptly.

His attention was distracted by an incoming call. Sahoo spotted it was his boss calling, "hold on Chhattar. Singh Sahib is calling… you just hold on," as he switched over to the other line.

"You may have jeopardised your chances Sahoo," boss already, from the beginning, was not sure of Sahoo winning in a direct 35 vs 1 fight.

"You don't seem to understand…" he stopped abruptly realizing the rude tongue, he rephrases in a flash, "Sahib…" dropping his voice to sound respectful, "Sahib we now have two seats in contest Panipat Rural and Samalkha, we may get to win. Still, a better prospect than to bank on just one and result in none. Who knows if we get to win both? Please we must not forget - Independent contestant from Samalkha does not have as many non-Jat votes as we have in the other three assembly constituencies. He is likely to win if my calculations are correct."

"If we win two Sahoo, any by-election in any of these 4, will get us 1 more… hmmm… good–I liked it!"

"Shukriyaa." Sahoo Singh felt relieved.

"By the way… your son is leaving no stone unturned to see you defeated," the new state party president said sarcastically.

"What happened Janaab… he is out only for a day… you may not know-"

But he was cut short, "Your He-Man has just bashed up some youngsters belonging to BJP MLA village. Villagers are angry, you may like to speak to them."

"What?" said a stunned aspiring lawmaker as he switched to the other line and yelled in rage, "If you could resist your urges for a day… Chhattar… no point beating men when you know every vote has become crucial."

"If I had not," Chhattar retorted, "who knows they would have stopped only once they have raped her."

Stunned father felt embarrassed to question his son, grappled to find the right words. Alleged Murthal rape case, during the 2016 Jat Aarkshan Andolan, had made the headlines in national dailies. Nervous, exhausted, a weary veteran on the last day of the battle of his life wanted nothing to derail his chances, said gingerly, "As you prefer beta… but just make sure they all get to vote."

Moments later, Chhattar settled himself by Dharma's side as he began to drive. Ismail Khurd was a few kilometres. "Will get there soon… should not take more than half an hour," assured Dharma spotting his friend lost in thoughts and losing momentum

"Would you have her number?" asked Chhattar, still pensive.

"Who… her?"

"The lady you just managed to rescue from the hooligans," He replied in a dead voice.

Dharma stopped the jeep, picked his phone up, and started checking the messages, "She promised she would text me… I guess she fears some of these bastards would follow her."

"Hmmm," murmuring, Chhattar looked up the latest messages on Dharma's mobile. Found one without a contact name, dialled.

"What are you up to?" asked Dharma, bringing the jeep back in motion

The phone rang and was answered on the second ring. A husky voice attended and said hurriedly, "All fine so far. Thanks to you Dharma… massive thanks and to your friend too to cover for us."

"We are also happy to find a woman safe," Chhattar started gingerly.

"Who? Is it not Dharma?"

"His friend…" Chhattar clarified.

"Okay," she found his ginger voice little out of place, "What is it?" she asked little wary at the prolonged silence from the other end.

"Well… have you and your crew driven too far… or still nearby?" Chhattar asked anxiously.

"Not sure, Chhatrapal… let me," he heard some voice in the background. She was speaking to her crew member, he guessed. After a few seconds, a voice emerged, "Have just reached the highway and moving towards Sonepat and Delhi," she said.

"Would you need a Secular Shot for your secular news channel," his voice had sarcasm. Ex-army man wanted a particular effect and the desired outcome.

"And what would that be…" voice at the other end sounded little cautious.

"Village Ismail Khurd you will have to come to… a few kilometres from where you are…"

"Okay, but what would I get to see… I mean to record… um… I mean just now we had a scary time so to come back…" The lady reported wanted to be sure of the gains.

Chhattrapal thought for a moment to gather the right words and then said in a steady and firm voice, "Some 100 Muslims are not getting out of their hamlet to cast their votes fearing what we do not know. We will escort them to the polling booth. Perhaps you will get a good shot you have been trying all day long, who knows maybe the best of the lot of the whole assembly election."

"Let me call you back," but before disconnecting, "you said... Ismailpur... right?"

"Nah–Ismail Khurd."

"Okay," She disconnected the call.

Dharma stopped the pickup, "What are you up to?"

Before Chhattar could reply, his phone rang, it was Baapu.

"Ji" said Chhattar answering the call.

Baapu broke the news of the hour, "Inderjeet and team are arranging a roadblock a kilometre outside the Ismail Khurd. They will not let you pass."

"And why?"

"Why?!...you have just thrashed some brutally... one is seriously injured and is hospitalized... the whole village is gunning for you and Inderjeet will make the most of it. And..." elderly stopped short of going berserk on a brazen bizarre attitude, held his tongue, "And... don't be naïve..." breathing heavily sounding as exasperated to Chhattar as if someone was standing right behind him and breathing on his neck, "you may get away fighting Chhattar..." teeth clenching tongue was biting every word being uttered, "but others are bound to lose... especially the women and children... they will not even get a chance to run," and thundered– "Do you get it?!"

Chhattar cut the phone.

"So, what's the next bad news?" Dharma was about to burst into a chuckle.

"Take a u-turn dost... we will take the longer route to Ismail Khurd."

"Already 2 pm raja Ji... voting ends at 5 pm and you know who is going to greet us and waste our time," Dharma was still grinning unaware of the dramatic evolving and a dangerous situation

"We will have to call SSP and ask for some sort of deployment of paramilitary near the spot Baapu mentioned Inderjeet is planning a roadblock." Chhattar said in a desperate voice.

"And who would call SSP... you... me... reminding him we are that... you know... of Sahoo Singh...you remember Sir... we who are out on the parole you know and trying this idea of democracy... you know," enacting a physical plea... holding back a chuckle all along, "who will pyaare Raja Ji... issuing orders one after another... uh?"

"Your pyaare Tau Ji," said Chhattar dryly, who had not altered his stern posture even for a second while others were going full throttle laughing-off the idea.

"Hmmm... sane advice... I thought you are preparing to argue and smack the police officer out of the sight first," winking said he as Chhattar dialled Sahoo Singh number. A brief was presented stressing on the need of getting paramilitary deployed to be sure of the security the plan could succeed on.

An hour later, all the participants of the show had reached the spot.

"Democracy on Road has been written by an American Indian casting a journey of the past 25 years of general elections... and here you see that on display."

The young lady was speaking at the top of her voice, with the camera rolling. The camera was trying to lay a visual canvas offering live feedback to the studio and possibly a nation glued in. Canvas had on the live roll a few tractor-trolley hauling some 100 Muslims wearing white topis, women in burqa clung to each other in the packed to hilt rickety relics, being escorted by a pickup filled with beaming Congress workers fluttering party flag while in the background was paramilitary keeping the shouting, booing, protesting BJP protestors waving Kamal bearing flags at bay.

Inderjeet was watching from a distance, terming 100 cannot sway results in Congress candidate favour. "Better to translate anger of the villagers into votes for himself," he murmured. When reminded of how urgent had it become to unleash some physical blows to the 'happy-to go-gung-ho-anytime', politician remarked to soothe and assure his supporters, "A matter of time before the court decides and gung-ho is caught napping in some jail... will play gladiator... don't worry," smirking he signalled the driver to move on.

100 votes were cast in favour of Congress, Sahoo was yet on tenterhook. First timer's nervousness or an eternal ever-present feeling of those goosebumps even a multi-term winner contender feels every time he sets out to campaign and fight to win another term?

CHAPTER 18

∽

"Why did you write even?"

"How else could I?"

"Where are your frustration and aggression, therefore?"

A pause, no reply, Anant looked straight.

"Militant outburst is expected post such a..." lady literary agent was putting her thoughts together.

"A trauma, if you like," Anant commented, sometimes lost, sometimes struggling to put together a sentence.

"Vivid stamps of Right-wingy nowadays all around, times under the rule, yet no aggression so far, wouldn't you like to end up doing some dhamaka... uh?"

Grappling for words he could only utter a whisper, 'Book has been written...'

Smirking, the lady literary agent taunted, "Writing a piece of paper won't take you anywhere, or would it?'

"So?" He certainly did not like the comment.

She smiled and said, "Do something, make them proud, let be the rule of the land by your side, they will oblige, I bet."

Her sarcasm was clear.

"We do not have perhaps..." he was still unsure of words.

Literary agent thundered - "Then what's that you hope to achieve this book with if you are not doing what your book seems to prescribe."

"Perhaps we do not have the spine and..." Anant was struggling to put together a sentence.

233

She snapped, "I'm Hindu I have spine not because I'm a Hindu but because for anything right there can have a spine found by anyone," pausing momentarily, "I bet, you need to look around and be truthful if that helps, it will I bet."

"They must know what they are up against?" he could say something finally.

"And then?" She could not understand much.

"Message can only be spread if it has a purpose and the majority is convinced." He sounded convinced.

"And you thought a book would be the right carrier?" The literary agent asked.

"Yes!"

"And this Tejo Mahalaya," said she as the manuscript was slung on the table, "I find laughable, and millions reading would I am sure."

"That is symbolic, semantic." Anant protested and tried to justify it at the same time.

"Still not sellable," she smirked.

He carried on in the same breath, "Tejo Mahalaya is a symbol no one wants to destroy - that is part of the national narrative, almost all believe in."

"Yet you have chosen it to be otherwise." Lady literary agent said looking away as she stretched her body and leaned back in the chair.

"As I said - symbolic - shows how utterly a lot, and If we find a majority I will not be surprised, are disgusted hence a powerful symbol as Tejo Mehalaya can only elicit an expression I and this lot want to." He said in a flash.

"You advise to destroy it?" Lady asked, looking straight into Anant's eyes, and intently so.

"Nah, neither does the story if you read carefully," Anant, the author, clarified.

"I have." She said, again leaning back on the chair.

"I doubt," Anant snapped, their eyes penetrating each other's, the glare, the stare, and the smirk, he added, "Taj Mahal..." but was cut short.

"There you go!" The literary agent snapped.

"Taj Mahal has been retained by the majority," the author argued, "It wouldn't have survived had this not been the case."

The literary agent lunged her body forward and asked, "Oh, I see, so?"

The author completed his argument, "So, it has an existence which all believe in and it's not going anywhere that's all."

"You are not confusing me now?" asked the lady.

Anant gushed out, "It is a rarity that it's part of the national narrative almost all have no objection on."

"One more - Now what is this national narrative?" The literary agent was certainly getting agitated.

"The national narrative is - We are a secular nation. Speaker and reader both conveniently forget about the demography. The majority must protect the minorities, minorities need state protection, and a cocoon in the guise of laws, welfare policies, relaxed rules which otherwise are very strict for the majority."

"Such as?" She was getting intrigued too now.

"Such as religious practices, minority especially followers of Islam receive as guaranteed," Anant stopped, pondering over…

"Aa-han! go on I'm listening…" A smile crossed literary agent's face, she leaned back in the chair.

"The majority since independence has been harsh on the other side. The Other side has always been tormented, oppressed thus not only the state must protect since we are a secular constitution but also we should have non-state entities to lend a helping hand and ensure minorities are not threatened, oppressed."

"So?" The smile widened on her face. The literary agent smacked her lips, she was readying herself now for a thump to floor the idiotic commentary.

Anant carried on describing the national narrative, "So, bring effective methods, tools, modus operandi to achieve the same."

She lunged her upper body forward and asked, "Which are?"

"Which we have been seeing - Gujrat riots must be condemned forever, that fact must never go out of print."

"Go out of print - nice metaphor."

Anant carried on, "With right-wingy on the seat - the true colours are on display - the narrative will say. The minority will be questioned, about their nationalism lies on which side? Will be labelled 'Pakistanis' for every small big coincidence; will be lynched on the name of a cow; the national narrative will make the state a protectionist - a hand in glove with the perpetrators."

"Which is true, no?" The literary agent asked.

Anant clarified, "This has been the case for ages, irrespective of who rules."

Lady thundered, "People have established gangs, operate under state protection, the perceived other side is being lynched and still, you are not convinced."

Anant said in hurried words, "Padmawat was a grand box office success as many wanted and hence watched it."

She intervened, "Because the majority of this country is Hindu!"

"The majority of those who watched the movie were Hindu - does not certainly imply islamophobia," he retorted. It was the moment he was waiting for the whole time to pitch in the crux of the argument. "Do not forget even for a second that the same majority was spoon-fed a distorted history in schools and colleges. It was a fact that to rule and rule with an iron fist many of the symbolic executions of sultanates and empires were to instil a sense of fear and thus impressing the supremacy amongst the majority Hindus. Yet, in modern times, years have passed since we have stepped in, liberals, leftists, communists do not find it necessary to underline this fact. Why? Just because some Hindu rajas' palaces might get un-earthed? The distorted fact is better suited than 'The Fact'? That the laborious work and grand successful execution will get exposed and the consistency be weakened?"

The literary agent was taken aback. "So, you are justifying the Modi regime?" She asked angrily.

"Neither have I or nor the story does." Anant was breathing heavily now, emotions had overwhelmed him.

"But that's what you just said."

"You heard carefully yet could not ponder over much ... you will have to." He said gently, his straight posture collapsing on the elbows which were now resting on the knees.

"I have you, why don't you then... I may still end up with the same belief pondering over for hours," smirking lady Literary agent said, "days... weeks... you know."

Anant took a long breath, collected his thoughts, and began.

"The narrative and its cult - they fear... make no mistake ... only for the cult believer at large! This truth is not told that it is not a fear to sustain the narrative, hence a mix here, and there must be the order now and then. So fear is if, in the times of right-wingy being in power, this narrative is not spoken widely and vehemently by the end of the tenure - the secular aspect of the majority will pave a way to communal, anti-minority belief and that will be detrimental to the social fabric - which has not been a secular as it is made out to be by the way - and that it eventually will lead to a 'Hindu' Pakistan."

The literary agent was pondering now.

Anant carried on, "This narrative is to protect and sustain the ecosystem - does not have widespread truth - is convincing to many because not everyone has the resources to sit back, think deep and look at the presented details in the right perspective."

"You are getting too complex for your readers to understand your point of view, Mr. Anant." Lady observed and said in a sincere tone.

"National narrative is thus a haze created beautifully, smoke screens of labour party PM, 1945... right metaphor?"

"Your story must teach your readers history, I guess." She commented as she picked up the manuscript and flipped some pages.

"This haze has sustained itself so long and so widely look at the textbooks in the schools, colleges - I mean - for an average countryman this is too hard to see through and not be affected of?"

The lady editor was still busy flipping the pages and reading stanza here and there. She took a few minutes before she came back to the conversation. Lifting her head, she looked straight and asked, "How would you like to summarize Mr. Anant?"

"Hindustan is alive, is solely basis and through its demography. Demography exhibits the spirit Hindustan is every day comes alive with. For some reason, this becomes and is very hard to understand though it is right in front of us my countrymen every day, every hour, in every hamlet, in every community, every dwelling in each corner, every strife - these nerve centres this land breaths. Regional identity howsoever small matters, social strife or harmony finds root in this identity alone and in turn, strengthens it more. Majority rules and thankfully at the regions and overwhelmingly so, thus letting Hindustan survive to defy the national majority - this is just as good as statistics can get - So, even when at the time right-wing is winning the race, nation appears to be in nationalism grip, regional power centres we must remind ourselves dictate the nerve! Kashmiri Muslims will and continue so to crush pundits - the minority, Punjab can only have a Sikh CM, Haryana's mere 25% population of Jats will keep dominating rest put together because they have a majority in state institutions and departments, Ahmedabad will keep the minority ghettos alive, Kerala will receive the most ME donations and make the best of it for the community and a number of them alike - could be the easy examples - you and I must realize - high time! Let the truth prevail! - No more leftist haze we must see through the propaganda - a narrative that country majority overwhelms and will eventually defeat the idea of India - this narrative fails, concedes hands down at these nerve centres.

And let me cite some incidents, madam:

15th August 2017 two attempted to unfurl the tricolour at Laal Chowk, Srinagar. Locals, the 'Kashmiris' thrashed 'Indians'. Police reported in time, 'kaafirs - the Indians' were saved.

September 2018, the Mizoram students group claimed to have pushed back dozens of immigrants trying to enter Mizoram 'illegally' from Assam. Alleged Bangladeshis had failed to show NRC, and identity documents.

Mizo Zirlai Pawl (MZP) just followed the steps of the Khasi Students Union (KSU) in Meghalaya, which routinely patrols the state border.

Every story needs an episode. Story of Hindustan has had innumerable... these times are merely another set, for a story to survive and continue to find the next set - next times."

Anant breathed heavily as he concluded, wiping sweat from his forehead.

The liberal across the table admitted reluctantly, "I believe instead of a few lines we could have a couple of chapters on Pandyan, Cholas, and Cheras."

"Precisely," Anant excited to hear the words, complemented in a flash, "if sultanate and Mughals can be taught in every other standard with a historical presence of 600 years put together."

"1200 years of Pandyan alone..." The literary agent added, then pulling herself out, in haste - "What else?"

"Answer me one question," Anant asked settling his breath and tongue, "irrespective of whether you accept the story and we go to print."

"Sure."

He said gingerly, "Taj Mahal is a national symbol. Story does not endorse destroying it, just carving out as easily as we could a dwar for whosoever is interested to visit whatever is underneath, but..."

"But?!"

He carried on, "A mob can have fanatics and can lead to an eventually no one wants."

"Finally, you understand," liberal pride had sealed her face, expressions shackled inside.

"Yet this cannot justify, to have an umbrella narrative in place which has been distorting all, our history and heritage must be taught as is - the haze is unnecessary!" Anant said in hurried words.

The literary agent was startled, "I thought you were to ask a question?!!"

Anant concluded, "This is the question we all must ask - majority and minority alike - this Hindustan - India to many!"

"I have been asked to...," Head of the Department's voice got sluggish as it approached the definitive words.

Patanjali Kapoor spotted, "I know… um… you need not say I've already been made aware."

"I… um… at a personal level… you know… um… feel sorry… but"

"I understand," she said with a look of stoic resignation writ across her face.

Head brought out the letter and placed it before her on the desk.

"Perhaps you should have avoided a fight head-on with them - the powerful."

She laughed, "Powerful? Nah, no more! Allegiance alters, affiliates to the one sustaining itself in power… BJP is back and powerful will have the days gone past them in a flash," her eyes were fixed in oblivion.

He could spot her, at ease and in peace.

Head tried to change the subject to something more prudent and practical one, "Where are you headed now? How would you survive?"

"You must not forget," she said calmly, "I am an Indian housewife too," and smiled.

"Oh yes," he noticed it was naïve, adjusted his specs, "Yes… yes, um… yes, you are right."

"About getting head on…," she said getting up, "No regret, they may have the power to dismiss me and others of the opposite ideology but for how long?"

"University has dismissed him as well."

"Who?!"

"Pandey!"

"Really but why?!" She was startled.

"Probably could be the reason you believe takes the course… Allegiance." Head of the department replied.

"Or the intermediate state before one fully submits itself?" She observed.

Head carried on, "His session, rather a concealed one to evade scrutiny on Kashmir and later on the Naxals did him… university authorities want to pursue a middle path."

"Imperative before–"

She was cut short, "Before they submit wholly to the ideology back in centre. I mean Modi, Shah, and BJP?" Head said.

"No Sir. Being in the centre is all we should be, I want. Respect all ideologies… do not pursue agendas… and um… respect whatever has been the legacy… our culture… okay," she stopped, "let me not say culture, Sanskriti, Vedant, and so on. Let's just say…"

She stopped again, mustering her thoughts as her face reddened in fury.

She resumed, "Give space to all that this land has seen… space in our textbooks… space in our discourse… read them… let them be written… our children will decide themselves… all that I want."

"But you seem to be tilted towards right-wing ideology. So isn't that bizarre and out of place you have just now vociferously preached," head said in an almost objecting tone.

Objection evoked her innermost emotions, she burst at that moment, "Left-wing ideology dominates intellectual life in our land, and for decades now. Since Indian Left had state patronage and a permeate hold on academia, they could and have been intolerant towards the opposite view. Leftist dominance over the intellectual establishment has its roots in the systematic 'ethnic cleansing' of all non-Left thinkers since independence. Consequently, not many non-Left academics remained in the social sciences field by the late eighties. Inculcating greater plurality of thought in our intellectual establishment was never allowed."

She paused for a few moments before resuming seething, "And they talk about plurality in society, Pseudo."

Fuming to the hilt, she had to stop for a moment or two.

"We, my generation and lot many before us, belong to a peculiar melee of twenty-first-century-second-decade of India. Confused by, and about identity - their crisis subconsciously, melee seem not to notice. A sense of insecurity has now begun to grip this melee. Seemingly an urgency to secure not to establish the majority identity."

She picked a glass of water and gulped the whole.

She continued, "And as to why - answers are mere guesses yet do strongly point to the disenchantment for the secular social orientation, millions gotten groomed by liberal, leftists' academicians and their textbooks in the last century and with the advent of social media, ever more urgent to address and nail. They feel entrenched and a majority should not any longer - but then how? - the confusion starts thence."

Her face glowed in content.

For the next few seconds, none uttered any word - hesitant, partly pensive. Professor got up finally and walked towards the door. Senior got his attention back to papers on the desk waiting for him. Near the door, she stopped and turned around, "I am going to Bengal… a fight at another level with TMC and of a different cause is ensuing… I must make most of the time," she waved the suspension letters, grinning, "Thanks–a blessing in disguise, I reckon!"

"Wouldn't that be tough for an Indian housewife?" asked he.

"If the paid leftist housewives can hit the streets, one more could," she replied, "Just that her endeavour will be self-funded."

"BJP is a rich party," remarked he, "she may not need to," smiling.

Patanjali Kapoor stepped out, resolve hardened.

Later in the day. She dialled her brother. She wanted to confide, perhaps.

"Anant?"

"Bahin," ecstatic he said, "kaisee ho? (how are you?)"

"Can I speak to…" overwhelming emotions froze her tongue.

"Who?" Brother felt something was utterly wrong, "Hua kya hai? (What has happened?)."

He repeated.

She could not answer, for long, returned after a while, gingerly–" Chacko must be knowing… um… someone in Bengal who may have switched sides… you know Bhai… many who joined BJP before May 2014 elections originally hail from the left parties…"

"Something happened at University?" he sensed.

"We have been fired," she could say finally.

"What?!! But why?"

"They have also been… Pandey, Elite, and others from the Left-wing."

Aggrieved, he gushed out, "Couldn't you go slow? be politically correct? Why Bengal now? What about the girls?"

She said nothing.

"I will speak to Chacko and let you know." Dejectedly brother disconnected.

CHAPTER 19

B JP retained power in the 14th Legislative Assembly.

Tyagi won from Samalkha. Sahoo won from Panipat Rural. MLA Inderjeet's political standing took a massive hit.

BJP leadership approached, Sahib Singh, now the part of Congress State President and part leader of opposition in the 14th state Assembly to resolve the Freight Corridor dispute.

Social Impact Analysis needed to be completed asap. BJP back in power in centre wanted to showcase its grip on development matters to the masses.

Just after the 2014 elections, many inside BJP remembered there was massive disillusionment among the Indian voters with Modi, for various reasons. Prime Minister perhaps did not want a repeat. Development projects of gigantic proportion and those which promised a sea change economically or socially were decided to be given impetus. Freight corridor construction of west and east were to come to an end by early 2020. The next big announcement, Freight Corridor of the North, was around the corner.

"You got to give us good compensation–we will get the farmers to agree," demanded Opposition leader Sahib Singh

"I reckon we do not even need to go in detail. The earlier announced compensation will be distributed," promised the BJP representative from the centre, calling over the phone, "Just get the SIA done."

"There are some Muslim peasants also, so-"

"All will get," BJP representative assured, "I can be sent the list if Singh Sahib you are not okay to deal with State leadership."

"Yes, bull's eye," Congress opposition leader said, "We are not, Congress is not. I will send sir you the list and special consideration that you erstwhile MLA promised us."

"Who?"

"Inderjeet. And he is also a proxy builder, by the way, Sire." Sahib Singh said.

"I will find out, who is that and what these terms were."

"Do you really need to? I thought you believe my words," countered the Congress opposition leader.

Stopping and thinking for a moment, BJ representative asked, "What is that special consideration?"

"Land adjacent to Imperial city… if you ever heard of."

"What is special about it?"

Sahib Singh replied, "Nothing just that my MLA owns that farmland and was promised a handsome compensation."

"Ah- you wasted many minutes, should have uttered at the start. Learn to keep things simple and brief. Now that you have become State President time would be money Singh Sahib. Good compensation for all farmers–done, handsome for one easy–consider accepted."

"I will send you the list." An ecstatic Sahib Singh said.

And BJP representative reminded, "And I need announcement from district collector of 70% SIA consent received."

"My word - you will get that Sire. In the next fifteen days, please announce the schedule for SIA team composition and visit dates in the region."

"Shukriyaa."

Multiple facets needed to be settled. Newly elected felt rattled and at a great unease while setting out to meet Khan Chacha in the Muslim dominated hamlet. It was already dark and though suited his purpose, MLA with his guards was feeling unsafe still.

'So, undulating has been the events, no one seemed sure of the end of the course,' he sighed for a moment. He realized he had sighed after a long time. 'Times-a-changing?' he asked himself. 'Laado must get married now, should be a fitting end to this crazy saga,' thought crossed his mind like a lightning. Dusty wide roads began to turn into winding narrow lanes as the small entourage of a vintage jeep and a pickup entered the village.

Minutes later they were sitting in Khan chacha's courtyard.

"You will get the compensation, you have been longing for and you Khan chacha…," said Sahoo Singh looking at the chacha sitting next to him in the cot, " could never get from that Samajwadi Yadav."

"What about those killed by your son?" Khan commented and suddenly so.

Sahoo Singh was quite surprised to hear brazen words, daring outlook. The seasoned politician took that one in his stride and replied, "They will also, didn't I say–all farmers will receive."

"They do not own land, they were daily wagers, sweating hard on the field for a Jat jamindaar."

"Hmmm," thinking for a minute newly elected MLA said, "2 small apartments in the Imperial city–will that do?"

Khan had no ready answer, he kept thinking, moments passed by, eventually, a node came about. Sahoo Singh was astonished to find easy acceptance.

He looked towards Khan, threw a manoeuvre in, looking for reassuring words before he could head back home with the deal sealed, "What do you need from this old man now?"

Khan said nothing. He signalled to one standing in the little veranda in front of two rooms dwelling. The man went inside and appeared with one in tow.

Sahoo Singh got up in surprise. Aide by his side, the veteran walked towards the one standing behind, stopped just close to his face. "Are you the one who killed SHO Saini? Are you the one police has been looking for?"

An aide pulled that lad in his 20s a step aside to make sure MLA was a distance. A swipe if attempted in desperation could be ugly if not fatal.

"I have given him the shelter Sahoo Ji," Khan pleaded, "he has committed a mistake," spreading out arms, looking at others standing just behind him, "we agree… but then-"

Elderly was cut short, the lad was fuming, "Was your son not spared? Wasn't he at my mercy that night Sarpanch?"

Sahoo walked back to the cot, sat down. He let a few moments pass by. Perhaps there was too much anxiety in the air.

He looked at the full moon, right in the centre of the courtyard. For a few moments, he closed his eyes, feeling the moonlight on the eyelids.

"Shukriya," said he slowly opening his eyes still gazing the eternal beauty, "You are a man of your word Khan. It was necessary for me to meet him and for us to settle the matter one way or the other."

It was until midnight a discussion took place. It was short of a heated debate, yet possibilities were actively probed, and options were pondered over - the aim was to settle everything once and for all, the bottom line was to secure as much as all the stakeholders could.

Sahoo Singh finally got up, "Are you happy? Can you turn yourself in? Behind bars you will be treated well, I can assure."

SHO murderer on the run kept thinking.

The question was repeated a few moments later, tone and manner intimidating for an answer.

"Well... who can doubt that," tauntingly replied Atif–the SHO murder accused, "... murderers are MLAs now."

Aide launched themselves to smack the disobedient on the ground. Sahoo Singh interjected held one's arm, stopping them midway.

"Think to save your ass, bachche," veteran yelled, "This is the last chance to grant benefits to your family and those of two paani chor. If you do not surrender and submit in front of the judge as I suggested–nothing will get in your hands," turning towards the gate, he made a swift walk, stopped at the gate, turned around, and said, "Khan?!!"

"Ji," Khan stood up, fearful... strained... nervous.

"Whatever he says and does in the witness box in front of the judge," pointing his index finger in rage on the murder accused, "will have an implication on the compensation your farming community will receive and in time. My word. And no patronage to shield him from Inderjeet's hooligans who are waiting to lynch him the day he comes out of hiding."

"What if..." an exhausted soul could not bear the cauldron any more

Word and voice rattled Sahoo, gushed, "What?!"

"What if a spurned Inderjeet files a case against your son for murdering... what you called them... yes paani chor and force us to turn witness?" Khan challenged.

"Then... deal with it," thundered Sahoo, "who started all this–your Samajwadi Yadav–and where is he now? In BJP? This is what happens when there is no political representation and you follow blindly someone who turns out to be at best a fly-by-night operator."

Member of Legislative Assembly and his entourage barged out - enraged.

One patronage established itself on the way out of its predecessor–feudality remained intact and to continue unabated.

Moon had begun its usual decline, gods no longer stop by to notice agony and the prejudice.

"You need to come to Panipat sessions' court." Chhatrapal almost ordered him.

"Am I your slave?" a shocked, IT manager retorted.

Chhattar did not answer immediately, let pass a moment or two, "Hearing is today, around noontime."

"Am I your slave..." he was fixed and seething, and tauntingly, "Sire?"

"One is a slave to his desires and responsible for one's actions." Chhatrapal taunted.

"There was no need for you to make a fool of me... it was fun for you to just go there and ridicule my intent... right captain?" Anant thundered.

Undertrial stepped aside, "All you need to say and stick to what you witnessed that night in the chowki."

"WoW... and what makes you think I will come over there even let alone submit as you order?"

"And what made you believe... you will walk into a village... accompanying an unmarried girl and show up at the police chowki?" Chhattar snapped, "Could I not see the agenda... the unlawful intent manager? Were you not leveraging her to realize your purpose?"

The manager was shut up. He realized his mistake. He had nothing to counter.

"You just need to utter what you witnessed that eventful night? You get that?" Chhattar thundered

Anant could say nothing.

"And in case you believe you do not even give a damn to all this," An angered farmer was yelling at the top of his voice now, "let me tell you one charge of the many I face is about an attempt to break in your... Tejo Mahalaya," he stopped short, let a moment pass be and then gushed out, "So come and deal with it."

And he cut the phone as the cell door was unlocked, the constable was there accompanied by Dharma.

Eyes met, everything had been arranged and minutely planned for, yet he was edgy, "it could still turn out to be a bad day," he mumbled to himself.

Dharma put his arm around Chhattar's neck. The touch and warmth assured friend. He felt lost still, though.

Hours later, at the Sessions court.

The judge had taken the chair. A revised charge sheet had just been filed by the police. The judge was meticulously reading the papers.

"Charge no 1?" the judge asked.

"Accused murdered SHO on duty the fateful night, section 304 be applied lord," declared the prosecution lawyer.

"Charge no 2…"

"My lord… An attempt to break in UNESCO Heritage Site Taj Mahal at Agra. Applicable section be applied, lord."

"Witnesses?" the judge asked, lifting his head and looking towards the prosecution benches.

"Ex-MLA Inderjeet and Mr. Yadav." The Prosecution lawyer pointed towards the politician sitting behind him.

"And for the second charge?"

"Head constable Munshi had appeared in the last hearing lord while the other witness was accused's friend Dharma." The prosecution lawyer argued.

"Call Mr. Inderjeet first and later Mr. Yadav." The judge said, going back to the papers laid out in front of him.

Inderjeet was standing in the witness box a few minutes later.

"Would you have anything more to say other than you submitted earlier?" Judge asked, carrying on with the paperwork.

"Judge sahib… I saw a group… accused was one of them…"

"In the last submission," judge flipped few pages backwards, "you said there were 3-"

"Yes Sahib–the accused, his friend Dharma and father Sahoo Singh."

"Hmmm," the judge wrote down a few points.

"Okay, call the second witness-" Judge stopped midway. A commotion had just erupted in the outer hall. A group of men surrounded one in the middle who appeared at the wide door a few seconds later.

Man is the middle, was escorted from that point by two policemen while the others took seats in the last benches.

Sahoo Singh and Dharma appeared at the door in the last.

"Call the second witness," the judge completed his call.

"My lord," the prosecution lawyer requested, "Mr. Yadav has requested the court to allow him to submit his deposition without having to be present in the court in person."

The judge consented, "If you can please readout."

The prosecution readout. The deposition was like the one submitted by ex-MLA Inderjeet.

"Now we move to Charge no 2 or..." judge looked at the defence lawyer, "would you like to cross-question the witness?"

"No My lord," said the defence lawyer standing up, "I rather request to hear an urgent plea from one of the defence depositions."

"And what is that?" The judge leaned back in the chair.

"Who is rather the person police had failed to nab so far..." defence lawyer claimed.

Murmurs thus far turned into voices and in din in no time in the courtroom.

The judge could barely hear the last words, "Who?" striking hammer endlessly, "Who are you talking about?"

Defence lawyer signalled to the policemen. The person, recently brought in, was moved in the witness box flanked by two constables on either side, stood outside, and circumspect.

"Who is he? Who are you?" asked the judge, turning towards the person in the early twenties.

Din had reached its zenith when the judge decided to get up to bring some order, "You all could well be asked to vacate if you continue to disrupt the proceedings," he thundered getting up from the chair.

As voices went down, the judge sat down and signalled to the witness.

"My name is Atif Khan. And I...," he stopped.

"Go on... I'm listening."

"I murdered SHO that night."

All hell broke loose, a commotion on the backbenches as a few ran out.

Inderjeet's entourage was on its feet mumbling, a few gaping.

Inderjeet sat calm and composed next to Tyagi who was sitting between him and newly elected MLA Sahoo Singh, on his right.

The judge was thinking, writing all along for a very long one minute, asked in the end asked the prosecution, "Anything you want to say?"

Prosecution lawyer was startled to the core, could only mutter, "My lord… um… perhaps next hearing…"

Defence lawyer intervened, "I would like to object my lord… the witness is pleading guilty. My client must be released. The murderer has been on the run for long, decided to turn himself in and there is he now admitting and pleading guilty in the lord's court. We request a learned judge to set my client immediately free."

The judge went back to the papers and started writing. A full minute was taken as Chhattar awaited Judge's next words with a racing heartbeat.

"Do you plead guilty," the judge asked finally.

"Ji…" as a youngster began, snapped the learned chair, "You must know the consequence… so submit only if you are sure of your submission."

"I did that… I'm the one… I plead guilty," Atif said in a low voice.

Judge reluctantly resumed writing. For the next few moments, there was pin-drop silence in the courtroom.

"But Chhatarpal," youngster shrieked, "Chhatrapal must be tried for murdering two on the canal!"

Another round of chaos, murmurs, accusation, and counter words followed.

The judge got up, ordered constables to push the backbenchers out, "And lock the door," thundered the chair.

Moments later, as the judge went back to his writing and stopped after spending many minutes, he passed his order, "Chattarpal Singh son of Sahoo Singh a native of Bawani Khurd be released only once a suitable bail application is filed by the defence citing the reasons and witnesses account in written."

Chhattar was relieved.

He cried, and so was his father and his friend.

Murmurs turned into a din.

The order further read, "Atif Khan be taken in custody immediately and police must file its investigation report. The defence is asked to file a case in this court, pressing charges against the accused before this case can be quashed."

Chhattar was un-handcuffed.

Anant, the IT Manager looked on. A manager was not needed for the moment. No Tejo-Mahalaya was needed. There was never an odyssey.

Minutes later.

Stretching his legs in a brand new SUV, MLA said in a warm voice, "beta, could that Merchant Navy lad be the right choice for our Laado?"

"She could only settle with a city dweller," brother sighed. They were sitting in the middle row.

"You are right, otherwise, I always thought of Dha..." old man stopped realizing Dharma was sitting in the front.

Chhattar looked at him, eyes saying, "Not any longer Baapu... Laado has ascended a few social strata."

CHAPTER 20

~ ⌘ ~

"I've been trying to know for long now, sir."

"What's the matter Sapna," Anant asked, "any issue with project delivery?"

"No Anant. Deliveries are good and have been so."

The manager was happy to learn that, said sighing a long breath, "We are happy to see you get mature and able to handle customers at the onsite. How is the weather in Jersey?"

She ignored the question and went on to say in a stark voice what she had been dying to know about, "No one seems to know where Chacko is and when he is expected back. It's been three weeks since he has not reported offshore and his phone is switched off."

Anant could hear notes in sometime trembling sometimes audacious voice, many layers were contrasting yet complete—a mark of an evolving confident persona.

"As I said," manager nudged and killed the narrative, "leadership is happy to note your consistent performance."

Sapna Singh was surprised but had to hold on to her tongue. She was no longer a trainee, speaking her mind at this juncture could be termed not-so-confidence-inspiring. She was after all there where she wanted from an eternity.

The manager in the meantime noticed an email popping up on the righthand bottom corner of his laptop screen. It was an e-Mail from the customer David addressed solely to him—the Senior Manager. Title suggested a complaint - an escalation in the IT world term.

"So…" he adjusted his posture to a comforting position looking out of the window of his tenth floor Billysoft sprawling office. The evening had fallen.

Gurugram business centre's glittering skyline was lying bare in front of him, "You were saying something about the customer… Sapna?"

"Sir, David has already asked twice about Chacko. I fear he may escalate his absence. Chacko should have caught the flight and be here last Monday."

"I agree," said the manager as he quickly typed the reply, "Apologies David for not being able to send you a note in this regard as early as I would have liked. Chacko has met a mishap. We have just come to know. God bless his soul. Naved is taking over, work and quality will not be impacted, Billysoft can assure you."

And clicked the 'send' button.

And next moment he returned to the conversation and a waiting subordinate, "Yes Sapna… we will see to figure out what has gone wrong. All you need to do is to make sure you are in touch with… um… what is his name…"

"Who? Chacko?" She said.

'Can't she forget him… poor lady,' he murmured.

Sapna could not hear the murmur, asked, "Who sir?" She sounded a little desperate.

"Naved, you both need to steer the deliveries while I find about Chacko, hope SK has not sent him to some other assignment while I was away for a few days." Anant shared the plan and disconnected the call.

She felt dissatisfied, a little angry. She realized the morning coffee had gone cold, she walked to the break-out area and put the mug in the oven.

'Uh…' she mumbled, 'First that Kashmiri, now this Naved…' She stopped. 'How does that matter even so long as she stays onsite?' She was perhaps telling herself, ensured her good self remains folded deep inside. There was someone behind her she felt and hurriedly turned around.

David was standing with a grim face.

"Good morning David." She said, barely managing half-smile.

"I have some bad news. Chacko is no more, just now received the message from Anant."

"Chacko is no more…" she was exasperated.

"Excuse me, I got to go…" David said, "a meeting is coming up… will talk later. Naved is coming in, we need to plan."

Oven buzzed, she lifted the mug out and took the sip - shocked, engrieved, and lost. She felt the hot coffee cold still… Chacko was none to forget. She felt crying a moment, was blank, emotionless - the very next! Her identity was stretching herself on the void left by Chacko while the inner self grieved. She could not decide which of her she belonged and pay heed to. She was definitely over the line now–no more struggle to strife with–no more stares to avoid. She was there where everyone is no one. And no one has time to stare at anyone. And there was no patriarchy to yield to.

All fine: The Summit has been reached,

Farther and Richer dividends, hereafter,

Are only to be grasped–just a matter of time!

Her phone rang, it was Bhabhi, she picked on the very second ring, would usually leave unanswered.

"How many times I need to tell you Bhabhi…" she shouted, "I'm not coming back and marrying that useless Marchant navy man…" eyes moist, urging the lashing to go on, "can't you get it? Feudal…" She spoke more in English than Haryanavi. She realized she was surprising her, "You need not call me every other day. You can marry him if this pains you… you are cursed… I do not know… but I'm not… I am not coming back to live in stone age confined for nothing…. you get it?!!"

"Chhattar bolu soo (It is me, Chhattar, speaking)."

She was terrified at first. Could hardly utter, "Bhai…" She had never uttered more than two words in one go to her big brother.

Something made her indifferent the next moment. Indignation born over the years justified to her, her indifference.

"If you are not keen…" he stopped midway - voice heavy and burdened - "I will let Baapu know… Laado… khush rah tu (you be happy)."

And the phone was disconnected abruptly.

For sure, she was not listening.

She affirmed that provincial life was over.

A successful professional sneered at the hurried groom.

"And the girls?"

"I have secured one job."

"That's wonderful," brother felt relieved.

254

"There is no worry. It was never, in fact," looking at him she was in peace, "He is quite supportive."

"Of course," brother agreed, "The support one needs to embark on sojourns you have ventured into so far."

Yet she admitted, "Bengal could be a risk."

Anant nodded.

"Chacko? Could you get anything about him?" She was eager.

"He is no more." Anant said in a dead voice.

Her body leaned back on the chair, fearful, "How? Some illness? But he was young."

"His father believes he has been killed. Left cadre had their revenge, others reckon."

"You mean no one is sure?"

"They were upstairs, eyewitness deposing before police said some circled him in the veranda and…" he could not utter any word, sighed. "He had a bright career… the change affects lives… and here we had someone wanted a drastic change."

None could say anything. Many seconds passed by.

"He wanted a break to canvassing for his childhood friend," Anant resumed suddenly, "And he was fighting as an independent."

"Yet, opponents could not accept it?" she asked. "He wasn't there for right-wing."

"Some say he secretly assisted the right-wing party," Anant said, "Some believe that independent was a proxy for the right-wing."

He came close to her, "That's why I advise you not to run too far."

"HOD Sir was correct."

Patanjali sounded content, brother could see in her eyes. "One needs a forum, a pedestal you know."

She was speaking in a low and firm voice.

"Here we need change as Chacko felt and I am assuming strongly so. And any change-maker would need patronage to sustain the efforts over a long time. Power brings Patronage, which in turn the Affiliation and later, Allegiance."

She concluded, "And any change takes time."

Promise for lineage in her activism was tangible.

Singh family gets twenty-eight crores for the fifty-one acres.

Inderjeet wants Khan to find a witness. A court case on two lives lost at the canal would come handy someday. Sahoo Singh has money for Khans, Atifs to lead a better life, and to desist–power, patronage come handy–every day!

Yadav lost the assembly election on the BJP ticket. He lost his cadre and the minority vote bank a lot earlier. He will go back to Samajwadi Party and to Uttar Pradesh to rebuild from where he started–Yadav vote bank.

Chhattar has one Imperial City flat registered for her little Laado. He hopes she will come back soon. Next Sarpanchi election Chhatrapal Singh aspires to fight.

Patanjali Kapoor is now a primary member of a nationalist party. Discovery at Rakhigarhi vindicates her long-held belief–She is not an Aryan!

Anant has spotted white marble at Safdarjung Tomb placed on a red brick plinth.